DAGGER AND VOW

JERRY AUTIERI

1

V arro stepped into the forbidden room. His sandaled foot glowed pale in the fluttering gloom that shrank an already small room to a dark hole. He set his weight down first on the ball of his foot, then rolled back to his heel. He felt as if crossing a rotten bridge over a mountain pass, daring each plank and praying to the gods he would not plunge to his doom.

With his first foot planted, he searched back over his shoulder to the atrium. His family had all cleared out to the courtyard at his father's orders. Golden light spilled into the atrium to flash on the pool at its center. The dazzling brilliance contrasted with the room he prepared to enter.

"Marcus, I knew you would come. Hurry, boy."

The haunted, strained voice of his great-grandfather whispered from beyond. He whispered back.

"Yes, Papa." He used the familiar term at his great-grandfather's request, but only when his own parents were absent.

Checking a final time, confirming only the atrium and the sparkling pool behind him, he committed to the humid darkness of his great-grandfather's room. The air inside carried a strange and pungent odor along with something else his young mind could not grasp. Something dreadful.

"Close the door, Marcus."

"Father says we must leave it open."

His great-grandfather lay on his bed, white sheets glowing orange with the lamp flame dancing on the small table beside him. His red-painted bed posts were chipped and split with age, perhaps as old as the man who lay upon it.

"That foolish boy," he said. "Do as I say and close it."

Varro snickered at hearing his own father called a boy. At thirteen, he was the only real boy in the house. But to his great-grandfather, every man from the farm villa to the gates of Rome was a boy. He was the most ancient person anyone knew, and held in great regard for his age. Varro loved him more than anyone.

The door clicked shut and he rested his back against it. His heart sped. For the last few weeks he could not see Papa without his parents. He missed their long walks and grown-up, philosophical discussions. Unlike other boys his age, he spent most of his time with Papa and learned a great many things other children did not. This filled him with pride.

"Sit beside me." Papa patted the chipped wood frame. "My mind is clear now. There is much to say."

"Papa, are you feeling better? You were coughing so much before."

His great-grandfather had outlived his own son, Varro's grandfather, by a decade. He had once bragged that he would outlive his grandson too. This pleased Varro, but made his mother unhappy.

Papa had never stooped to the weight of his prodigious age. He walked with purpose and his eyes flickered with delight whenever he debated with Varro. He could lift him onto a cart and the two of them ride through the countryside together. He never seemed old, not like Old Man Pius did with his bent back and stiff legs. Papa had fought more battles for Rome than even he could recall, but no old wounds hobbled him. He was all strength and vigor, even if his hair had gone white and his yellow teeth fell out. To Varro, he was ageless.

But as he sat on the bed frame, he realized Papa was not much bigger than himself now. In the space of two weeks, he had shriveled. All his hair fell out. His brown eyes now seemed too large for his head, which seemed too large for his body. He hid himself under sheets drawn to his neck. Yet Varro could see the shadow-filled gaps between his straining muscles. Worse yet, his scent had changed. That same sour, clinging odor that filled the room wafted up from Papa's body.

He smiled with thin, bloodless lips. His eyes were ringed in black, couched in delineated sockets. Dark spots blotched his face.

"Marcus," he said in a long sigh. "The gods have returned my sense for this one purpose. I am glad they have sent you to me."

"I lied to Mother about feeling sick. I'm supposed to be in bed."

Papa cocked his head and gave a sly smile. For that instant, he seemed as strong as he always had.

"A sly boy, and rebellious too. You shouldn't lie to your parents. Though it is well you did."

Varro would have denied all of it, but Papa began to cough. Not a normal cough, but a wet and violent explosion of coughing that forced Papa's head back into his feather mattress. His eyes widened in horrified terror and Varro jumped off the bed to hover beside him. He sought a bowl of water or a cup of wine, anything to ease his great-grandfather's suffering. There was medicine here, but he had never paid attention to where his mother placed it.

At last Papa stopped and collapsed deeper into his bed with a groan. He stared for a long time into the dark. Sweat beaded on his splotchy forehead. He looked at the palm of his hand, which he had used to cover his coughing. With a snarl of disgust, he wiped it on his sheet. Varro saw the streaks of blood left behind.

"There is so much to tell," Papa said. "There will not be the time for all of it."

"Be well," Varro said, returning to sit by his great-grandfather. "We can talk when you are better. Maybe I should open the door again?"

His great-grandfather waved his hand and shook his head.

"Marcus, you are young. Still a boy. But you will not always remain so. Papa cannot be with you forever. I have angered the gods with my great age. For it is more than any man I've ever known, or that other man can reckon. Now I am dying. Our time together is at an end."

"Don't say it." Varro put his hands over Papa's. Hands like ice shifted under his own.

"Listen to me, Marcus. I must tell a story I have never told. Someone must hear it, and someone must learn from it. Let it be you. You are the youngest and the greatest hope of all my progeny. My grandson is lost, and may never find his way again. But you have a finer mind and a finer character. You will carry my story."

As Varro made to protest, Papa devolved into violent hacking and coughing that left him prone and stunned at its end. All Varro could do was wring his hands and search between Papa and the door, hoping his father would not enter in a fury.

"You remember our talks about nonviolence and peace between men?" His great-grandfather's icy, skeletal hand slipped trembling over his.

"Of course, I do, Papa. But Father said it is nonsense and Mother—"

"Do not listen to them!" Papa's eyes grew wide and fierce, his voice full and stern. "Listen to me, Marcus. Listen to why I have spoken to you about these ideas, so unsuited to the times we find ourselves in. It is important."

Varro lowered his head, his face turning hot. His great-grandfather was the wisest of men, and the kindest of all he knew. He quailed at having angered him.

"It was a long time ago when I was young." Papa's voice weakened and his eyes seemed to look through the ceiling above. The lamp spilled its flickering light and shadow across his sallow face.

"We had fought a terrible battle that day. So many of my friends had died. I can see them now, lined up on the grass, bloody corpses side by side. So many. Horses too. I'd never seen so many dead horses and their riders piled up in a lake of blood. Flies everywhere and a stench unlike anything I had experienced before."

Varro grew still. Papa never spoke of his time in the legion, except to have once described the appearance of an elephant. Today was a rare chance to hear a story.

"We called that day a victory." Papa rolled his head to the side and closed his eyes a moment before continuing. "It was a near thing, but I suppose it was a victory. Yet seeing my friends killed, it was not enough to know we had won. So I gathered others of a like mind, and we roamed into the countryside. We came upon a village we were certain had aided our foes."

Papa opened his eyes and tears glittered in them. Varro's hands turned as cold as his great-grandfather's.

"We dragged them out, poor families all. Dragged them out and killed them. Marcus, it was bloody and violent murder. Not just the men, but the women, the old, and the young. I dragged someone's grandmother by the hair, and I sawed her throat open for her grandchildren to watch. Then I turned to those children and hacked them down. I can still see their tiny arms crossed before their faces. When it was done, the village flowed with blood and the same flies that crawled over my friends' corpses now swarmed over the village. We burned their homes after stealing what pitiful wealth they had left us."

Tears reached Varro's eyes as well. He shook his head, not

believing this kind man who taught him peace could have done the evil he just described.

"But that is one story of so many more like it, Marcus. From that day, I turned the grass red wherever I travelled. In war or peace, at home or in the field, I settled all debate with violence. For that is the great allure of it, Marcus. Once you take up such a path, you will fly along it into ever greater evil. To even raise a fist in anger is an invitation to the cruel beast that dwells in all men's hearts. Better to never call it forward, or else you will live in a red world."

"I don't believe you, Papa."

"Believe me." He closed his eyes again, then swallowed. "Violence begets violence. If your great-grandmother were alive, she could tell you what kind of man I was. She carried the scars of my untamed rage. How I regret all of it."

"Father said you were a hero of Rome. I believe it. Why are you telling me these stories, Papa? I don't want to hear them."

"Hero? My centurions felt that way, certainly. And you must hear these stories. Of all my blood, you are most like me. But you are also unlike anyone else in our family. You can break this chain. You can become what I failed to be. Marcus, you can know greatness."

"Papa, I want to be just like you."

The words sent his great-grandfather shooting up from his bed. His eyes blazed with madness, the flickering lamplight two orange points within each. The bedsheet slipped away, revealing a wasted, waxy torso gleaming with sweat. Veins stood out on his thin neck. His hand shot forward, grasping Varro by the arm and crushing it.

"Promise me, Marcus, swear to it before all the gods and all our ancestors. You will not live the life of violence that I have lived. You must not, cannot, become what I was. Learn and keep the ways of nonviolence. Make an offering to Pax and ask her to remember you. Swear this now."

Varro recoiled and pulled against Papa's icy grip. But he was set in place, able only to shake his head.

"Swear it! Before the gods!" His great-grandfather hauled him closer. His grip trembled. They were locked together, and Varro read all the fear and hope in his great-grandfather's penetrating stare.

"I swear it, Papa. I swear to you and all the gods that I will not raise my fist in anger, and never to commit murder."

His great-grandfather cast his arm aside, but smiled. He collapsed back into his bed and his eyes drifted out of focus as his face softened.

"That is well. Remember always this vow and never forget what I have told you this day. You are my..."

But Varro did not hear the last words. Instead, they swished together into a long, dry exhalation of sour breath.

Varro waited for Papa to finish. But he remained staring at the ceiling.

At length, he shook his great-grandfather's shoulder. But he neither stirred nor blinked.

With his message delivered, Papa had died.

2

Varro heard the scratch of footsteps along the path before him and paused. To the left, fields of barley stretched toward hills studded with brush and pale rock. To the right, branches of high bushes nodded over the path, casting blue shadows across tan earth. The curve and bushes blocked the view of the path ahead. At the elbow of the turn, a waist-high statue of gray stone stood guard. It once depicted a legionnaire. Yet birds had smothered the head and shoulders with waste, and time ground the details to rounded lumps. Varro stared at it, searching for a warning in what had once been its face.

More gravelly crunches and laughter met his ears. This was a natural point for thieves to ambush the unwary returning from market. Varro looped an empty wicker basket over his left arm and clutched a pouch of coins in his right hand. His palms were sweaty as he clamped down on the hard edges of the coins. Thieves might chuckle after springing their trap. Not before.

Still Varro thought of running.

The brilliant sun in a cloudless sky of blue prickled his skin. He ran his tongue along his lips and shifted backward. If he ran, where would he go? The farms were packed tight between the folds of hills, but none were so close for him to reach one in time. Even if successful, what would he say that would not disgrace him as a coward?

He was not a coward, he reminded himself. He was a believer in peace and nonviolence. The difference could not be more fundamental, yet Varro despaired of ever finding another capable of grasping this distinction. He lived in a red world of conflict, no man realizing all could exist in peace if they so desired.

What approached from the corner on this humid summer day was only violence. He did not need to round it to know. The laughter was familiar enough. Better to avoid the abuse and preserve his beliefs.

Indecision left him with no choice. The source of laughter and grinding of sandaled feet emerged from the blind spot on the path.

"Well, look at who we've run into boys. Marcus Varro, the delicate lily."

Varro's grip tightened on the coins and his stomach burned. The giant boy standing at the center of the path had two cronies to flank him. They all wore plain gray tunics. The smaller two had blotchy stains on their chests.

"Good afternoon, Falco," Varro said to the brute obstructing his path.

"Such courtesy! But we can't expect less of our farmer-philosopher." Falco then looked to both his friends and all laughed together.

Caius Falco had been a scourge from birth. Varro's mother said when he and Falco were newborns lying together on a blanket, Falco had managed to gouge Varro's eye. Varro's mother claimed he cried the rest of the afternoon. Relations only deteriorated over the past seventeen years.

"I'm in a hurry," Varro said. "I'd stay and chat, but better move along."

"In a hurry," Falco repeated, spreading his arms wide. The three laughed again.

Falco was strong for his age. The swell of muscles was clear under his dark skin. He was not unhandsome. He carried himself in the manner of a leather-necked brigand who had yet to spoil from a life of dissolution. Varro suspected he was smarter than his heavy brow and deep-set, black eyes made him appear. Were he not a giant, other boys might torment him for his brutish countenance. Yet instead here he was blocking Varro's path with two younger boys at his call.

"It's just like you to grab the matter," Varro said. He held the pouch close to his thigh and stepped ahead. "See you all later."

Falco remained as settled in the path as the time-worn statue behind him. Varro steered right, the bush branches raking his face and catching the curls of his brown hair. One of Varro's flunkies, Tullas, shifted to prevent Varro from passing. The other boy, with a long, crooked nose and weak chin that earned him the nickname Ibis, ranged out to the left.

"Sorry to keep you," Falco said, folding his arms. "But I didn't give you permission to pass just yet. We've got to talk."

Ibis, whose real name was so seldom used that Varro struggled to recall it, slipped behind him. He crushed down on the pouch of coins, their edges biting into his palm through the cloth. Why had he let himself become surrounded? Bushes blocked his right. The golden barley fields to the left were chest height, only offering concealment if he ran at a stoop. The barley might as well be the very walls of Rome keeping him on the path with these three fools.

"We have nothing to say, Falco. You don't know how to speak."

"Really? Then what am I doing now? Are you saying I'm just a hot wind blowing across your pretty face? That's an insult to me,

Varro. What have I done to deserve such hostility? Me and the boys are just out for a stroll, and we happen into my old pal Marcus Varro. All I do is say we're not done talking, then you insult me like this? Your father would be disappointed in your behavior. But I bet that's a familiar feeling for him, wouldn't you say?"

Falco's voice had grown as dark and gravelly as the path he blocked. His beard was thin, but better than anything Varro could grow. He might have already begun shaving. Combined with his deepened, threatening voice, he gave the impression of a much older man. The squeaking snickers of Ibis and Tullas was such a stark contrast it broke Falco's spell. He knew it, too.

"The two of you shut your fucking mouths. It's nothing to laugh about when a grave insult has been so carelessly thrown in my face. And by my lifelong friend, no less."

The laughter ceased. Varro sighed.

"Look, I know where this is going," he said. "I don't want to fight. I just want to go home. I'm expected soon. If you're insulted, then I'm sorry."

"Sorry! You're sorry?" Falco stepped back, running his thick hand over his face. "By the gods, you have no spine at all. You never did. Just want to run away and cry to your mother. Always been that way. Isn't it true, Tullas?"

"Yeah, always running away." Tullas tittered again, and Varro thought he sounded like a girl.

"The three of you are a disgrace," Varro said. His voice cracked and he winced. Anger and rage labored his breathing. "You are the reason good people cannot live in peace. You don't know how to exist as humans. You're brutes, no better than wild boars."

Tullas's smile twisted into anger. Varro felt Ibis drawing closer behind him and heard his sandals drag across the grit. But Falco folded his arms once more and nodded with a smile.

"There you go. Finally, some sign of a spine. I knew you must have a reason to be standing upright rather than crawling on your belly like a worm."

"Falco, step aside and let a real man pass. Animals belong in pens, not on paths made for human feet."

"You're going to pay for that, lily!" Tullas raised his fist. But Falco barred his younger friend with his arm.

"See? Nothing but insults from you. That's why it comes to fists, Varro. You shit on my name and reputation, and all I've done is stand in the road. You think I'm an animal, eh? Well, what kind of animal am I? Have you thought about that? A boar, you said. No, I'm stronger and better than that. I'm a fucking lion. Everything from here to Rome is my prey, and you just kicked a lion in the mouth. Well, what do you expect when you do something like that?"

Varro had taken enough bruises through the years to know the answer. He had no choice.

He ducked off the road, sprinting for the edge of the barley fields. He could cut through the fields directly, and head for Old Man Pius's house.

"You little bitch!" Falco shouted after him, and Ibis and Tullas squealed with the joy of the chase.

The barley slapped Varro in the face as he broke into the rows of plants. He had no better plan than to avoid the confrontation. With luck, one or all of them would trip on the uneven ground to aid his escape.

The soft earth slid beneath his feet and he skidded. The barley rustled and thrashed at his arms and neck. Falco and the others howled with laughter as they raced after him.

Varro prided himself on speed. He often ran to both test and improve himself. If he were to uphold the tenets of nonviolence, which seemed known only to himself, he must be a champion runner. So in a short time he was pulling ahead into the barley field.

Yet the error of his impetuous decision was soon apparent. He trampled a path for the others to follow. They did not struggle with the barley or wonder if their next steps would land in a ditch.

Sweat sprung across his brow and ran down into his eyes. The sun lashed at his back. The basket on his left arm swung wildly against his side. He looked back.

Falco's long legs were the answers to Varro's practiced speed. The brute was nearly upon him, and he had that grin. It was the slack-jawed lolling of a moron bent on violence for the love of violence. How often had he seen it. How he had wished Falco would bite his own tongue while it hung slack in his open mouth. But the gods had never granted him that favor.

"Got you now, lily!"

Falco tagged him with a light punch to the back of Varro's right shoulder. Yet with his forward momentum, he crashed forward. Barley whipped across his eyes, spraying him with seeds. He slammed face-forward into the earth. The mineral smell of it crushed into his nose as he slid on his right cheek. He crushed the empty basket under his chest, but held tight to the coins.

For a moment, he saw only shadow and smelled only earth. The violent crash had rocked his senses, and he lay motionless. A dull ache in his shoulder reminded him of why he had fallen. But he flipped aside too late.

"I knew you'd run," Falco said, seizing Varro by his left arm and hauling him onto his back.

The brute was a black shadow against the sun in the cloudless sky. Tullas and Ibis arrived huffing beside him.

"Break his stones," Ibis said. "He ain't ever going to need them."

Tullas laughed again like a little girl.

"Let me have at him," he said. "I'll teach him."

Varro kicked and wormed to break free, but Falco's grip dug into his arms.

"I'm the one who was insulted. I give the lessons today."

Varro crushed down on the coins in his hand. They were weighty enough to smash into the side of Falco's head. The blow might knock him back, maybe even knock him out. He was not weak, and a solid blow would take Falco out long enough for him to deal with the two others. He was outnumbered, yet bigger and stronger than either Tullas or Ibis.

But he had his principles.

A man's promises were the measure of his honor. To strike now, where his life was not endangered, would be against all he had promised to uphold.

"I've a lesson for you," Varro said, ceasing his struggles. He looked into Falco's dark eyes. "But you're too stupid to understand. Every time you strike me, I show what real strength means."

Falco paused, as did Ibis and Tullas.

For a moment the dark shadows seemed contemplative.

Then Falco snorted.

"What the fuck does that mean? Philosophy was for the fucking Greeks. You're no better than the rest of us." He yanked Varro off the ground. "Here's a lesson about not being a snotty prick."

The blow to Varro's face snapped his head back. White flashed across his vision. Before he could cry out, another blow crashed into his cheek.

Ibis and Tullas cheered. Varro clenched his teeth so he wouldn't bite his tongue as the blows rained down.

Falco was merciless.

He held Varro by his tunic and pummeled his face until tossing him aside like discarding a rag.

"You made my knuckles hurt, I'll give you that."

Varro's face was numb and throbbing. His vision swam and his left eye resisted opening. Hot fluid leaked from his nose, a tinge of salt blooming as it ran between his lips.

Falco at last grabbed Varro's hand and pried the coin pouch from his fingers. He held it before Varro's opened eye.

"Did you think I was going to steal this? I'm a thief to you? You should know me better."

"How much did he have?" Ibis asked as he and Tullas both crowded around their leader.

"Nothing for you two scraps of waste." Falco emptied the coins into his palm, the silver chiming merrily. He threw the pouch into Varro's face.

"You shouldn't have run. You wrecked Old Man Pius's barley field. Don't worry, though. I won't tell him what you did. But you shouldn't have run. I wasn't going to hurt you, not till you insulted me."

"Liar," Varro said. Just moving his lips hurt, but he struggled not to show it.

Falco shrugged. "Believe what you want. I had some news for you, but I'm not in the mood to tell you anymore."

"Lies," Varro said. The blood leaked onto his tongue now, spreading the taste of copper along with hot salt. "It's always about fighting with you."

"Heh, that might be true. But nothing galls me more than seeing you run like a scared lamb. Can't blame me for wanting to pound you for it. I hate your peaceful philosophy. Or maybe you can't fight and are just covering it up."

"I can, but choose not to. That's the difference between us. I can control myself," Varro said. He at last sat up, and blood flowed out of his nose to patter on the front of his tunic. "Give me back my coins."

"Coins? I seem to have misplaced those."

Falco flung the coins into the barley field. Varro watched them gleam against the blue sky, then vanish. He glared up at Falco, who sneered alongside his two flunkies.

"I'm sure when you open up that other eye, you'll be able to find all of them. Come on, boys. We're not refined enough company for Marcus Varro."

He watched the three push an alternative path through the barley, deliberately damaging more of the field as they left. Their laughter trailed behind, leaving quivering stalks in their wake.

Varro gathered the emptied pouch. He sat with his face throbbing and hot, staring at the ground but seeing nothing. His hands balled up and rage seethed through his heart. But he gathered his breath and waited for the anger to pass. He controlled his emotions, and not the other way around.

The coins were somewhere in the field. He had the afternoon to find them and escape before Old Man Pius caught him out here and dragged him back to his parents.

He mustered the will to withstand a single humiliation today, but not two.

On hands and knees he padded through the barley, searching for the silver coins he had lost.

3

Varro slipped down the narrow entrance hall. The orange flash of late-day sun ignited the mosaics lining both walls and accented the shadows where pieces had long since fallen out. He emerged into the atrium. Sunlight slanted in from above to sparkle on the pool at the center. But Varro's eyes skipped across the water, looking toward the courtyard and kitchen beyond.

He hugged the walls like a thief and found the small vase stand where he set the pouch. The coins clinked as they settled. The scent of onions reached him from the kitchen. His mother would be fussing over the night's meal. Doubtless she had wondered at his long absence. So he preempted her questions. Still leaning against the wall, he called out in his most cheerful voice.

"I'm home, Mother. Coins are beside the vase here. I'll just be in my room."

"Marcus?" His mother's voice echoed across the atrium. Her shadow stretched across the open door to the kitchen. Varro's heart raced.

He ducked into his room, closing the door behind him. His cubiculum was the smallest of the rooms lining the sides of the atrium. The sun did not reach this side of the house in the late afternoon, and so his eyes failed at the sudden darkness. Being his room, he could navigate blind. He felt around for a clean tunic hanging on a wall peg. But his mother's voice was already clear in the atrium.

"Marcus? Where have you been all afternoon?"

He had washed his face in a stream before returning home. But blood had splattered his tunic. His nose, while not broken, remained crusted with blood that when washed away bled anew. His eye had opened but was swollen. With no hope of concealing his condition, he hoped to forestall his mother's reaction until Father could save him.

The knock on his door was a thunderous jolt. While his mother respected his privacy now that he was older, she was still his mother. Varro knew too well that to deny her was to invite terrible anger.

"Marcus, open this door. What are you hiding?"

He threw the bloodied tunic at the rope netting of his bed. It caught on one of the wooden posts and instead of bunching up now unfurled as if on display. Varro hissed.

"What is the matter with you?" His mother pushed open his door.

Golden light spilled in, splashing across Varro's pale, young torso and spotlighting the bloodied tunic suspended from a bedpost. He smiled.

"Sorry I was late, Mother."

Varro realized his mother was considered a great beauty. Being his mother, he could never see her otherwise. Though his father told him a thousand times or more that he was luckier than any other man to have her, Varro did not see what lifted her among other women. But now he understood how men reacted to her, and how their rough speech shifted to courtesies whenever she appeared.

She stood framed in the doorway. Only a hint of gray stained her black hair. Her dark eyes glinted with irritation. Firm arms emerged from her sleeveless white stola and rested against the doorframe as if to block Varro's escape.

"Look at you," she said. "What happened?"

Varro waived his hand. "Just a squabble with some boys. It's nothing, Mother. Please, the coins are on the table."

His arm hovered as he pointed to where he set the coins painstakingly recovered from Old Man Pius's barley field. But his mother's eyes glided past him to rest on the tunic hanging from his bedpost.

"Marcus Varro, you look like an elephant stepped on your face."

Varro laughed. "What does that look like? I've never seen an elephant."

His mother clucked her tongue and folded her arms. Her eyes narrowed at Varro, and she called over her shoulder.

"Arria, I need your help."

A muffled voice replied, sounding irritated and bored. Varro let his shoulders drop, then picked up the clean tunic he had hoped to wear in time to convince his mother he was not so bad off.

"I don't care," his mother shouted back, again never letting her sight off Varro. "Your brother is hurt again. Bring a water bowl and cloth."

"It's nothing," he said. But after wearing his tunic, he sat on the wood frame of his bed to await treatment. His plans had failed.

Arria's pile of styled auburn hair appeared over his mother's shoulder. He could hear his sister now.

"For pity's sake, this is happening too often. Marcus, when are you going to fight back? You won't have a face if this keeps up any longer."

"There was no need for fighting, Arria. Why don't you go back to staring at yourself your hand mirror?"

Arria inhaled to argue, but his mother cut her off. She turned to accept the cloth and bowl.

"Thank you, now go tend to dinner or your father will be in a mood when he returns. I've got to take care of your brother."

"I don't need you to take care of me." But he slipped aside as his mother set the bowl of water and white cloth on his bed. She sat beside him.

Her smooth hands were cool against the hot bruises on his cheeks. She firmly shifted his head from side to side, examining with a critical eye. Creases had formed at the corners, and a deep line ran over both her eyes. She bit her lower lip as she felt his nose and prodded the wounds. Though it stung, Varro resisted showing any pain.

"Well, at least your nose is not broken. You have a fine nose, and it'd be a shame to let some—some boys—ruin it for you."

Varro had heard this talk too often. Arria had been right, in that he had worn his lumps too prominently in recent days.

She worked with sharp, silent motions, dabbing and stroking. When she washed the bloody crust from his nose, her eyes narrowed again. More blood flowed, but she shoved the cloth into it and pressed. They sat in awkward silence. From the atrium beyond, no sound came. Sunlight shifted with the late hour, and soon lamps would need to be lit. He enjoyed that task, but tonight it would fall on Arria.

"I don't understand," his mother said. She shoved the cloth harder, as if she wished to hit him rather than stop more bleeding. "This foolishness of yours, it's gone on too long. One day you are going to really get hurt. I know who did this. Caius Falco. Am I wrong? If it wasn't him, it was the Tullas boy."

Varro dropped his gaze and said nothing.

His mother waited as if timing her next words. She looked from him back to the door.

"This idea of yours. If there was one thing I could erase from your mind—"

She bit her lip.

"Mother, I know you think I am weak. But I can defend myself."

"Can you?" She remained pressing under his nose, staring out the door to the atrium. "Then why don't you? I don't think you're weak, Marcus. It takes the rock-hard stubbornness of your father and his family to keep your code. But how often and how badly do you have to be beaten before you fight back? Is there no circumstance where you will defend yourself?"

"Only to defend my own life, or the lives of those in my care."

His mother laughed, punching her small fist into her thigh.

"Marcus, how do you know when your life is in danger? Today you let someone beat your face. But he might have killed you, even if he did not intend it. And you would lie there and let him do it? For some promise you made to—"

Now a sob choked off her words. She pulled away the cloth, tossing it into the bowl. Water sloshed over the side to splash Varro's feet. His mother stared out the door, then covered her face with both hands.

In the past, she might shed a tear or let her voice quiver, but never broken down sobbing. Varro was more stunned than when Falco had struck his head. She leaned forward, elbows on her knees and face buried in her hands. He slipped his arms around his mother's shoulders.

"I am fine. Look, the bleeding has stopped. You don't need to worry."

"Don't I?" Her voice was muffled behind her hands. She let

them slide to her lap. Her eyes were red and cheeks stained. She stared at the floor as if she had lost their farm.

"Mother, I'm fine."

"One day, Marcus, soon. One day, your peaceful philosophy will lead to grave trouble. They call you a coward. If you let people strike you in the face, then they will see you as a fool. They will take everything from you, because they believe you'll let them. And wouldn't you? As long as they're not threatening your life, you would step aside."

He had explained himself a hundred times to no avail. Explaining once more would not change his mother's opinions. Her father and brothers were war heroes. She traced a lineage of proud warriors, and to find that her own son rejected violence for the sake of violence was intolerable to her. She would never state it. But Varro suspected she cried more for herself than him. So he sat at the edge of the bed, arm looped over his mother's shoulder, and said nothing. He had to endure this, for she would not listen to reason.

"Very well, Marcus," she said at last. "You've no broken bones. So I suppose this was not as bad as it could've been. The coins are on the table, you say. Thank you for running to the market for me. Now I must see to Arria and how she's coming along with dinner."

She stood, retrieved the bowl and cloth, never looking at Varro. At the doorway, she paused and turned her head over her shoulder.

"Your father will be home shortly. Clean up before you present yourself to him."

"Yes, Mother."

"Marcus, those tears were not for myself."

Varro straightened up. Had his mother read his thoughts? His eyes widened and he shook his head. But his mother did not face him.

"You will understand soon enough. You will have to change, my son, or else you will be—"

Once more she bit her lip, then raced from his room. Varro stared after her, wondering why this time was so hard for his mother to tolerate.

As directed, he combed his hair, changed to a clean tunic, then cleaned the mud and dirt from his sandals. The house felt strangely quiet, despite his mother, sister, and a slave working in the kitchen just across the atrium. When he felt ready, he lay on his bed. Yet the pressure on his wounded face was too much, and he ended up waiting for his father outside his study. He paced the atrium, and now that the last of the sunlight sparkled on the pool, he decided to light lamps.

Arria traveled back and forth from the kitchen to the dining area. But she did not look at him, and he avoided her.

At last, the front door opened and his father returned home.

Varro and the rest of the household greeted him in the atrium. His mother, Arria, and their slave, an old woman named Yasha, lined up before him.

Varro's father was old, soon to turn forty-seven, but still strong. His hair was full and wavy like his son's, but had faded to iron gray. His hazel eyes were alight with intelligence and wisdom. Varro adored his father's learned and cultured demeanor. Every farmhouse for miles around recognized him as a wise and noble man.

But as he looked from face to face, his hazel eyes settled on his son. His father had a thin scar on the left side of his face. Whenever he tightened his jaw in anger, it pulled tighter and deeper. Now shadow filled it so that it seemed a black line ruled from eye to jaw.

"Marcus, I will speak with you in the tablinum."

The three women melted away, heading back toward the kitchen. Varro stepped aside to let his father pass, then followed him across the atrium toward his father's office. As he crossed the tile floors, he was aware of the funerary masks of his ancestors watching him. These stone busts were said to be made from casts of his ancestors' faces. Some were stern, others meek. Varro saw them every day and thought nothing of them until this moment.

They were watching and judging.

His father took his seat behind his desk. The office was small, for there was not too much formal business conducted in the countryside. Decorative vases, small painted panels, lamps, candleholders and a dozen other fine decorations filled the room. Several chests and bookshelves crowded the small space. Varro took his seat across from his father.

"I am sorry, Father. I have disgraced you again."

His father folded his hands on the table and gave a weak smile.

"It is no disgrace to hold to a noble belief. You acted according to your principles and morals. There are few so young as you who would do the same. You felt the rage, didn't you? You wanted to strike back, but did not."

"I did, Father." Varro leaned forward, both fists on the table. "I had a sack of coins in my hand, and I could've flattened Falco if I wanted to. It was a struggle to do what was right."

His father smiled, and the scar on his cheek slackened. But he also sighed.

"Marcus, while it is noble to promote peace and set an example for others, you must preserve yourself. Caius Falco is not as bad as you think."

"He's a brute, Father."

His father held up a hand. "He is made to play that role. His father... has problems. You know this. That violence passes along to his son, and he cannot help his nature. You cannot teach him peace. He has to learn it the hard way, or at least learn he is not welcomed if he brings violence with him. If you allow yourself to be beaten, then you only encourage him. Further, if you are seriously hurt, then how will you carry out your mission of peace? If your jaw is broken and your teeth scattered, how will speak your wisdom?"

Varro had considered this many times, but each time he had no satisfactory answer.

"I have made a promise. I swore before the gods and our ancestors. I swore it to Great-Grandfather, that I would never raise my hand in violence."

He felt the emotions whirling up in him. His great-grandfather had lived an unnaturally long life, nearly a hundred years. He loved Varro as his greatest joy and treasure. The two spent every day of Varro's first thirteen years together, exploring the world and learning from his wisdom.

His funerary mask sat outside the tablinum in the second to last alcove before Varro's grandfather. He looked at peace, unlike that final day four years ago when all the muscles of his body were wrenched out of place and his eyes bulged. Sweat gleamed on his pale, naked torso. He leaned forward from his bed and grabbed Varro's arm, squeezing as if to pour all his life's strength into Varro's body before he died.

His eyes gleamed, half-mad, and bored into Varro's own.

"Promise me, Marcus, swear to it before all the gods and all our ancestors. You will not live the life of violence that I have lived. You must not, cannot, become what I was. Learn and keep the ways of nonviolence. Make an offering to Pax, and ask her to remember you. Swear this now."

And so Varro had.

That vow had remained strong for four years, and boys like Falco, Tullas, and Ibis tested that vow nearly every day.

He looked to his father, who remained with a patient smile. His eyes flitted toward the funerary masks.

"I remember the promise you swore," he said. "My grandfather was a hero of the legions. None of us since have matched him. He is the reason we have the modest wealth we enjoy today. I have a deep respect for him. But he was confused and angry in his later life. I'm certain when he asked you to be a man of peace, he did not intend you to be beaten daily and do nothing about it."

Varro's throbbing face warmed, and he looked down to his fists. His knuckles had whitened.

His father cleared his throat.

"Your mother will have dinner ready soon. Find a pleasing topic to cheer her tonight."

"She is embarrassed by me."

"Never say it," his father said. "She is proud of you. She is proud of all her family. But she is worried you will be killed trying to honor your promises."

"I am not a fool, Father."

"Of course not. But soon, soon, you will have to make a hard choice. It will change your life forever."

4

Horsemen arrived at the farm at the height of the day. Varro saw the dust clouds on the horizon and guessed a half-dozen riders approached. He had fetched his father back from their barley field, and now the two stood ready before their house.

Unexpected visitors were always a cause for stress, either for the danger they represented or the stress of necessary hospitality. But his father was calm and ordered Varro to clean up and be ready to greet the riders. His mother, sister, and Yasha were sent to prepare drinks to welcome these visitors.

"Father, you never mentioned guests. You should have warned us."

His father ran his forearm along his brow. His hair curled with sweat that trickled down the back of his neck. Varro saw the stain at the edge of his tunic. But he paid no attention to his son and shielded his eyes to watch the approaching riders.

Varro joined his father, also shielding his eyes against the glare. There were only four men, moving at a trot down the unpaved track that led to their villa. As one of the wealthier farms, they had set themselves back from the main road. Yet they were not so wealthy as to maintain even a single horse. Whoever these men were represented significant wealth. Brigands would not be mounted and were not a problem this close to Rome. Still, Varro's lip curled at the thought of mounted men trampling into their courtyard.

Flies buzzed around Varro's head. He stood in his father's shadow as the riders drew closer. His mother emerged from the house, searching between the two of them.

"Quintius, is it... them?"

His father nodded. "I can't be certain, but it seems so."

Varro's mother grimaced. She looked to him with a strange expression. She seemed fearful but somehow hopeful. The oddity of her look made him cock his head, but this seemed to chase her away. She vanished back into the house.

"What did that mean?"

His father did not reply. The beat of the horses' hooves thumped in the distance. They had slowed, raising less dust as they approached. Thick gray clouds scudded through the blue sky behind them. Beneath this was the golden sea of barley that spread everywhere. To the outsider it might seem as borderless as a veritable sea. Yet all the farmers in the area knew their boundaries. All supplied Rome with its endless demands for grain. Varro considered these men might be on business from Rome. He could not guess. His father never involved him in the business of running the farm, even though he would inherit it after him.

Varro's face still throbbed from Falco's beating a few days ago. He had not gone far from the farm since then, instead remaining close to supervise his father's slaves in the field. He had spent a day repairing a wagon axle. Though he had used a mirror to check the growth of his beard, hoping it would spring up full like his father could grow his, he avoided looking at his injuries. He could see himself yet not see anything in his sister's bronze mirror.

At last the horsemen arrived within hailing distance. The four men drew their horses up, then dismounted. Two were junior to the others, as they aided the older men from their mounts, then gathered each two horses to lead behind the others.

Varro's father walked to the edge of the path. He raised his hand in greeting, calling out to the men.

"Ave! Ave!"

The two senior men waved back and smiled. Varro felt relief at this amicable greeting. He looked back to the house, and his mother and Arria were both peeking out from the darkness of the door. His mother strained to look down the path, but bushes likely blocked her view.

His father and the four riders spoke out of Varro's hearing. Then he gestured them back, and the men followed.

Varro waited, suddenly aware of the swelling over his eyes obstructing his vision. An intense stab of humiliation made him wince. He should have pounded Falco's head when he had the chance. He would not look like an embarrassment before his father's guests, and no one would have to lie about how he had fallen and struck his face. Gods curse Caius Falco and his lot! Why did they have to be neighbors and why was his father so friendly with Falco's father?

"You'll remember my son, Marcus," his father said as they arrived before Varro and the house.

The lead man was older than he appeared from a distance. He stood straight and walked with the looseness of a much younger man. But up close his hair showed gray and wrinkles bunched around his eyes. He had a nose like a gnarled root, broken and cut more than once in his life.

"My, he has grown, hasn't he?" The man held his palm down just below the belt of his white tunic. "He wasn't even this high when I was here last."

The other man beside him smiled patiently. He was closer in

age to Varro's father, perhaps shy a few years. He too was dark and had a dominating nose similar to his older companion's. But his smile was less genuine and more practiced. The two boys leading the horses stared at Varro. Each was around his age, sharing similar features to the older men.

A family, then, Varro decided. He inclined his head to the older man.

"This is Titus Bodenius," his father said. "My old centurion from years ago. You met him once when you were too you young to remember."

Titus remained with his hand measuring the ghost of Varro's past height.

"An active boy, if I remember. Seems like he's still active." He tapped his own cheek where Varro sported his bruises. "A bit of a scrapper, then. Runs in his family, I suppose."

Quintius, Varro's father, laughed. If no one else heard the nervousness in it at least Varro did.

"Please come inside and we will have a drink," Quintius said. He stretched his arm toward the door. Varro's mother, who had been peering out of the door, leaped back inside when everyone followed her husband's gesture.

"Unfortunately, we are not here on a social visit. I wish I were, for I rarely come out this far from the city."

"Then no matter the reason, stay and share a jug of wine with us," Quintius led the older man by the arm. But he remained firm and, at least to Varro's mind, his good humor diminished.

"As I said, we cannot. I'm here to bring you news. My circuit must finish by sunset, and I have several farms to visit before I am done."

Quintius inclined his head. "Very well. Marcus, come forward and stand with me."

The shift from friendly banter to solemnity was as fast changing as an ocean storm. Titus straightened his tunic and cleared his throat. The other man waved flies away. The two boys and their horses seemed to vanish.

Varro felt as if his vision were closing around Titus and his companion. His throat constricted and heart pounded against the base of his neck.

"Don't delay," his father said. "You heard what Titus said. Now stand beside me and close your mouth or else you'll eat a fly."

His sandals dragged over the ground, and he walked as if dreaming. But he did as instructed and stood next to his father, who straightened Varro's shoulder before indicating Titus should speak.

"Ah, well, yes." Gentleness returned to the old man and his shoulders relaxed. He again cleared his throat and continued.

"Marcus Varro, being of the age suitable for service, you are summoned to appear three days hence in Rome before your tribune for selection into the legions. Given the present need to raise an army for the safety and betterment of Rome, the dilectus is invoked. I need not remind you it is your duty as a Roman citizen of sufficient wealth to report and serve if selected. This is an honor, one you should hold in highest regard. I expect to see you in three days' time."

Varro blinked.

Fear had chewed at him for days, ever since his father had warned him he would one day need to make a choice about his vow of peace. He knew this would happen. Yet he would not admit it to himself. His mother knew, too, which was why she had cried so hard on that day. He stared at Titus Bodenius's dark, stern face.

What was he supposed to do?

"I thought the Comitia voted against war?" Varro asked, hoping to see Titus and his father laugh at revealing their terrible joke. But Titus shook his head.

"The first vote failed. Surprised you know affairs in the Senate so well, young man. Well, Consul Galba wanted his war with

31

Macedonia, and so brought the matter to the Comitia again. King Philip has besieged Athens. Something must be done, and so the vote passed. Now, you will report in three days. Understood?"

Varro nodded. But Titus turned as dark as a storm cloud and drew up his shoulders as he shouted.

"That is yes, sir! You address a centurion as sir! Am I clear, Varro?"

"Yes, sir." Varro staggered back, hand on his chest.

Now the laughter came from both Titus and his companion. The kindly smile returned.

"Just a bit of fun, young Marcus. But you had best get used to that. Ask your father how I trained him."

The throbbing on Varro's face intensified with his embarrassment, yet he tried to laugh. It sounded more like a hack, and he looked to the two boys his own age. They too laughed, but it read as derisive.

"I knew of the second vote," Quintius said. "We do get news out here, old friend. You always said you were going to settle a patch of land and grow grapes. Will that day come soon, I wonder?"

"Well, farming is a lot of work," Titus said. "And grapes are even harder work than barley. So, I'll let you enjoy that life. But I'm glad you knew of the dilectus. Perhaps these other farms in the area also know. Makes my job easier."

"Such news travels," Quintius said. "You might still have time for a drink yet."

Titus held up his hand to refuse. Yet it lingered longer than needed, and both Varro and Quintius grew still. At last the older man cleared his throat yet again, sniffed, then squared up to Quintius.

"People are tired of war. A lot of men are returning from Africa, and they've done their duty. Jupiter knows, they've done more than anyone could ask. So they're being excused for the time being. We need every man, old friend. I expect to see you in three days."

Varro looked to his father, a gasp trapped in his throat.

"I've done my sixteen years. I've fought enough for Rome."

Titus raised his hand. "Don't stain that glorious service with denials now. You are forty-seven, just at the end of eligibility. You're being called for the dilectus. If you are selected, it'd be as an evocatus. You'd not be expected to fight."

Quintius snorted a laugh. "You've seen what happens when the ranks need to be filled in the field."

"I'm sorry," Titus said, no longer a commanding whirlwind of a centurion, but just a weary old man. He seemed to shrink. "Your name is on the roster. Be in Rome with your son three days from now."

The scar line on Quintius's face deepened as his father's jaw clenched. His gnarled, callused hands flexed. He stared at the old centurion, who did not flinch. Varro felt as if his face would burn off. His swollen eye grew hot and dewy. But his father remained rigid and silent. This was the violent side of his father's temper, something Varro had hardly ever witnessed. He seemed to struggle to contain it.

"Yes, sir."

The words could have frozen the Tiber River. But they seemed to satisfy Titus. The corners of his mouth bent and he gave a curt nod. The man standing beside him gently touched his elbow. It was enough to break his lock with Varro's father. He guided Titus back to the boys, who offered assistance in mounting their horses.

Varro stood beside his father, both silent, and watched the group return to the road. When again clouds of dust rose behind them, Quintius turned to Varro.

"You've got three days to prepare," he said.

"Will they take me right away?"

"Once you've been given your assignments, you'll return home,

33

then wait for deployment. But expect little time. If you've got something to do or say, do it before we leave for Rome."

Varro stared at his father's hazel eyes, searching them for comfort. What he had heard is father say, though without words, was to do whatever he needed to do before leaving for Rome because he would never come back.

His father expected him to die in battle?

Before he could voice the question, the door of the house exploded open and Varro's mother raced out. Arria was fast behind her.

"What did Titus mean? You're not going to the dilectus? You've already served enough."

"Father, you can't leave us alone," Arria said, leaning on her knees as if winded. "Who will take care of the farm?"

In the afternoon light, his mother's black hair shined. But had it turned grayer since this morning? To Varro, his mother being bent over and teary-eyed seemed to age her a decade.

Flies buzzed around Varro's head, echoing the confusion that filled his thoughts. His father stood before them, the deep line on his cheek taut and filled with shadow. His brows furrowed and his hands flexed.

"I have a duty to Rome," he said. "As does Marcus. We will leave in three days. Depending on the outcome, I will have time to plan for the farm."

"We can't manage alone," Varro's mother said. "It's not like when your grandfather and father were alive. It's just us. Who will do business while you are both gone? We can't afford your absence. The farm will collapse. We—"

"Silence!"

Varro jumped along with his mother and sister. The command echoed across the fields. Though it was only a summer breeze that rippled the barley, to Varro it seemed his father's shout had done it. No one moved.

"Do not talk of money here, Cassia. We will discuss this in private."

"They are our children. They have to know."

Quintius stepped forward with his hand raised to strike Varro's mother. Arria screamed and Varro thought his heart had stopped.

But Cassia stood ready to accept a blow that did not fall. Instead, Quintius glanced at Varro, then lowered his hand.

"I have business to prepare," Quintius said. "I am hungry, and expect to eat well tonight."

He strode off into the house where the door hung open on the shadowed interior.

Varro's mother adjusted her stola, then helped Arria stand straight again. She tutted at her.

"Stop acting so foolishly," she said. "Go bring your father a cup of the wine we prepared. He likes you best. So try to ease his worries."

Arria nodded so that her pile of hair wobbled as if it might fall off. After she followed her father into the house, Varro's mother rotated toward him. Her dark eyes glittered with a cache of tears. She placed cool, smooth hands against his hot face.

"My son, my dear son. I knew the day would come. I have dreaded it, but I am also proud of it. You are following the path of great men."

"Father doesn't think I'll survive."

He expected his mother to cluck her tongue and dismiss his fears.

Instead, a tear released then rolled down her cheek to patter on her chest.

5

"The penalty for not appearing at the dilectus is death."

The words bounced around Varro's head with the rocking of the horse-drawn cart. Varro sat in the back on a bench of faded gray wood, worn smooth by the years. He stared at the ruts in the tracks the cart followed on the way to Rome. The planks shook and clacked and the wheels squealed as they turned. Barley fields were long vanished behind dun-colored hills, now replaced by grassy plains and copse of dark trees. To Varro's disappointment, the sky remained blue, and a hawk flew through the warm summer day. Rain would not delay the dilectus, even if only for a day.

He wondered about death, both as the penalty for fleeing his summons and as the end point of life. What came after it? When would he meet his own? Would it hurt? Would he be afraid?

The cart struck a stone, the carriage slammed and shuddered.

"Sorry," Old Man Pius called over his shoulder from the driver's seat. He waved in apology without turning around.

"You'd think the roads would be flattened by now. How many pass this way, and still a stone!"

Varro looked out the back of the cart again. He did not want to see the two men sitting across from him in the cart, Sextus Falco and his son Caius. He would rather imagine he was on this long journey toward death alone. It was bad enough the heat from Caius Falco's knees warmed Varro's own.

"No one ever stops to pull it up," Quintius said.

He sat next to Varro, as even-mannered and comported as always. How he could remain so calm when he was being dragged toward a fate he should not have to suffer? Varro's own mind was a whirlwind of conflict. Trees rolled by and in the distance he saw others cutting across footpaths on some errand. They were points of white tunics in the late afternoon sun. Were they headed to the dilectus as well? They had to be close to Rome now, for Varro's back and hips were sore from jolting in Old Man Pius's wagon for so long.

Conversation ebbed and flowed throughout the long journey. Sextus Falco had brought himself a gourd filled with wine, which now filled the wagon with its sour odor. Varro heard him swishing from it, belching, then offering it across the cart to Quintius. Again, his father politely refused.

Falco's presence was like sitting next to a hot stone. He felt his heat and pressure across from him. Like Varro, he passed the time staring out the rear of the wagon. But he interspersed it with long stares that made the side of Varro's head itch. He had toed him several times by sliding his sandaled foot across the cart floor. But Varro managed to ignore him.

At last, he seemed to have expended all his patience.

"How's your face doing, Marcus?" He always called him by his first name when Varro's parents were around. His pretense of friendship sickened Varro.

"Eh? What's this about Marcus's face?" Sextus belched as if emphasizing his point. A sour puff of air followed it.

"It seems our sons had a disagreement," Quintius said. "And Marcus lost the argument."

"Is that it?" Sextus asked. "I thought his face looked funny. His eye's not quite right, is it?"

Falco laughed that hyena laugh which always set Varro's ears on fire.

"A bit more than that, Father. But Marcus's face is a lot harder than it looks. I wore out my knuckles on it."

"I wonder what kind of disagreement could lead to such a violent end?"

Varro turned to his father, who was picking a wind-blown leaf from his shoulder as if he had merely asked out of curiosity. Perhaps he had.

"Well, sir," Falco said, straightening up. "Marcus got a bit testy and said some things I didn't much care to hear. So I gave him a good push, and, well sir, I remember little about what happened after that. I guess we came to blows and I got the better of Marcus."

"It's not what happened," Varro said. "You and your two friends set out to ambush me, which you did. I tried to avoid a fight, but you chased me. You could've just walked off. I said nothing to insult you."

"It's not how I remember it." Falco tilted his head back and grinned.

"All right," Sextus said, barring his son with his arm as if Falco would stand up though he had not moved. "Just a bit of sport, that's all it was. Bound to happen between boys. Got into scrapes all the time growing up, isn't it true, Quintius?"

"Certainly. I suppose it was all good-natured fun that got out of hand."

Varro looked at his father, who refused to meet his eyes. He felt his hands trembling. If he could get away with it, he would rattle his father until he admitted what Falco did was wrong. But once again his father sided with these so-called old friends who did nothing but torment his son. Sextus Falco, besides being entertaining as a drunk, offered no other redeeming qualities. What could be the deep connection with his father besides the proximity of their farms?

Rather than complain, he sat back on the bench and looked at Falco and his father. The two shared the same aggravating smirk, though Sextus's nose was already red from his wine. He shared the same prominent brow as his father, who was more handsome than his son in every regard. He was whip-thin but strong. His skin was still clear and his sandy hair thin but holding its color. His chin was prominent and cleft. Caius Falco looked more like his mother, who others called Medusa out of Falco's hearing. She had small, close-set eyes that she had given to her son, but hers were bright with madness that could freeze a man in place when she stared at him.

"Was it you two who wrecked my field?" Old Man Pius called back over his shoulder. "You'll owe me for it if it was."

"Wasn't us," Falco said. His father drained the wine gourd rather than answer. Quintius smiled and nodded as if he heard nothing.

Varro was content to let this lie go unchallenged. Old Man Pius could be a bastard when he was angered, particularly toward those younger than him, which seemed everyone within miles.

The cart trundled on and the conversation drifted away. Sextus talked to Varro's father about harvest and commodity prices, a topic that reliably drove Varro's mind into a fantasy world. But now with Falco across from him in the cart, he had no escape.

"Eh, Varro," he said, leaning forward and lowering his voice. "Sorry about your face. It does look better now though."

Varro ignored him, instead following the cart's shadow as it flickered over bushes growing beside the road.

"Hey, you know where we're going, right? I mean, your father told you, I hope. We're going to become soldiers. How's that going to sit with your little peace plans? You let a Macedonian do you like I did, and you're in the shit. He won't be hitting you with a fist. It'll be the sharp end of his spear. Maybe you should vanish when we get to Rome. You know, run off and never be seen again. You can live in a cave where no one will ever threaten you."

"It's a death sentence to avoid the dilectus."

"Ah, so you have thought about running." Falco sat back and folded his arms. "I knew you'd fucking shit yourself. That's what I was going to warn you about, that day you decided you were better than me and I had to teach you otherwise. Yeah, my father heard all about it. I was going to tell you to run while you had the chance. But now look at you. You're here with me, going off to fight the Macedonians."

"Maybe we won't be selected. We're still very young."

Falco laughed, oddly timed with a laugh from his father's conversation.

"Very young is when you don't know to shit in a pot. We're men now. At least I am. Can't be sure if you're really a man."

"What are you saying, Falco?"

"You're not deaf. A real man can stand up for himself. You just flop around like a gasping fish."

Falco imitated what he must have considered a flopping fish, but Varro thought he seemed more like choking on food. The imitation continued. Falco now bought in his own flourishes, such as weeping and protecting his crotch as he flopped in the wagon's corner.

"Oh dear, a bad man his going to hurt me. If only I could run away and cry."

"Stop it."

"Why am I protecting my balls?" Falco's voice rose higher. "I don't fucking have any. I'm not a man."

"I am a man! I know more about honor than you do."

His shout halted their fathers' conversation. It echoed around the grassy fields, bouncing back from the hills. Varro's hands dug into his own knees. His eyes throbbed and he wished he could tear Falco's throat out. Falco himself paused under the grown men's glares. For a moment, only the squeak and clatter of the wagon made any sound.

"What's this about?" Sextus asked, frowning at his son.

"Just asking him a question, Father. He got all offended."

"It seems you were doing a little more than questioning," Quintius said. He nodded toward Falco's crotch, where he still cupped himself.

He straightened up and put his hands to his sides.

Sextus shifted around to face his son.

"We're trying to have a conversation here," he said, gesturing to Quintius. "What are you going on about, throwing yourself around like a baby?"

"Sorry, Father."

"Sorry? You better be! You shame me by acting like a child."

Sextus smashed his wine gourd over his son's head.

Falco fell back with a shout, both hands reaching up to ward off his father. The gourd thumped his head again, making a hollow clop then shattering. The pieces fell over Falco's shoulders. Red wine dregs spilled out over his face and stained his tunic. He cried out, then spit the sour wine.

Yet Sextus did not stop.

At first, Varro enjoyed seeing the beating delivered that his oath forbade. The bits of gourd still in his father's hand landed on Falco's head and face, and soon he crawled into the corner.

But then he felt embarrassment as the blows continued. Sextus now stood up and hammered at his son, all the while ignoring pleas for mercy. He crushed the remains of the gourd into his son's face, grinding it in until Falco's head turned aside. Still, Sextus continued to punch his son's head.

The cart struck another stone, perhaps on purpose, and rocked enough to knock Sextus back to his seat. He too was splattered with wine stains. Falco suffered more than that, as blood trickled from his mouth to dribble on his tunic. Tears trembled in his eyelashes.

Varro looked to his father, who watched without reaction. Though the thin scar line on his face was taut and straight. Whether from pity or disgust, Quintius shook his head.

Wishing he could escape, Varro shifted to look out the back of the cart. Would that he had never witnessed this, for Falco would be certain to torment him for it. Before the day was done, Varro would suffer for Falco's frustrated humiliation.

The outburst silenced everyone, including Sextus, who remained slouched in the corner where he had fallen. The cart rolled on, and Varro made a careful study of the path flowing out from behind the cart. The wheels squealed and the horse snorted ahead of them. Old Man Pius encouraged the beast with gentle words Varro could not distinguish.

He realized the horse received better treatment than Falco had from his own father. Here they were, old enough to be called as men to die for Rome, and his father humiliated him like this. Varro had heard stories of Falco's poor family life. But he never wanted to indulge in sympathy for the brute. It was another matter to see the abuse firsthand.

After what felt like a journey to Mount Olympus, Varro noted the change in the path the cart followed. Soon they were on paved road and the ceaseless rocking and shuddering eased. Old Man Pius called back.

"Here we are, boys, not long now." He gave a dry laugh. "How I remember my days. First time I was so excited to be called. Of course, now I know a lot better. Can't believe you two old goats were summoned, too. Is it that bad?"

"I know as much as you," Quintius said. "They need all available men."

Pius shook his head. His wispy halo of white hair seemed turned to fire in the late sunlight.

"Glad they didn't call me. It's a young man's task."

"They probably didn't think you were still alive to call," Sextus said.

While this did not strike Varro as funny, the whole cart burst into laughter. The tension had been seeking an escape and the lame joke was enough to send it spilling out. He joined in, but as the seven hills of Rome lifted ahead of their cart, he could not help but think of what lay ahead.

He was rolling toward death. Once they gave him a sword and put him in the ranks, he must uphold his promise or fight. Could he kill? His life would be in danger, so he would have to. But would he hesitate? Most likely, and so discover his undoing. To hesitate in battle, as his elders insisted, was to invite death. So he would die, probably in his first encounter with an enemy.

Rabid animals like Falco would survive and flourish.

So they laughed as they passed into Rome, as merry as a bunch of drunken revelers, though Varro less sincere than the others. Sextus for one was truly drunk.

Rome had an odor. Spending time in the countryside, Varro enjoyed the clear and crisp air. But once within the walls and rolling down crowded streets, the air became stale with odors of waste and rot. People were pressed in together, living in tiny buildings with only the barest of natural light.

Varro now spun around to hang over the side of the cart and watch Rome pass before him. He had been here several times, though on many of those occasions he was too young to remember.

People crowded the streets, dressed in tunics and togas. Women wore stolas of fine cloth, while bare-backed beggars hid in the shadows of alleys. Pack animals clogged the roads, hauling crates and bales and a myriad other goods Varro could only guess at. Not everyone here was Roman, for people came from everywhere to experience the city's greatness. A hundred different accents fluttered up from the crowds. Colors of the rainbow spangled the endless procession, as people wore clothing of all designs.

Alongside their cart, scores of men walked the same path toward their destinies. Varro could not help but wonder how many were making this walk the last time in their lives. He counted himself among the dead already and was building peace with this fact. But these other men, most were cheerful and laughing. Some were Varro's age, and could be forgiven their carefree demeanors. But the older men should know better.

Then Varro sat back from the cart, startled at his realization. These experienced men likely did know, and had come to accept their destinies. Their stomachs did not bind in knots as his did. Their hands did not quiver. They did not feign laughter, but laughed genuinely, for they were resigned to whatever might befall them.

"I must learn to be like that?"

His father looked to him, brows raised. Varro waved him aside.

"It seems we're not the only ones afraid of being late."

Quintius laughed. "You do not want to be late to this. Besides, there will be many old friends here that people will want to meet. Tomorrow there may be more than a few bleary-eyed fellows called to service."

At last Old Man Pius rolled the cart to a stop. Makeshift tents dotted a large plaza. The grand columns and statuary surrounding this scene did little to relieve the haphazard organization. The plaza glowed with rose sunlight and buzzed with a hundred different conversations. Somehow, Varro thought, they would cull an army out of this sprawl of men and their tents.

"I drove you here," Pius said. "But I'm not making the tent for you. Besides, I've got my own business to attend. You boys are good here if I leave you?"

"Thank you for your kindness," Quintius said. He looked to Varro, who was quick to join his father.

"Thank you, sir."

Sextus and his son had already begun wandering into the plaza. Probably looking for more wine and a drinking partner, Varro thought. Even though this meant he would erect the tent for the night, he was glad to see Falco leave.

With Old Man Pius and their cart gone, Varro and his father carried their tent and poles toward an open spot in the plaza. If there were guards about, Varro did not see any. He assumed his future officers and commanders would be present. But these were not common men to sleep in a plaza overnight. They would have rooms or friends to put them up.

Varro and his father found the Sabines, which was Varro's ancestral tribe. Varro's family were not the raucous mountain men most thought of as Sabines. Rather, they descended from Sabines that had lived close to Rome and assimilated to it decades ahead of their wilder cousins. But now all Sabines were united, and the old divisions merely points of conversation. Tribes favored their own, and so Varro and his father set up among their own folk.

The evening passed and Varro wondered about their dinner. Deep shadows were filling the plaza and soon it would be dark. Before he could mention this to his father, as they stood before their tent, a man approached.

"Ave, Quintius Varro."

Quintius turned at his name.

The man emerging from the crowd swaggered toward them as if about to order them into a marching file. He had short black hair with a fringe of gray. His round head was heavily creased, and his blue eyes looked out from beneath untamed brows. He was

45

taller than Varro, and shorter than his father. But the man carried himself as if he were a titan.

Varro's father stiffened at the man's approach. The scar line on his face drew tight. An icy wave ran across Varro's back and tingled his nape. The man's bearing and his father's reaction spoke of threat, but he had only offered a greeting and a smile as genuine as a cobra's.

"Manius Latro," his father said. "Have you gotten lost?"

"You sound hopeful about that," said Latro. He stood before Quintius, head bobbing as his smile twisted to a sneer. "I should ask you the same question. What's an old fox like you doing here?"

"Same as you, I imagine."

Latro nodded and said nothing. Quintius folded his arms and his jaw flexed. Varro stepped back, wondering if he should vanish into the crowds surrounding them. But the man called Latro pierced him with his brilliant blue eyes.

"And you brought your son. Now that's something. A whole family. Or maybe you have another boy back home?"

Quintius did not answer, but remained with his arms folded.

Latro gave a coughing laugh. "I didn't think so. It's a terrible risk your family is taking. But there is no higher honor than serving Rome. Isn't that true?"

"Yes."

"Well, it's just me and my girls. They don't miss their father much, and my wife could stand some time away from me. So this is just the thing. I love serving in the legions."

Quintius sighed and shifted his weight.

Manius Latro's head bobbled once more, and he narrowed his eyes at Varro.

"I just love the legions. I love the job of killing Rome's enemies. No better living. You're going to find out, lad. Your father will tell you. It's all blood and killing from today forward. You're going to love it."

"We were just thinking of getting dinner," Quintius said.

Latro looked up expectantly.

"Without you. So good evening, Latro."

The round-headed Latro clicked his tongue and left without another word. Varro and his father watched him vanish into the crowds of men loitering in the plaza.

"Who was that, Father?"

"Trouble."

6

V arro broke down his tent while guards shouted at him
to hurry.

"You're not at home, fools! Be quick about it." A
soldier shouted close to Varro.

Though his commands were aimed at two men who stumbled
over their gear, Varro redoubled his efforts to stow their tent and
blankets into Old Man Pius's cart. The soldier set a long spear
across his shoulder, looping his arm over it as he strolled among
the crowds. His helmet gleamed with morning light, and a short
sword hung at his right hip. Varro expected him to carry a shield
or his helmet to be set with feathers, but he saw neither. He strode
past them, shooting Varro a vacant glance.

Flocks of pigeons flew over the plaza. Beneath them, scores of
men rolled up whatever they had slept in the night before. New
arrivals, probably locals or those living just outside the walls,
flooded into the plaza. Even after a full night in the city, Varro still
smelled the rank sweat of the crowd mixed with the more foul
odors wafting in from the crowded streets.

"You can't even see the flagstones," Falco said. He and his

father had been missing most of the night. Both of them still wore their wine-stained and blood speckled tunics. More of both seemed to have accumulated overnight. Yet neither seemed to remember their scuffle of the prior day. They were chatting and stretching, looking as if they were preparing for a friendly race.

"We better report to our tribune and at least be noted for showing up," Quintius said.

Varro rolled the last tent pole, then shoved it into the cart. Old Man Pius sat on the driver's seat, turned around and smirking.

"Come on, son. Don't turn green and throw up on your tribune. You'll be fine."

Falco laughed. "Don't worry, Marcus. They need cart drivers for the baggage trains, too. I'll be in with the real men. Probably never see each other again."

"What a pity," Varro mumbled. Pius chuckled, then frowned at Falco.

"You've got a big mouth, but that won't get you in with the men. You're too young. You first-timers will be in with the velites."

"I don't want to throw javelins and run off. That's for cowards like Marcus."

"Shut up," Sextus said. "There's plenty of brave men in the Velites. You'll think twice before picking a fight with the best of them. They've got to run right up to the enemy without anyone supporting them. See if you have the balls to do that when the day comes."

Falco lowered his head and walked to the edge of their small camp space, turning his back to everyone.

Varro returned to the world of his horrified imaginations. Running up to an enemy and hurling a javelin at him sounded horrible. What if he missed? In his mind, a giant Greek hoplite thundered out of the vagueness of a half-imagined battlefield and impaled Varro on a massive lance.

Yet what if his javelin hit? Now he envisioned a boy much like himself folded over on the grass. Bright blood sprayed from his punctured stomach and he screamed in agony. He looked up to Varro with tears in his eyes, calling out for his mother as he struggled to hold back the blood. In Varro's imagination, the blood sprayed like a geyser and painted him red with gore. Over all this the words of his great-grandfather boomed.

"Promise me, Marcus, swear to it before all the gods and all our ancestors. You will not live the life of violence that I have lived. You must not, cannot, become what I was."

"Marcus!" His father grabbed him by the shoulder. "Stop daydreaming. It's time to begin."

Leaving Old Man Pius, who offered him a cheerful pat, Varro followed his father and Sextus into the gathering of candidates. While a gentle murmur hummed through the crowd, Varro noted how muted the lively conversations of the earlier morning had become. Smiles flattened and laughter turned to polite chuckles. One man seemed to summarize the entire scope of feelings Varro sensed drawing over this crowd. He was close in age to Varro's father. He wore a pale blue tunic and a straw hat. His mouth had fallen into a thin line, and his weathered face looked about to slide from his head. He leaned on a walking stick, following the flow of the crowd but none too eager to lead the way. He kept looking over his shoulder, as if expecting someone.

"Maybe you just want to go home," Varro mumbled to himself.

A table had been erected and many of the Sabines were gathered there. Quintius pointed it out and led the small group through the crowd. Men moved at all angles, crossing each other and at time running into each other. A young, dark-skinned woman bungled about the group, looking frightened and confused. She had a red scarf and head-covering and wrapped her arms tight around herself.

Sextus chuckled. "Guess someone bought themselves a bit of fun last night."

The woman vanished, and Varro found he had appeared before the registration table along with his father.

They gave their names, which were recorded on a wax-coated board. The man seated at the table etched with a stylus while resting his chin on his left fist. When done, he looked up as if wondering why Varro was still present.

His father caught him aside as Sextus and his son gave their names.

"Well, this is it. I know you're worried. It's natural to be afraid, Marcus."

"I'm not afraid, Father. At least not afraid to be selected. I'm afraid of dying."

Quintius laughed. "Who isn't? There's no shame in it. We'll be going different ways from here. So you're on your own."

His father paused, put both hands on Varro's shoulders, and looked him over. He had never seen such a conflicted expression in his father before. His lips quivered as if either about to cry or shout with joy. His eyes narrowed and blinked. He squeezed Varro's shoulders.

"Whatever may come, you are a man this day hence. I'm proud of the hard choices you've made. Life in the legions will only make those choices harder. Remain true to yourself always, and fear not for tomorrow. Now go on."

Varro wondered why this talk happened now. They would return home after today. Certainly there would be a better moment. But his father turned before he could ask. He wiped at his eye with the back of his wrist and headed off toward the gathering point for older men.

"Hey, boy, you lost?" one soldier by the registration table shouted. Varro looked around and found no one behind him. The soldier remained staring at him.

"Don't play dumb," the soldier said. "The tribunes will know it and won't take kindly to trying to escape your duty."

"I wasn't trying to escape my duty."

"I don't fucking care what you do, boy, as long as you go to where the other boys are. Like you were told."

"No one told me, sir." He recalled old Centurion Titus's admonition and was sure to add the respectful term. But this just made the soldier angrier.

"Get moving or else I'll kick you over. What a brat."

Varro felt isolated, even with men pushing and sliding around him. Had everyone grown taller and stronger than him while he was not looking? Had color seeped away from the world, fading all to tints of gray? Even sounds were muted and mumbled as he bounced through the crowds to his assigned gathering point. Falco was already there. Even he looked colorless and fearful. His eyes met Varro's but he did not seem to recognize him.

Gathering men by age groupings seemed to consume the entire day. But Varro noted the sunlight still slanted into the plaza from the east, leaving most of it in shadow. Pigeons lined the vaulted rooflines at its edge like spectators at a chariot race. Hardly any time had passed.

Another soldier approached. He might be the same soldier that Varro was seeing over and over, but his mind was in such a state he could not remember anything.

"You, the thin one with the wavy hair, go stand over there." The soldier's forearm was covered in thick black hair. He pointed opposite of Varro. "Yes, I'm speaking to you. Got wool in your ears? Stop wasting time and get over there."

Varro's face burned at again failing to respond. He tipped his head and scurried toward where the soldier indicated. Others of his age were gathered already, and other soldiers were leading men to this spot.

He did not recognize any of them, and none seemed to have a friend. All stood holding their arms or else turning sideways to each other. Despite the coughing, shouting, laughing, and clomp of hobnailed boots on flagstones, the plaza seemed a dreary and silent place. Varro's face remained heated as he stared out over the crowd, wondering what would happen next.

As if to answer his thoughts, a soldier motioned that their group should gather close to him.

"Listen up, men." The soldier leaned on his left foot and put both hands on his hips as he waited for attention. "You lot seem barely growing your beards. So I'm going to explain this to you in case you don't know what to expect. If you do know, then I expect you to listen like you don't. 'Cause none of you know shit about anything unless I told it to you. Understand?"

Varro nodded along with the others. He was fortunate enough to be standing in front of the soldier as he addressed the group. He did not want to mishear something and then make a fool of himself.

"You've been grouped by size and age, as best as we can figure. Every swinging cock in Rome is here for the dilectus, so it's going to take some time to sort this out. Always does. So just relax and stay put. Wander off and you'll delay the whole process, which will make me mad."

The soldier paused to scowl. Varro stared back intently, listening for his next instruction. Someone behind him snorted and drew the soldier's stare. As they were not yet sworn to the legions, the soldier could only glare until the silence grew uncomfortable.

"All right, once we're settled, the tribunes will come down to the plaza. There are four of them, one for each legion. You'll all line up, and I'm going to call you out four at a time. For the geniuses in this group, that's all your fingers but not your thumb. Four, one man for each tribune. The tribunes will have a look at you and each pick the man they want. You will not address the tribunes, look at the tribunes, or breathe on the tribunes. I suggest you just hold your breath until they're done. If they ask you a question, answer it and call them sir. It's possible, but not likely, that you'll be sent back. If you are, don't go home just yet. We'll keep going until we have four full legions. You just might not be anyone's favorite pick at that moment."

Varro prayed he was not anyone's favorite pick and that he would be sent back to his normal life. Even if it was just to delay a year, he would welcome it.

"If you're chosen, you'll join your tribune's legion and await instruction. Not too hard, eh? Just follow directions and keep your mouths shut."

With his instructions given, the soldier turned his back to Varro and the others. Their tight group broke up, and again Varro was aware of the stinging loneliness of his ordeal. Some met his eyes, looking desperate or hopeful. Other than a few raised brows or muffled smiles, no one spoke.

By the afternoon, Varro's feet were sore from standing. Many squatted on the flagstone, but soldiers would shout at them until they were again standing.

When the command came to fall in line, everything proceeded as described to him.

He now stood in a long row of men about his own age and height. The soldier that had instructed them stood at the end of this file. Rows of other men lined up ahead and behind them. Varro looked for his father but despaired of finding anyone familiar in the thousands gathered in the plaza.

As he awaited his turn, he began to feel feverish. His eyes ached and his mouth dried. He looked at his feet, not wanting to see the tribunes or the end of this line drawing closer. But the soldier at the end of the file shouted, and he shuffled sideways. This repeated until Varro was at the soldier's side. Not only had he reached the end, he was the very last man. Was this a sign of something? Perhaps he would not be picked. He stared at his shadow stretching across the flagstone.

The soldier snorted as if to spit, but swallowed instead.

"Next four, present yourselves."

He grabbed Varro's arm and pulled him out of the line, nudging him ahead. As Varro stepped forward, he reached behind him for another man as if he were unloading sacks of barley from a cart.

The four tribunes lined up before him. They were stunning men. Each wore a bronze cuirass, all shaped into the image of a muscular torso. Two wore helmets with a fore-to-rear crest of red horsehair. The other two had their helmets tucked underarm. Their swords hovered at their hips, and their red cloaks swept across their shoulders. They wore their tunics short in the style of all soldiers, at mid-thigh level. These were fringed with purple to show their senatorial rank.

More impressive were their keen and noble features. Each was like a bird of prey examining a mouse. Their eyes swept over Varro to the others lining up to his left. One tribune had a clay slate and stylus, which he consulted.

Behind them other men in white togas chatted. These were older men, though some were not as old as Varro's father. He wondered who they might be, for none seemed much interested in the proceedings.

"It's my turn," said the tribune to Varro's left. The other three nodded that he should come forward.

This tribune was one who had removed his helmet. The impression of the helmet remained on his short black hair. He frowned as he looked each man over.

"Sabines," he said. Varro was not sure if it was a statement of fact or intended as an insult. He just remembered to hold his breath.

"You'll do," he said, pointing to the first man in line. The tribune had not even come down the line far enough to review him.

The next tribune narrowed his eyes and scanned the group. He pointed at the man beside Varro.

"I'll take you. Join the men of the Second over there."

A moment of panic struck Varro. Second? What was second? Would the next pick be the first? If so, he had half a chance to be sent back. If they were counting down then nothing would fall after the first. He had hope.

"You," said the next tribune while pointing at the other man. "Join the men of the Fourth."

The tribunes who had already made their selections were looking at the next round still in line. The final tribune rubbed his chin as he considered Varro.

"We'll be here all day if I send you back," the tribune said. "Would you like to go back?"

"No, sir! I wish to serve Rome, sir!"

The tribune smiled and extended his hand toward a group of men. "Then welcome to the First Legion. Go that way and they'll sort you out."

He stumbled away and headed for the men of the First Legion.

"I had a chance," he mumbled to himself. "The tribune offered me a chance to go back."

Varro settled among the others selected for the First. He blinked as if they were all imaginary and could be dismissed with a shake of his head. But they were real, and of every age and size. Varro had been with the younger and thinner set. He was not as short as some, not as tall as others. Now he was amid what seemed superior men. Each one seemed taller, stronger, more confident. They chatted with their new companions, each one a commander in his own right.

Varro felt faint.

"Well, this is a fucking disappointment. They let you in here?"

He turned to find Falco approaching him.

"The gods have no mercy," he said. "How did we wind up together?"

"Don't worry," Falco said as he picked his nose. "You and I won't end up together. They'll put me in the hastati. Once they figure out you won't fight, they'll probably have you milk goats or something. You'll be no use in a battle line."

"You won't be in the hastati. You'll be a velite. Old Man Pius knows what he's talking about."

"That old prick hasn't served in over twenty years. What does he know about a modern army? Besides, look at me. Are they going to waste my strength on throwing javelins then running off? I don't think so."

"Whatever you say." Varro turned from his hated enemy and tried to find another familiar face. It seemed every man was a stranger and each had another friend to occupy him. He was alone with Falco.

"Where's your father at?" Falco asked at length. "Mine probably got thrown back. Who needs a drunk in the ranks?"

Varro considered a drunk would be useful to throw at an enemy as a diversion. Yet he shrugged and kept quiet. He wondered about his own father, but hoped they would see his age and understand the farm needed him. He was certain all would end well for his father.

This was a call for young men like himself.

After an endlessly uncomfortable silence with Falco, soldiers shouted to form up. Some men seemed to understand this better than others. Varro had no idea how he was to react. So he followed the older men. Even Falco lost his swagger.

They formed into a wide block, with Varro and Falco both at the center. Taller men in front obscured the action. Varro heard muffled speech and eventually the tribune of the First Legion stepped up on a platform. He called another man from the ranks to stand with him.

"You will now all be sworn in." The sun was lower in the west, having passed the bulk of the day to this ordeal, and the stark shadows of the buildings surrounding the plaza now cut the opposite direction. The tribune's burnished cuirass shined with the light and he wore his helmet with its long red tail. He seemed like a god above the men.

"All of you raise your hands and listen."

The men around Varro extended their hand right hands forward and palms out. He followed along.

The tribune then began to speak, addressing the man on the platform with him. But the words were muffled.

"I can't hear him," Falco whispered.

Someone behind hissed for silence.

Varro's hand felt like he wore a lead cuff. His entire body trembled. He was being sworn into life as a soldier. He would be given a sword and made to kill. He would have to break an oath that had cost him dearly to uphold. But he would have no choice.

It was either make this oath or die himself.

The tribune spoke with the boredom of a man who has done the same thing too many times. His voice rose and fell, at times clear and at others lost.

"...swear to uphold your duty, and to act on behalf of the Roman republic. You swear to obey your officers to the utmost of your abilities, and too... even unto your own death."

Varro wished he knew what he was about to swear himself to do even unto his own death. But no one else seemed confused except for Falco. But he was a fool from the start. He should have told the tribune he wanted to go home. As a man sworn to peace and nonviolence, he had no place in an army. He would be a liability and get others killed. Surely the tribune would have understood. But instead he had shouted cliches that he thought would please the tribune instead. Falco might be a fool, but Varro declared himself the bigger one.

58

"I do so swear," shouted the man on the platform.

Now the tribune guided the newly sworn soldier aside. "I'm not going to repeat that for one thousand men. The rest of you answer with 'As do I.'"

"As do I!"

Varro shouted it along with the hundreds gathered into his legion. Applause and cheers followed, but the tribune held up a hand for silence.

"In one week's time, I expect you all to report outside the eastern gate. We will take you to your training camps from there. Dismissed."

The tribune leaped off the platform and disappeared behind a hundred heads between him and Varro.

"Well, we're legionaries now," Falco said. "How's it feel? Better warm up to some violence. Hey, I'll give you a rematch when we get home. I'll even let you take the first punch. You're going to need the practice."

Varro felt ready to vomit. He turned aside from Falco to leave.

Then stopped short.

The crowd of the First Legion was still breaking up, and as it did, the departing men revealed Varro's father Quintius among them. His face was pale and the thin scar line on his cheek was taut and straight. He stared ahead to where the tribune had been, eyes fixed on something Varro could not see.

The tribune had selected his father to serve. Their farm would have no men at home to protect and run it.

Varro bent over and vomited on the flagstone.

7

On the morning of Varro's day to join the legion, rain plastered the land. Varro stood in the villa's doorway as gray rain hissed down so hard mud splashed back up at his knees. He let the coolness of it trickle over his legs and feet. The earthy scent of the downpour filled his nose. The new summer heat abated to the black clouds, and he wanted to enjoy it before having to step onto the path in such miserable conditions.

"Just like I feel," he said. "Do the gods mock the obedient sons of Rome who leave today for their deaths in a far-off land?"

"Marcus! What are you saying?"

His mother's voice sounded down the short entrance hall. He turned back, seeing her slender figure framed against the atrium beyond.

"Just enjoying my last moments at home. I'd rather it not have rained so hard. If the fields flood, the barley will rot."

"Don't curse us. Now, come inside and spend some time with your mother before you leave."

Varro stared a moment longer at the empty green fields before the family villa. The violent rain obscured the hills beyond. He turned his back to the sheeting, hissing storm and joined his mother in the atrium. They hugged the sides as rain fell in from the central opening to refill the pool in the center. It made a merry sound, like a happy baby splashing in a bath.

His mother had dressed plainly for the foul weather. Varro noted her green cloak draped over a chair in preparation for their send-off. His father was occupied in his office across the atrium. Arria and Yasha were nowhere to be seen.

"Let's go to your room," his mother said. "I have something for you."

His room no longer seemed his own. He had packed all his belongings, either for travel or storage. He had rolled up his blanket and now his bed was just netting and a wood frame. His mother gestured he should sit there, and she pulled up a stool.

"Mother, I don't want you to worry for me while I'm gone. I will be fine. I'm worried about you and Arria, even Yasha."

She gave a weak smile that seemed more like she was sickened.

"My dear Marcus, do not worry for home. You will have more important things to consider. Dear old Pius will help with farm business. Sextus Falco's eldest brother will check in on both our farms. We will get by."

Varro thought he hid his dark expression at the mention of the Falcos. But his mother frowned.

"Mother, that entire family is mad."

"Mind yourself," she said. "Our families have been friends for generations. You and Caius have been companions since you were just babies."

"You've forced that on me." Varro discovered his hands gripped the edge of his bed hard enough to hurt. He released and sighed. "Mother, I just want you to be safe while Father and I are away."

She closed her eyes and nodded.

"How is Father?"

His father had said nothing after being selected and had

remained quiet and aloof after returning home. Varro had heard him and his mother shouting the night he brought back the news. He had blocked his ears against it. But Arria had listened and informed Varro that Father was outraged at being called again, and that Mother was upset at his attitude. She did not like it either, but wanted him to bring honor to their family.

"He is busy with last-minute arrangements."

They sat in silence. Varro was not sure what to say. Even with a whole week to think on this, he still could not accept the day had arrived. He was leaving home, possibly forever.

At last, his mother shuffled her stool closer and spoke.

"My son, I want you to be brave. Remember your family and your ancestors."

"I will," he said, swallowing. He remembered his great-grand-father above all. His mother seemed to realize this too and winced.

"You must defend yourself, even if it means hurting another."

"The Macedonians will be trying to kill me. So of course—"

"That's not what I mean," she said, putting her hands on Varro's knee. They were cold and trembling. "I'm talking about your fellow soldiers. They will test you. If you let them think you are weak, they will take advantage of you. If you let them think you won't fight, they might do worse. They may try to remove you altogether."

"Mother, you mean to say I'll be murdered for not starting a fight?"

"That's not what I said." Her hands pulled back and she sat up straighter. "You must finish a fight if someone starts one with you. You used to be able to do that before you made—that promise."

Varro heard the disdain in his mother's voice. It hurt, but he was determined to not leave his mother in anger. So he simply nodded as she continued.

"You have to be strong with your own fellows, or there will be no trust between them and you. If that happens, Marcus, you will not live long."

Varro sighed, then rubbed his face. "I've been thinking of this for days. You're right, of course. I've been foolish and naive. Great-Grandfather would understand this."

"He was a different man in his last years." His mother again patted his knee. "He would not want his only male heir to die in disgrace. He was a famous soldier himself, a true hero. You can be the same."

Varro forced his smile again, which his mother seemed to accept as genuine. He could not imagine himself involved with anything heroic. He just wanted to survive this campaign and return home. If Rome needed six years' service from him, then let it pass without heroics.

"Now, I have something for you. I'm surprised you didn't notice it already."

He had noticed the linen-wrapped object left on the small table in the corner, but had thought nothing of it. Now his mother stood from her stool and retrieved it. Varro stood to accept it from her.

"I've kept this for you. It's time you took it."

She set it onto his upturned palms. It weighed heavier than it seemed. The cream-colored linen wound around the length spanning both hands. He took it in one and unwrapped it with another.

"It's as if time never touched it," his mother said. "I've kept it oiled and sharpened."

As the last of the wrap fell away, Varro held a sheathed pugio in his left hand. The leather sheath was worn at its edges. The straps showed the stress of long use. But the dagger handle was wrapped with fresh leather.

"Draw it," his mother said. "It belonged to my eldest brother. I collected it from his belongings before he died. He had talked to me about passing it to you."

He had vague memories of his oldest uncle. He had been handsome, but his aunt had a huge black wart with hair sprouting from her chin. That was all he could remember other than their five daughters. Varro wondered where they were now.

"Mother, I'm not supposed to bring my own weapons. I will buy them from the quartermaster. That's what Father said."

His mother clucked her tongue.

"Pack it in your bag and no one will know. I had it blessed at the Temple of Mars. You must take it."

While Varro was a man of peace, he could not overlook the craftsmanship of the pugio. He drew it halfway from the sheath. The dagger blade was sharp and triangular. Even in the low light, its edge shined white. Whorls showed in the metal, offering distorted reflections of the room. He snapped it back into the sheath.

"My brother carried this pugio for all his years in the legions. It will serve you as it served him."

"I will keep it close to me," he said, setting it on his bed.

His mother's eyes filled with tears. Whatever she wanted to say came out as a squeal. At last, she turned away to dab her eyes with the back of her wrists.

"Your father should be ready," she said. "Time to go."

They all gathered in the atrium. The rain continued to slash down into the pool. It no longer sounded happy to Varro's ears. Arria had donned her green rain cloak, a match to her mother's which she carried over her arm. Yasha wore a simple cloak and cloth over her head.

His father shouldered his pack over his rain cloak. He seemed more relaxed than he had been in days. Perhaps like Varro, he was now at peace with what must come.

Varro fetched his own cloak and pack. He admired the pugio a final time before hiding it among his clothes and other belongings. He slung the sack over his shoulder then joined everyone outside the villa.

In the rain, Old Man Pius's cart trundled ahead. Varro had never seen a sadder horse. Pius was covered in a black cloak. The two Falco men were already seated in the wagon.

"Be safe," his mother said to his father.

"There are more instructions on my desk," he said. "Keep those guarded if you should need them."

She nodded, then they shared a fleeting hug. His father gently set his mother aside and turned to Arria.

She sniffled, trying to hide her face beneath her hood. She started to sob after her father embraced her and kissed her head.

"I'll be in the cart," his father said. "Don't make us wait."

Rain thrummed over Varro's hood and dripped onto his feet. He already felt miserable and wet. His feet squelched in the mud as he went to his mother then hugged her.

"Be safe," she repeated. But she folded her arms over him and would not release until he pulled back.

He took a long look at his mother. Perhaps this was the last time he would see her.

He repeated the same for his sister, who was now unabashedly weeping.

"It's going to be lonely without you here," she said.

"I will bring you back something from Macedonia," he said. "Something pretty. I promise."

She nodded and turned aside.

To old Yasha he smiled and inclined his head. She was a slave, but had always been kind to him. The old woman offered a strange smile but said nothing.

He rounded to the back of Old Man Pius's cart. His father pulled him up, and Pius goaded his horse back around the track. Varro did not look again to his mother or home. He could not think of a worse memory than his mother and sister standing forlorn in sheeting rain.

"The gods are cruel," Pius shouted over his shoulder. "This rain is a burden no one needs."

As in the journey to the dilectus, Varro once again sat opposite Falco. His knees were covered in his brown rain cloak, which hid his face. But his heavy brow still protruded from the dark shadow.

"Good thing it's raining," Falco said. "Better to hide your tears."

Varro ignored the jibe. If his father Sextus was drunk, no one could tell. He seemed asleep against the corner of the cart, with his rain cloak pulled tight and over his face.

"It's a blessing for you to drive us in," Quintius said. "I'm grateful for everything you're doing. I've left instructions in my office. My wife has savings for your expenses as well."

Pius waved his hand in dismissal.

"I owed your grandfather my life. It's all I should do for you. Plus, it's no trouble looking in on your lovely wife. She might tire of seeing me around so often."

Quintius laughed. Varro decided that if his father could smile and laugh, then so could he. He forced himself to chuckle.

Both of the Falcos said nothing for the entire journey.

The rain never abated. Ruts and mud harried them all the way into Rome, yet they never mired the cart.

"The eastern gate," Pius announced. "You boys jump off here, but I'm going into the city to dry out and pass the night."

Varro and Falco both sat upright to get a better view from the cart. Neither of their fathers stirred. Ordered rows of large white tents bobbed with the wind and rain. They seemed organized into sections, with a defined square pattern. He could see the black dots of men moving between tents, though the heavy rain erased details.

"No break even for rain like this," Sextus said. "Some things never change."

"The legion never changes," Quintius agreed.

Pius finally delivered them to an acceptance station, which was a long desk with bored men sitting at it beneath an awning. Rain ran off the awning to wear streams into the muddy earth. Only one of the dozen men seated there even looked up at their cart.

Varro stepped into cold mud that sucked at his feet. His bag felt like someone had replaced the contents with rocks. He slung it over his shoulders.

Old Man Pius stood on his driver's seat and put his fist to his heart.

"Gods be with you boys. Serve Rome and come back."

Varro felt a lump in his throat. This old man had once done as he was about to do. Pius had served Rome, as was every landowning citizen's duty. He returned the salute, then followed his father to the station. Rain did not reach them beneath the awning, but struck it with such force Varro could have mistaken the thumping for falling stones.

They were sorted by legion first. Falco's father had been assigned to the Fourth Legion, whereas everyone else had been selected for the First. His camp was far on the other side of where they stood.

"Seems like I've got a hike," Sextus said. He looked between his son, Quintius, and Varro. "Well, you all stay alive. See you in Macedonia."

He hefted his pack, adjusted his rain cloak, then turned into the rain.

Varro blinked after him. Not even a word between him and his son? He looked to Falco, who frowned after his father.

"The First Legion is this way," Quintius said. "Best get moving before we're dragged off."

Falco, rather than stare after his father, followed the posts that indicated the paths to the legion camps. Even in the rain, dozens of arrivals were tramping through the rain to their assignments.

Falco ranged ahead without a backward glance. His brown cloak swiftly faded to gray as he melted into the rain.

"He must be eager to get started," Quintius said.

Varro pulled his hood tighter, sending water sliding off his head to splatter over his chest. His shoulder ached from the weight of the pack hanging over it. He and his father followed after Falco.

"Father, before they separate us, I want to ask you about the farm. What were the instructions you left Mother? Is there trouble?"

His father sighed. "When is there not trouble? The harvests for the last two years have not been what I've needed. Barley prices have declined. Competition for buyers is increasingly difficult. With my being away, I'm worried. Your mother is a capable woman. But she cannot command the markets or the competition."

"Why haven't you said anything to me?" Varro asked. The track they followed dipped into puddles like brown soup that someone had placed boards over at one time. The boards were now flooded. His father stepped over them first.

"There's nothing you could do. I had thought after Carthage we would have peace, and I could have spent this summer bringing you into the business. So you see where we are at. The farm could be in trouble. All the small farms are these days. There's nothing to be done for it now. Pray and sacrifice to the gods. I don't want you to worry for it. You focus on your first year in the legions."

Varro crossed the flooded dip. The boards offered solid footing, but water still flowed out of his sandals. They now traveled uphill. Falco had disappeared.

"Here's what you'll need to buy your equipment." His father offered him a sack of coins as they walked, as casually as offering an apple.

"It's heavy," he said as he took it into his hands. "I'm going to spend all that?"

"Eventually," Quintius said. "One day you'll own most of what you need, like me. I need a new helmet, though. You'll be able to afford everything you require and still have coin. Don't gamble the rest away. You'll need to pay for repairs and other things along the way."

"I don't gamble, Father."

"You don't now, but you will soon. There's no tent in the legions without dice. There'll be precious else to occupy your free time. So be wise."

At the top of the rise they found Falco again. He was in a long line of men at a low table covered in an awning. They shuffled down its length, speaking to various men seated behind it.

A soldier in full panoply held a faded red cloak tight at his neck and shrugged his shoulders against the rain. He frowned out from beneath his hood.

"You, boy, in this line. You go that way, old man. Hurry up about it!"

The soldier indicated Varro should follow Falco, who was already halfway through the line.

"This is it for a long while," Quintius said. He patted Varro's shoulder. "Make me proud."

"I will, Father."

Quintius squeezed his shoulder and smiled. Rain formed a gray halo around his hooded head. He wished he had a better look at his father before he turned away to continue along the track.

Others were arriving behind them, splitting off to different tables. Varro for now seemed the last for his assigned spot.

"Another father and son send-off. Are you going to cry?" The soldier in the red cloak sneered at him. "Get in the fucking line. You're blocking my beautiful view of Rome, boy."

So it begins, he thought.

He stepped up to the table and the first tired man looked up with a welcoming smile.

By the time he reached the end of the line, he understood the smile better. He had spent what seemed half the coins his father had provided only a moment ago. In return he was the owner of a number of receipts written on bark strips. These apparently would convert to equipment and rations and a slew of other things.

At the end of the line, another cloaked soldier glared at him. His face seemed as if it were folded in half beneath his hood. He screamed at Varro for his name, which he provided.

"Varro, stop staring at me like I'm your first love. You'll be assigned a maniple and contubernium in due time. Officers will suss that out. I get a first look at you though."

The fold-faced soldier searched him up and down, dripping rain off his pointed chin.

"Should be a velite, could be a hastati." He rubbed beneath his nose with the back of his wrist as if scrubbing a tile floor. "Well, for now it's the velites. That could change. Now get over with them."

"Thank you, sir."

The soldier laughed, but then immediately shouted the same lines at the man following Varro.

He joined a group of young men his own age beneath a large awning. He did not see Falco, which was a relief. Perhaps they had assigned him to the hastati as he had expected. The rain pattered on the awning and splashed into long ruts in the mud. The air here was thick and musky. The men looked to each other with searching expressions. Some seemed eager to make friends, and others glanced aside. Varro decided to stay with his pack slung on his shoulder and his receipts clutched in his fist.

At last someone tapped him from behind.

He turned, expecting a man his own age. Instead, an older man glared at him.

"I recognize you, boy. Quintius Varro's son."

The older man had fierce blue eyes that seemed to burn with madness beneath his untamed brows.

"Sir? Have we met?"

The man nodded his round head.

Varro stared harder at him. Realization struck. Here was the man from the dilectus, the one called Manius Latro who his father had cautioned against.

"I'm going to enjoy breaking you, boy. When I'm done, you'll either be Rome's finest soldier or you'll wish you were dead."

8

Varro struck again. He drove the weighted wooden sword at the dummy tied to the post. Its point punctured the straw-filled sack body at about the height of a man's stomach. His heavy wicker shield crashed into the rest of the dummy's body, sending a shudder up his arm. Amber straw spilled out of the wound, and Varro imagined the horror when this would be real entrails gushing over his hand.

"Varro, you fool! Are you asking for your leg to get cut off at the knee?"

The bright snap of a vine cane delivering a stinging blow to his left shin filled the air. Varro slammed his mouth shut against the hot pain. He recoiled from the strike, interposing his shield before the next blow. The cane struck the heavy wicker shield with a thud.

Optio Manius Latro glared at him over the top of the shield. Behind him, scores of other recruits just like Varro lunged and struck at their posts. They wielded the same weighted swords and heavy wicker shields. Like him, their tunics were dark with sweat at their collars and beneath their arms.

"You thinking of buying yourself some greaves?" Latro asked, his demeanor shifting to companionable conversation. "So you won't have to worry about protecting your shins. A good idea. I'd wear at least one on the lead leg here."

He tapped Varro's left calf with his vine cane as he walked behind him. Varro himself stood at attention and did not look at his officer. He had learned better over the last weeks what that would earn him. All around, recruits grunted and thumped against their training dummies, ignoring Latro's latest victim. They would all get a turn at it, but Varro seemed to get one more often.

"The problem with your idea, Varro, is that I can still—"

A whistling crack of pain exploded across the back of his left leg, nearly sending him to his knees.

"Cut your hamstrings."

Varro again stifled his scream. Sweat flecked from his face as he recoiled. His hand crushed down on the wooden short sword, wishing he could drive it through the optio's opened mouth. But he remained at attention.

"And if I cut your hamstrings, you'll be face down in a heartbeat. You don't want your last look at the world to be bloody mud, do you? Because when you're facedown on the ground, I'll be putting my sword through your kidney."

The final blow struck him where promised, and now Varro stumbled and fell. He landed on the wicker shield. Hard-packed dirt abraded his palms where he had tried to break his crash. A black shadow spread over him.

"Lying down during sword drills?" Latro leaned over him as he screamed. "I should have you flogged for it. Stand up, soldier."

Varro scrabbled to his feet. His stomach ached and he felt as if he might vomit. But he gathered his shield and sword, both drooping in his exhausted condition. To his front, recruits continued to drill while experienced soldiers inspected their progress. Varro alone had the honor of an officer's attention. Everyone else ignored the scene.

Latro circled back in front of him. His blue eyes seemed clear in the sun. It was a strange color that Varro had never seen in another man. His unruly, dark brows were a stark contrast. His wrinkled forehead glistened with sweat.

"The others will be breaking up for the day. But you've done so poorly, you'll practice until twilight. I don't want to see your effort flagging, either. Attack this post as if it were Hannibal himself. I'll be watching, and if I see you even pause a moment, I most certainly will have you flogged. Now get back to it, soldier."

"Yes, sir!"

The wooden sword, filled with lead, and the weighted wicker shield seemed to double their weight at the thought of continuing the drills. But Varro did not doubt Latro's malice and did not want to be flogged. He had not seen a flogging yet, but had been given such a vivid description that he would do anything to avoid it. To his mind, every breach of regulation in the army resulted in either flogging or being beaten to death by your fellow soldiers. That there were any soldiers left alive to face an enemy was a tribute to the numbers Rome recruited into the legions.

Latro wandered off, vine cane clasped behind his back. Varro attacked the dummy.

Within the hour, the other recruits ended their drills and returned to their barracks. Latro remained to ensure Varro continued. Once he appeared satisfied, he followed after the rest of the men.

So the drill continued into the late afternoon. He had been ordered to attack this dummy for two more hours. He had no idea of where he could draw the needed strength. The pain in his stomach was dull compared to the brightness of the stripe across the back of his leg. How much worse would a whip feel?

With the threat of flogging to fuel him, Varro attacked the post for two more hours. He stood alone in the field at the center of this enormous yet monotonous fortress. He lunged for the flanks, attacked for the head, cut for the hamstrings. He did all that he had been shown and repeated it until he dropped his sword from trembling fingers. But he snatched it from the dirt and continued, wondering if Latro still spied on him. He might even be behind. So he dared not ease his effort.

When twilight arrived, Varro could hardly see from the sweat stinging his eyes. The summer humidity meant every drop of sweat clung to his body and drenched his tunic. He continued to drill even as Latro approached. He would not allow the bastard a chance to punish him for stopping before ordered.

Latro stood to the side with both hands folded behind his back. Varro shouted and stabbed. The dummy was emptied of straw and was now just a sack hanging from the post he had set this morning.

At last, Latro stretched and yawned.

"Stop," he said. "You still look like a country boy playing with a stick, but you're getting better. That's enough for one day."

Varro pulled back and stood at attention. His inclination was to throw off the shield and drop the sword, then collapse. Instead, he straightened his shoulders and looked toward the row of barrack houses. His bed was there and he sorely needed it.

"There are forty posts here," Latro said, looking around. "But tomorrow we will be on a day-long march. These posts will only be in the way of the others. Dig them up and stack them out of the way."

Now he did look to the optio.

"Sir, that will take half the night."

Latro smiled.

"I'm in a good mood, so I'll just believe that you spoke out of turn to your officer because you've been under the sun too long. I will overlook your insubordination. This time."

Varro blinked. "Thank you, sir. Sorry, sir."

Latro searched him from head to toe, looked down his nose with hooded eyes.

"There's some truth to what you say, though. I'll send the rest of your contubernium to help. I'm sure they won't mind cutting their evening meal short."

"Sir, that won't be necessary. I can do it alone."

"Again, Varro? Do you think because you have a little more money than the rest of the hastati that you are some sort of special person?"

"No, sir." He stood straighter and looked ahead. The sun was going down on the long, narrow rows of barrack houses. Men were outside preparing their meals for the night.

"Then why do you continue to flout the most basic rules of military discipline?" The optio now drew close to his face, so Varro felt the heat of his body.

"Sir, I did not mean to. I'm an idiot, sir."

"I brought you into this century, Varro. I feel a great deal of personal responsibility for your success. You speak like this to one of the centurions, and you'll be pissing blood for a month. Do you understand me?"

"Yes, sir!"

Latro pulled back, then grunted. "You have your shovel. Get to work. The others will be along soon."

He was glad to have cause to leave Latro and grab his shovel. The other soldiers had taken theirs, and Varro realized that they had probably wondered why. Every soldier set up and took down their own posts. So Latro had been planning this from the start. The optio had departed without another word. Varro fantasized about braining him with the shovel.

For a man sworn to peace, he had never entertained so many violent impulses as he had since beginning training. He took a slow and deep breath while holding the shovel. He closed his eyes and let the anger drain away. Latro was just baiting him. But he was a master of his own emotions and did not need to feel like this.

When he opened his eyes, he turned his attention to digging out his post.

The fortress smelled of meals of porridge and meat being simmered over hundreds of cooking fires. While the tribune and his staff ate in the main fort with slaves and servants in attendance, the common men cooked as if they were on the march. This was all part of training.

His shovel crunched into the dirt and widened the space around the post base. He shoved it down with his sandaled feet. He wore the hobnailed sandals of a solider now, and it made him feel proud. They were far more comfortable than anything he ever owned and made him feel as if he could walk up a cliff face.

He had dug up three posts when he heard voices approaching from behind. He levered up the fourth post, and it thumped to the ground just when the chatting voices closed on him.

"Thanks for the assignment, Varro."

A line of seven men with shovels gathered around him. These were his tent-mates, and future comrades in arms, his contubernium. Eight all together, they shared the same tiny barracks room. They were of the same ages and came from all around Rome. None knew each other, with a single exception. The man who had just addressed Varro, Caius Falco.

To Varro's chagrin, when Manius Latro picked him out of the velites and placed him with his own century in the hastati, he had paired him with Falco. Neither of them were excited for their reunion, for they had only been separated for less than an hour. Yet Latro seemed pleased.

"It'll be good to have a friend in the legion," he said with a smile that somehow showed he knew of the bad blood between them. "You two Sabines ought to get along just fine."

Also to Varro's surprise, training and drilling had robbed Falco of the energy to harass him. At the end of the long march from Rome to Brundisium, their current position, neither of them had energy to clash. But something in Falco's voice tonight threatened to revive his old ways.

"It had nothing to do with me," Varro said, returning to the post. "You can all sit down and watch, if that pleases you."

"Come on, boys, it'll be faster if we all help out." Decius Panthera was a nice man, Varro had decided. He was quick to smile and to mediate disputes. With their quarters so cramped, Panthera had a full docket of quarrels. Unfortunately for Panthera he sweated profusely leading both to an unhealthy sheen and body odor. Some others called him The Fountain behind his back, including Falco.

The others sighed in agreement with Panthera, then spread into the field. Varro did not thank them, which would make it seem he had a part in their assignment. This was all part of Latro's plan to harass him and turn the others against him. But these men all knew Latro was a bastard. Thank the gods at least Panthera had sense to just power through this chore.

Falco did not have any sense. He continued to lean on his shovel as Varro dug.

"You can't seem to stay out of trouble, can you? You've got to act all mighty and smarter than anyone else."

"I didn't do or say anything. Latro has it in for me, that's all."

"Well, at least here's a time when your little phil-os-o-phy"— Falco sang the word—"finally has some use. No chance you'll punch the optio."

"I'd consider punching you if you don't find something better to do." Varro blushed at the words. He did not look up from the shadowy ditch he spaded out around the post.

"I can't fucking believe it," Falco said. "You made a threat of violence."

Varro continued to dig, shame bright on his cheeks.

"You'd hit me?" Falco stepped back, hand on his chest in mock surprise. "Your childhood friend? I can't believe the great thinker, Marcus Varro, would do more than piss himself and run away at the first sign of a proper fight."

Varro groaned, then stopped shoveling. "Look, Falco, your little followers aren't around to impress anymore. Tullas and Ibis are off searching for a new boss by now. So either put your shovel to work or leave me in peace to finish."

"What does that mean?" Falco flung his spade to the ground. The closer of their contubernales, Panthera being closest, turned toward them.

"It means you're either going to help us or be the rock-headed ass that you usually are and do nothing. Either way, it means stop wasting my time."

"Wasting your time? It was our fucking dinner that got interrupted because of your stupidity."

"Falco, I have to believe behind that gigantic brow of yours there is something capable of thought. Does it not occur to you that Optio Latro wants all of you to hate me?"

"My gigantic brow?" He touched his forehead, missing his brow entirely.

"I could hang my sandals from it."

"That's it, you fucking shit!"

"Hold on, boys." Panthera dropped his shovel and ran for them, hands raised as if waving down an out-of-control cart.

Falco landed his wide-arcing right hook against Varro's head. The jolt of pain snapped him back. Sweat showered after the blow and trailed in the air as he collapsed back.

He struck the ground. The sky above had shaded to purple with the onset of night, and the first hints of stars shined. As far as blows went, he had endured far worse. But after being whipped and beaten at Latro's hands, then drilling all day, sheer exhaustion had felled him. He considered lying on the ground and napping.

"Falco! What have you done!" Panthera's voice rose in shock. Out of the circle of Varro's vision, he heard the others shouting. Some seemed encouraging and others were angry.

"I'm giving the little shit what he deserves!"

Varro heard a brief scuffle, Panthera's shout of surprise, and then Falco appeared over him.

Sweat dripped off Falco onto Varro's face. He was all deep shadows, though his brow still evident. The gathering darkness emphasized the swell of his muscles, bulked up through weeks of hard drilling.

"I'm going to beat an apology out of you, Varro!"

But the blow did not land.

Panthera had jumped him from behind and pulled him back.

"Fighting is forbidden," he shouted. "You're going to get us all in trouble."

"Teaching a lesson isn't fighting."

Varro jumped up. Latro's warning about lying on the ground during a battle seemed applicable here. Panthera had Falco's arms locked from behind, but Falco was stronger. He had already wrestled free.

The punch was not his choice. Varro just found his arm shooting forward, pointed straight at Falco's exposed stomach.

He too had grown stronger from constant training. Despite his wearied condition, rage filled him with power. The blow slammed just beneath Falco's ribs, knocking his breath from his lungs.

"Not you too!" Panthera shouted. By now the others had gathered around, but no one else seemed to know what to do. Panthera grabbed Falco's arm to pull him away.

"Get off me." Falco twisted free.

But Varro was not done.

Astonished as he was to have struck back, he wanted more.

80

Falco had this coming. Four years of bitter blood had to be repaid. All this drilling, all this hatred from Latro, exhausting heat and crowded barracks, all of it spilled into the next punch.

His fist crashed into Falco's face. To Varro it seemed as if everything had slowed to show him Falco's mouth deforming and ripples of force tearing across his cheeks. Spit and sweat sprayed to the side, catching the final rays of daylight.

Falco staggered, but did not fall.

Varro pounced, driving his knee into Falco's crotch. He doubled over, and Varro decided that the kidney punch he had endured earlier would be a fine treat for his hated enemy. He seized Falco around the head with his left arm, locking him underarm, then pounded on his kidney with his right fist.

He delighted in Falco's choking screams. He yanked up on his neck to choke him further, redoubling his blows.

"Gods, Varro, stop it!" Panthera shouted. Sweat streaked from his face as he danced around them, looking for an opening to break up the fight. "You fools, help me out!"

The others had surrounded them, dumbfounded at the sudden fight. None of them likely understood what Varro was venting. To them, he must have seemed a madman.

To Falco, he must have seemed possessed.

He rained a dozen blows and kept Falco locked. He struggled and bucked, but could not get leverage. Varro stared to laugh, even as his knuckles sparked pain whenever he struck.

"What is this!"

Varro recognized the voice.

Optio Latro had returned.

The other contubernales jumped clear of Varro and Falco, standing at attention. Varro froze, even as Falco continued to struggle.

"Now you are fighting?" Optio Latro stopped in front of him.

He still carried his vine cane. "I leave you for an hour and return to find you in a fight."

Varro released Falco, who shoved him before standing to attention.

"Yes, sir, as you've seen, I was delivering a beating to Falco here."

He was in serious trouble, yet he felt better than he had in years.

Latro laughed, pointing to Falco. "You seem to have suffered quite a beating tonight. Given your size, I'd have expected a better showing from you. Though Varro here is no weakling."

"Thank you, sir." Varro regretted the stupidity of his comment the moment he spoke. His head felt ready to burst into flame. Optio Latro inclined his creased, round head.

"No, really, I saw your potential from the start. A sturdy country boy, you are. You've acquitted yourself nicely tonight. Very good. Very good."

The hot night grew colder. Varro stood at rigid attention as Optio Latro smiled and spun his vine cane in his palm.

"Of course, you know fighting among the ranks is forbidden. There is a very stiff penalty for it. I'm afraid, dear Varro, that tomorrow morning you will demonstrate for the entire century what that penalty is."

He leaned in, his smile widening.

"Of course, it's a flogging."

9

Varro lay on his bunk, staring up at the darkness of the rafters. In the lightless barracks room, he could not tell the hour of the day. Normally it did not matter, as he passed out when reaching his top bunk. Yet he had tonight endured a night without sleep or rest. Every moment stretched out into the black room in tedious succession with only random worries interspersed.

The others had all fallen asleep. Their snoring rarely mattered, but tonight it tormented Varro. He had never shared a room with others and being thrust in with seven other men disturbed him. He suspected some others also disliked the crowded quarters. For all of them, this was their first time in the legions. They had to all be worried for battles and enemies, and none had considered the trials of daily life.

So he listened to the snores, each one distinct to the man producing it. Panthera blew little puffs. Falco groaned and mumbled to himself. He had bunked beneath Varro. The others all just blended into a general hum.

He wished for a bath. After all day drilling and digging posts, he was rough with grit and sweat. The odor from his underarms wrinkled his nose. The others only added their odors to the stale, unmoving air.

"Varro, you awake?"

The voice whispered across the dark from a top bunk opposite his. He peered into the black, still unable to see anything. Though he knew the voice and man as Lars Gallio.

"I never slept."

"That was some fight," Gallio said. "You looked like you wanted to kill Falco. Hey, Falco, you awake?"

"He'll be sleeping just fine," Varro said, though both waited on Falco's next snore before continuing.

"What did he say to you?" Gallio asked. "You don't strike me as a brawler, but maybe I'm wrong. My father always cautioned me not to trust the ones who smile too much. But you don't smile much, either."

"What's to smile about? Optio Latro has decided he wants to ruin me. I've broken my vow."

"Vow?"

"Never mind that," Varro twisted onto his side to face the darkness that hid Gallio. "Do you think I will die today?"

"I don't know," Gallio said. "Depends on how much they flog you. I doubt they'll kill you for a shoving match."

"But it seems the penalty for every rule infraction is execution."

Gallio chuckled. "Seems that way. So what's the fight about? I thought Falco was a friend of yours from home?"

"He's no friend of mine."

"That's not good. We've got to support each other. What'll happen when we have to face the Macedonians? You two can't be fighting. We'll all get killed."

"I don't want to fight anyone." Varro snapped louder than he intended and tucked his head down, expecting curses from men awakened. Yet the snoring continued. "I don't even want to be here. Like everyone else, I have to be here if I want to live as a Roman."

"Don't put it like that. This is our duty. Plus, have you heard what that bastard Philip has done to his own people? He's a monster that needs to be stopped. The Macedonians will treat us like heroes. You'll see. They won't fight more than they have to. So, are you going to keep dodging my question?"

Varro rolled onto his back, realizing that he might be unable to do this for weeks after his flogging.

"Falco has been tormenting me since we were children, and it has been a lot worse since we both got older." He paused to confirm Falco was still snoring. He heard the light drag of his breathing and continued. "I made a promise not to act in violence unless it was to save my life or the life of another. He took advantage of that to pleasure his own base desire to hurt others. I did nothing to make him hate me. He just does. And I've never struck back, no matter how much I've wanted to. If a man can't keep a promise, then he's worth nothing. Yesterday, I'm not sure what happened, but it all broke free. I lost control and regret what I did. I wish none of it ever happened."

Silence stretched into the dark, and Varro regretted sharing so much. But then he heard a long sigh from Gallio.

"That's hard. We've both got to live with him. I don't think the others much like him. He's never got a kind word, only a bite. I think he likes to fight."

"That's Falco for you."

The lull drifted off to silence, then Varro thought he heard a light snore from Gallio. He continued to stare up, imagining the pain of a flogging. Would his father hear about his disgrace? Would it harm him in anyway? They were in the same legion, but not even in the same class of soldier. Many triarii trained the young velites and hastati, but Varro had not seen his father since they parted at the eastern gate. Presumably he was in the same camp here in Brundisium, which was large but not enough for his father to vanish.

He might have fallen asleep in his wondering, but in the next instant Optio Latro was shouting through the door of the barracks.

"Are you waiting for an invitation from the tribune himself? Get out here now!"

Varro lurched, feeling a hot ember drop into his stomach. He bolted upright, but as a top bunk man he had to wait for those below to exit first. A thin light spilled in from the door, lighting a knife shape into the bunk room. The men of his contubernium flitted through it as they left. Falco sat at the edge of his bed, rubbing his face. He was the last out, finally allowing Varro space to drop down.

They stacked all their training gear in the front room. Huge wicker shields and a stack of wooden training swords were all they owned now. In time, this room would store all their gear. Varro wondered how any of it would fit in such a confined space. He waited his turn to lace his hobnailed sandals, then fell out with the others.

Morning was a bare white stripe leading into a clear orange haze. A half-moon was still visible in the sky. Yet all around the hastati of Varro's century were lining up for a morning inspection by their two centurions. Optio Latro, it seemed, had been detailed to Varro alone.

"I've filed my charges already," Latro said, smiling in front of Varro. "You're to be flogged. The centurions want to see you first before they decide how many lashes. After that, you'll get your gear and join us on the march."

"Yes, sir!" Varro shouted and stared straight ahead. He hoped the flogging would render him unconscious, though doubtless Latro knew a way to revive him before the march.

Each century had a centurion in charge and an optio as a

second. Two centuries formed into a maniple that would work side by side in battle. Varro had not much interacted with either centurion. His own centurion was named Protus and the other was Drusus. They seemed remote and too high up the command chain to bother with him. As he watched the two officers now, dressed only in gray tunics though wearing their short swords, he realized they must be too busy to pay attention to young recruits who were unlikely to survive their first day of combat. Varro did not even count himself likely to live out this day.

When Latro went to report to the centurions, Varro shot Falco a dark look. He seemed unconcerned, standing at the far end of the line and dreamily scanning the field between barrack houses. Panthera stood next to him like a parent nervous for the behavior of an overactive child. There was truth in that image, Varro thought.

"I'm sure it'll be fine," Gallio whispered, standing beside him. "Probably just wants to scare you."

"Then he's done a fine job of it."

All eight soldiers of the contubernium stood at attention while line after line of others were dismissed to prepare for the day ahead. At last, Latro had caught up to the centurions and pointed toward Varro. Both offered curt nods, and one broke away with Latro while the other continued inspections.

"Here he comes," Varro said. Sweat was already trickling down the back of his neck. The morning was not so hot, but his skin was already aflame with fear.

Centurion Drusus was a squat man with thick muscles and a violent white scar running up his right arm. He seemed bored and irritated. His black eyes looked through the men arrayed before him.

"Sir, this is the culprit, Marcus Varro. Caught him fighting, sir."

"Fighting with himself, Optio? Who was the other?"

Latro's face shaded red, and Varro wished he had the courage to smile. Instead, he stared ahead.

"Caius Falco, this one, sir."

The centurion looked between them.

"And who was the aggressor?"

The question seemed pointed at Varro, and he was not sure if he should risk an answer. But in the next moment, he had no need.

"It was me, sir. I own total responsibility for all the trouble."

Falco had stepped forward, keeping rigid attention.

"That's not what I saw." Optio Latro drew up to Falco. "Are you calling your officer a liar?"

"Let him speak, Optio." The centurion looked to Varro. "Is that true? Was he the aggressor?"

"It was both of us really, sir."

"Shut up, Varro!" Falco shouted. "It's my responsibility, sir. Flog me, sir. Varro is an idiot."

The centurion clasped both hands behind his back and raised his chin.

"Very well, Caius Falco, you are sentenced to ten lashes, reduced to five for making this easy. But don't mistake me for a kind man. The next time I will not ask for details but will double the lashes for both of you. And I'll remind you that to break the same rule three times is grounds for execution. You've got one more fight each before the next one sees you dead. Understood?"

"Yes, sir!" Falco and Varro shouted together.

Centurion Drusus looked Varro over.

"You get one week of barley and water only. If I find you've been fed anything better, I'll have the entire contubernium flogged to death."

Varro repeated his acknowledgement.

"Let's get this done before we march. It should encourage the men."

Latro glared at Varro but turned to Falco, grabbing him by the arm.

"Five lashes. Aren't you the lucky one?"

Falco stumbled out of line, towed along behind the optio toward the center of the field. Varro and the others stood at attention, never being dismissed.

"Why would he do that?" Varro asked aloud. "It makes no sense."

"It was the truth," Panthera said. "I saw all of it and he hit you first."

"But I hit him while you held him. I was equally at fault."

"Then be glad he's taking the punishment for you," Gallio said with a laugh. "A week of barley and water is hard, but it's not going to leave a mark forever like Falco will have."

He watched Falco being dragged toward a post set up toward the end of the open area between barracks. He had wondered at this, and figured it was used for sword practice. But now he noted the iron rungs and the ropes. Latro had summoned the help of another to tie Falco to the post. He had removed his tunic, leaving him stark naked. His buttocks shined in the morning light.

"Do they have to shame him like that?" Varro asked. "That's not right."

"Sure it is," Gallio said. "If they lash him with his shirt on, it'll get stuck in his wounds and go bad."

"Stuck in his wounds? How bad is a flogging? It's just five lashes."

Gallio narrowed his small eyes at him. He was shorter and wider than Varro, with dark skin and hair. No matter the lighting conditions, he always squinted as if looking into the sun.

"You're in for an education this morning."

The two centurions and Latro conferred behind Falco, who hung his head as he awaited his sentence. Varro felt a pang of sympathy. He seemed so pale and fragile, so incredibly young. He had hated Falco and had endured so much at his hands. Only a day ago he would have thought a flogging was the least Falco deserved. But to see him naked, head lowered in humiliation, was plain cruelty. He was suffering this fate because Varro had broken his vow. This was terrible.

"Gather around!" Latro shouted to the men of the century. The order was not strictly needed, as most were gathering of their own accord.

Varro drew his breath and joined the gathered. He arrived at the edge of the assembled men and paused at the back. He wanted to hide from Falco. But he could not be such a coward. He forced his way to the front so he could witness this unobstructed.

"Caius Falco likes fighting," Optio Latro shouted to the assembled soldiers. "You were all told the rules the very first day of your training. No fighting in the ranks. Save it for the enemy. Ten lashes for Caius Falco, reduced to five for compliance with the investigation. Take a good look, boys. Next time you think of fighting, think of this."

Centurion Protus, the actual commander of their century, handed Latro a long, black whip then stepped back to join his fellow Drusus. Varro's hands chilled at the optio's loving familiarity with it. He coiled it into his hands and turned to Falco. The rest of the soldiers, Varro included, instinctively backed away.

Latro raised the whip so that it reared like a striking cobra, then released with a whistling crack.

The lash snapped across Falco's naked back, ripping a bright red cut through his pale skin. He crashed forward onto the post and screamed.

"One," Latro counted.

He coiled up the whip. Young soldiers of the two centuries stood in utter silence as Falco moaned. Varro's fists tightened and he clenched his teeth.

The whip hissed and cracked again. Falco hugged the post and screamed. A second line of bright blood appeared on Falco's back, forming a bloody cross.

"Two."

Another snap, this time across Falco's lower back, and he collapsed against the post. Yet he had been bound so that he would remain upright even if he passed out.

"Three."

The next two lashes thundered out in rapid succession, the first tearing a bloody line from shoulder to hip. The second scored the backs of both Falco's legs. Latro gave a small smile at that one. It was a malicious strike to spread the pain all over Falco's back.

He turned around, collecting his whip into his hands.

"I could do that all day. But we've got a march planned. I want all of you worms back here in full gear. Hurry."

Latro cracked his whip over the heads of the soldiers, causing everyone to jump. The centurions laughed but chided Latro for his antics.

Varro did not move with the others. Falco hung on the post, blood pouring out of his cuts. He rushed forward, but Latro stopped him.

"Got wax balls in your ears? Go get your gear."

"But sir, he's hurt."

"That was the point," Latro said, shoving Varro back. "Get your gear and get Falco's too."

Centurion Protus, not the one who passed the sentence, interrupted.

"Actually, let him take Falco to the hospital. The two might settle their differences."

"Falco can march, sir." Latro seemed like a child who had his toy sword snatched away.

"Not with that lash to the legs. You were sloppy, Optio. Besides, a march now would be fatal. If we had wanted to execute him, we'd have just done so." Protus addressed Varro directly. "Take him to the infirmary, get your gear, then catch up to your contubernium."

Varro acknowledged the order, ignored Latro staring at him, then went to untie Falco.

The knots had bit into his wrists and tightened. He thought of cutting him free, but then figured he might be flogged himself for wasting rope. Nothing in this damned army did not come with a threat of violence behind it.

Falco moaned. His eyes were tightly closed, and blood from his shoulder had splashed across his cheek. His face was pressed to the post.

"Hang on. I'll get you down."

He picked at the knots until they loosened. Falco himself was like one of his sister's dolls. Once released he flopped into a pile.

"Can you stand? I can help you."

Falco opened his eyes, looking far more alert than Varro would have guessed.

"Latro still here?" he whispered.

"No, they've all gone. Are you all right? Does it hurt?"

"Of course it fucking hurts, you stupid shit. But I can't feel my back right now. Help me up to the infirmary. At least I get to sit out that stupid march."

Hoisting Falco to his feet might have been a struggle a month ago. But now Varro surprised himself with his own strength. He hooked Falco under his shoulder to support him. Hot blood rolled off his body to merge with Varro's sweat.

"Don't forget my tunic," Falco said.

"I can't get it without dropping you. Just forget it. I'll bring it to you later."

While Falco belittled his pain as they limped toward the hospital, Varro realized it was mostly an act. The cuts were deep and the blood flowed readily. Falco hissed and flinched, but just growled at any attempt to console him along the way. Finally, Varro just dragged him along without another word.

The doctor at the hospital did not even raise a brow at the naked, bleeding man Varro presented.

"He's been flogged, sir," Varro said, feeling stupid for stating the obvious. What else should he say?

"Quite so," the doctor said. "Over there, please."

Varro helped shuffle Falco to a cot by the side of the room. One other man lay at the far end, on his side and facing the wooden wall.

"All right, the doctor will take you from here." Varro examined the cuts. The red lines were not all broken skin, but blood streaked out all along the length where the flesh had been torn away.

"Thanks."

Varro kneeled beside him so their eyes were level.

"Why did you do it? At the very least, we both should've been flogged."

Falco stared at him. His heavy brow shaded his eyes, revealing only faint points of reflected light.

"I had to take the punishment. You'd just fold up like a fucking lily and die. Your parents would never forgive me."

"Thank you, Falco."

The words felt as if someone else had spoken them. Yet he just met Falco's dark stare, who gave a barely perceptible nod.

He left Falco on the cot with his blood running over his sides to drip to the floor. On the way out, he addressed the doctor who sat at a desk reading a clay table.

"Sir, please see to him soon. He is bleeding badly. I'd hate for his condition to worsen."

He left to find his gear and join the march.

10

The soldier stepped into his punch, crushing the metal boss of his shield into his opponent's face. Varro cringed, feeling a tingle of empathy through his own teeth. The soldier staggered, dropping his shield out of position. His bronze helmet wobbled on his head as he spit blood from his mouth.

The spray of red elicited cheers from the rest of the hastati. One hundred twenty soldiers of the maniple lined the edge of the training ground. Some raised their fists in triumph, and others hid their faces in disappointment. The four officers, two centurions and two optios, sat on stools in the shade. Latro leaned forward on his knees. Even from this distance, Varro could see the bloodlust in his face. The two centurions sat with their arms folded, but Drusus stared off at a point beyond their field.

The victorious soldier, wielding his short sword, stabbed at his exposed opponent. Yet he skirted away, only his tunic tearing from the point.

An amazed cry went up from the spectators. Gallio, who stood at Varro's left, snorted like a mad boar and raised both arms in victory. Falco, who stood to his right, moaned.

"Come on," he said. "You're a head taller, you bastard. Finish him."

Varro said nothing, but watched the duel with interest.

Two months of training were on display. No, not training, physical torment. But Varro admitted he was stronger and sturdier than ever before. After practicing with wicker shields and lead-filled training swords, the real shield and sword were feather light. They were also conditioned to wear armor, which was a bronze pectoral, a simple bronze square over the chest. Soldiers of more means wore muscled chest pieces.

Varro adjusted his own square pectoral as he watched.

The beaten man now slipped around his enemy's shield. Blood flowed out his nose and he wobbled on his feet. But he had not yielded. He had been stunned and caught out of step. Now he returned the punch and stab.

He succeeded where his opponent had failed. Shorter than his enemy, most men had laughed at their match. Varro did not, for he saw himself and Falco in these two combatants. But now the shorter man showed his larger opponent's reach meant nothing.

His punch folded the other man to the side, exposing his ribs. His bronze pectoral meant nothing now. The stab landed on the protruding ribcage. The taller man cried out and collapsed atop his shield. His opponent followed him down, controlling his strike to not kill the other. Yet he scored the flesh and drew dark blood. The fallen soldier's helmet rolled away into the grass.

Gallio's mad snorting only worsened as he danced as if he had won the duel.

Falco spit on the ground, then shouted over Varro's head.

"Shut up, you fucking sow."

Gallio either did not hear or else ignored Falco.

The victor raised his sword to the centurions and the optio. The officers clapped and nodded approval. Then he bent over his defeated foe and leaned to whisper to him.

"Even without coin, it feels good to win that bet," Gallio said. Regulations strictly forbid gambling on the outcome of these matches. These were not games, but the culmination of training. After a duel, win or lose, the officers considered formal training complete. They said you could learn much from either result.

"Luck," Falco muttered.

Varro did not agree with that assessment. The shorter man relied less on physical strength and more on cunning. Being smaller, he had to train to fight with his wits while his bigger enemy trusted his strength. He noted the lesson, as it might one day save his life.

The rest of the contubernium lined up beyond Falco. Panthera, who seemed to have appointed himself as Falco's keeper, was next in line. The rest spread out into the long ring of hastati. Varro had developed a friendship with all in his contubernium to various degrees. Only Falco seemed unable to fit with the others. Strangely, he had adopted Varro as his only so-called friend.

Such a thing could not be, for Varro did not feel friendship for him. He was not sure what their relationship was after Falco's flogging. But something had changed.

The two combatants left the field arm in arm. Despite the viciousness, neither seemed to bear ill-will. The centurions claimed that after these duels your opponent would become your dearest friend. As dubious as that statement felt, the dozen fights he had watched seemed to bear it out. Could such violence lead to a better understanding between men? Varro wondered.

"Your turn has got to come soon," Falco said, as if reading his thoughts. Across the field, the officers conferred with each other between matches, consulting wax tablets and scanning the soldiers.

"I am ready for it," Varro said. "There's no choice."

Falco laughed. "Just a few months ago I was pounding your

face off at Old Man Pius's barley field. What are you going to do now? Your life isn't in danger. So you're just going to hide behind your shield until the enemy gets you. I'll be watching right here, laughing until my sides split."

"I have to fight, or Optio Latro will have me flogged to death. My life is in danger."

He shifted a glance to Falco, who fell silent at the mention of flogging. For all his bravado, Varro suspected Falco never wanted to experience it again. While recovered, he was still unable to sleep on his back even now.

"They'll pick the signifier from the winners," Panthera said. "So give it your best. Maybe you'll carry our standard."

Varro had not heard of this, though a signifier had yet to be chosen. As he waited for the officers to summon the next pairs, he searched beyond the ring of hastati. The more experienced soldiers watched from a distance. Men clustered in the shadows of buildings out of the noon heat. He wondered if his father was among them and if he could see. Somehow the thought of his father watching made him uncomfortable. It was as if his great-grandfather were watching. He could still see his bulging eyes, the veins straining at his temples as he grabbed Varro's arm.

Promise me, Marcus, swear to it before all the gods and all our ancestors. You will not live the life of violence that I have lived. You must not, cannot, become what I was.

What had his great-grandfather been? By all other accounts, he was a hero of the legions. But by his own account, he had been a monster and committed acts of intense personal shame. Varro had accepted this without question. Now that he had taken his first steps along the path his great-grandfather had walked, he wondered at the exact nature of those acts.

"Marcus Varro!"

Optio Latro stood at the center of the field, searching for then finding Varro. He wore his chain shirt over his tunic and had his short sword at his right hip. In his only acknowledgement of the heat, his head was bare. Though the centurions seated in the shade wore their helmets with feathered crests.

Falco shoved him forward. "I can tell the future! Get out there, lily. But don't fucking embarrass us, though I'm ready to carry you to the hospital. I owe you the favor."

"Go on, Varro," Panthera said, clapping his hands. "You'll do great."

"Don't get killed," Gallio said. "No offense, but I'm betting with Falco on this. You don't have it in you."

He gathered his shield and helmet, which rested against the barracks wall behind him. Slipping the bronze helmet on, he pulled the scalloped cheek pieces tight. He ran his finger along the leather thong that clamped the helmet to his head. Sweat already bloomed under it.

He glanced at his companions as he walked to the center of the field. They raised their fists in encouragement and shouted his name. Falco's heavy brow shadowed his eyes as he grinned.

"Keep that shield up," he said, then mimicked cowering behind one.

Encouraging cheers and polite applause followed him out, as all had done for every combat. No man here was an actual enemy. Optio Latro stood with his hand on his hip and his vine cane in the other. After Varro presented himself, Latro gave him a sneer.

"I suppose you think you're a regular soldier now? Well, you haven't died. So I'll credit you there. But time enough for that yet."

Varro did not answer and adjusted his oblong shield. It nearly covered his entire body, being concave and fashioned from birch wood. He tightened his fingers on the leather-wrapped iron grip. It was covered in lamb felt and reinforced at top and bottom with iron. When he ordered it, the smith asked if he wanted it painted for an extra fee. He had it painted green and white.

He admitted the shield made him feel safe. It was a heavy wooden wall between him and the enemy. For today's purposes, he only needed to stagger his opponent and force him to yield. The shield could do most of that work without undue violence to a man who was only fighting because he was ordered.

At his right hip hung his short sword, the gladius. Suspended with a clever four-belt system, he could draw it without ever exposing himself from behind the shield. Like shield and armor, this was his own sword bought with his own coin. It was sturdy and sharp, and Varro took pleasure in its maintenance. Unlike the other soldiers, he would only use it sparingly. The guilt of injuring a fellow soldier would tax his already strained spirit.

He wanted to win the match. He did not want to break his vow. Both seemed possible, renewing his confidence. He set his hand on his sword while Optio Latro scanned the other hastati.

"Ah, there's an excellent match for you," he said. He extended his vine cane across the field. "Nonus Flavinus, come forward."

Across the field, another soldier like Varro detached from the line of onlookers. His companions handed him his shield, then he donned his helmet. They patted him on the back and cheered, then he ambled out into the field to join Varro at the center.

He smiled, but Nonus did not return it. Of course, they were about to fight. Varro shook his head at his own foolishness. Nonus raised a shield unadorned with any decoration, remaining the off-white of the skin cover. He had a dark complexion and a short, deep scar beneath his left eye. His face was nicked with shaving scars, but otherwise glowed with youth. Yet he looked resigned, defeated even. Had this been a different situation, Varro would have wanted to cheer him.

Now he had to flatten this man and get him to yield as soon as possible.

"You two know the rules," Latro said. "First to yield or to take a serious injury loses."

Nonus stared hard at Latro before nodding.

"Let's not have a serious injury," Varro said. Levity was out of place, and his own smile vanished. Nonus did not even look at him, instead ground his hobnailed sandals into the dirt.

"Yes," Latro said, looking to Nonus. "No serious injuries. Now, when I give the word, you begin."

Varro stepped to the center of the field, and Nonus followed him. Yet he seemed to be looking more at Latro than him. The officers were all behind Varro, and he could not see if perhaps Latro was mocking him. It seemed unlikely, but he stared with such intensity, Varro wondered. Perhaps this was a mental game designed to unbalance him.

Now they squared off, swords still in their leather scabbards and shields raised. The sun gleamed off Nonus's bronze helmet. His eyes settled on Varro's. They were dark and void of hope, like a man facing death.

Nonus must know Varro's weakness, and so preyed on his conflicted conscience. While his companions had a vague idea of his vow, only Falco knew the depth of it. Had he said something to Latro, who then passed this on to Nonus? That had to be the cause.

In his wandering thought, he did not realize Optio Latro had called the start of the fight.

Nonus leaped forward, shield up. The crowd around the field cheered. Varro, realizing he had to escape his own thoughts and concentrate on the fight, skittered back.

He pulled up his shield while drawing his gladius with an underhand grip. The blade scraped from the sheath and with practiced ease he rotated his hand, then drew back to aim its point at Nonus. The unrelenting drilling and practice rewarded him. When he first tried the technique, he had dropped his sword to the grass. Now it was firm in his grip as Nonus's shield swipe skimmed past him.

But Varro was on the wrong foot. Nonus had used his initiative well, and while drawing his own sword also dominated the battle space.

Another shield punch followed the first. Per their training, Varro had been expecting a follow-up sword thrust. But Nonus was not drilling. He was trying to win this duel.

The shield collided with his own, and the slam of the wooden bulwarks echoed over the field. As the first real blow of the fight, the onlookers hollered in delight. Varro could see nothing but Nonus and his dead eyes staring at him over the top of his shield. Sweat glistened on his face.

Varro pulled back and circled.

"Get on the attack!"

Falco's voice was clear above the others. Even in the heat of battle, having Falco cheer and encourage him chagrined him.

Nonus again struck with his shield. He seemed intent on battering Varro to the ground rather than trying to force submission at sword point. But now Varro was prepared and slipped back, then skirted to the flank.

With all the strength earned from drilling and marching, he exploded forward into Nonus's extended position.

His green and white shield, so heavy and sturdy, connected with Nonus's left shoulder. The boss thudded hard against flesh and Nonus gasped. He staggered to the side.

Cheers roared out, filling Varro with pride.

Before he knew better, his training took over. The gladius struck hard and fast. It was the automatic reaction of a thousand drills. The edge flashed as it flickered for Nonus's exposed side.

But Nonus had trained equally well. He swiped with his shield, batting the sword off course so its point sliced his tunic. Yet Varro felt it drag through flesh.

"Gods, I'm sorry!"

He blurted out the apology as automatically as he had made

the strike. Nonus had already backed up behind his shield, and Varro hoped he had not heard it.

They circled once more, and the drama of their confrontation drew ever louder cheers from the audience.

"It's not a fucking dance!"

Again Falco's voice dominated the others. He would make a fine centurion.

Nonus charged. Not the step-punch of their drills. But the charge of a mad bull, only with a massive shield before him. Varro thought to slip aside, but then decided he should brace. The indecision cost him.

With a heavy wooden crack, he was sailing backwards. The shorter but equally strong Nonus had plowed him over so he lay sprawled to the sky. Cheers and groans erupted from all sides.

Well, now all Nonus had to do was touch his gladius to Varro's gut and he would yield. Too bad he had not done better. Hopefully his father was not watching.

But the touch did not come.

He heard thudding footsteps, then a guttural snarl.

Nonus, eyes now gleaming with rage—or was it tears?—had dropped his shield and now held his gladius overhead with both hands. He was not striking for a submission. He was going to impale Varro to the ground.

The sword stuck down, and Varro froze in disbelief. He only jerked aside at the last instant. A massive thump to his chest pressed the air out of his lungs. But the bronze pectoral had turned Nonus's sword.

Shouts and cheers greeted the fresh development. Varro's vision turned brown from loss of breath, then darkened as Nonus fell over him. His body fell across Varro, pinning him.

"What are you doing?" he gasped. "Gods, I yield. Don't kill me."

He made to shove Nonus off, but he resisted. His breath smelled like sour wine, and Varro felt him scrabbling.

Then a hot pain pierced his side, followed by a wet heat spreading out across his back.

Varro cried out and bucked.

He had been stabbed in the side.

Nonus now sat back, staring hatefully into Varro's eyes. But Varro saw only his own blood on the pugio Nonus gripped in his hand.

"You fucking bastard!"

Varro kicked him off, then scrambled aside to regain his feet. Nonus rolled over, but was faster to recover.

Barreling into him, Varro stumbled back. But he clasped his arms around Nonus to haul him along. His helmet loosened and slipped forward over his brow.

The pugio struck up again, gliding along Varro's chest to carve a furrow from his left side to his just below his pectoral, which again stopped the progress of the blade.

He screamed out, a raw and angry cry. This was no duel. Nonus was trying to kill him.

Varro drove his knee into Nonus's face. He swung his arms around to arrest the pugio. The sharp blade pricked at him, but Varro controlled it enough to continue smashing Nonus's face. Knee after knee crashed into Nonus, gouging Varro's knee from colliding with the cheek plates. But soon the helmet popped out and fell between them.

Explosive cheers met the violence. Blood slicked Varro's side, mingling with the cut from Nonus's earlier wound. The world around him was going blurry. Voices were becoming sludgy and indistinct.

"Put him down, lily!"

Falco. Again Falco with the jeers.

Something tore open in Varro.

The pugio found him once more, slashing up and cutting his right forearm.

But Varro felt far away, as if watching it all from the sky.

He and Nonus were locked together, with Nonus wielding the only weapon. Varro hurled himself backward, using momentum to flip Nonus over and away.

Springing to his feet, he searched for a weapon. Nonus's shield was closest. He snatched it off the ground and stalked forward.

Nonus was already regaining his footing, spinning around to face Varro.

He swung the shield with both hands so that the iron reinforcement struck Nonus in the face. His head snapped back, spewing teeth and blood from his mouth. He collapsed onto the grass.

The cheers were like a rush of air passing over Varro. Nonus, who now lay flattened and vulnerable, stared skyward. The sun glared from his pectoral, which was flecked with Varro's blood. His broken-toothed mouth hung open.

And Varro was going to kill him.

He raised the shield in both hands, then slammed it down on Nonus's head. The shield shivered with the impact. His entire body flexed and he groaned. The roar of the crowd extinguished like a snuffed candle flame.

Varro raised the shield again. Blood covered Nonus's face, obscuring his features.

"You want to kill me? We'll see about that!"

The shield swept down, dragging against the wind.

But a blur from the left collided with Varro. The heavy hit tore at his wounds, setting them afire with pain. In the next instant, he stared at the grass, each blade like a forest tree in his vision. Nonus's shield spun away. Sandaled feet were rushing toward him.

Someone pulled him over.

He stared up into Falco's face, white and panicked.

"All right, lily, you've made your point. Don't need to kill him."

Varro blinked.

"Dear gods, Falco. What did I do?"

11

Varro lay on the hospital bunk, staring at the gloomy rafters above. It occurred to him that every room in the camp seemed the same. The buildings were all new and still smelled of fresh timber. Yet they were functional buildings, not meant to last and built to this degree just to keep soldiers occupied. It seemed a calculated monotony.

These were the musings Varro indulged during his rest in the hospital. He did not want to think too deeply about the day before.

He hoped to put it forever from his mind.

The doctor was a Greek. He spoke in a low, husky voice to his assistants. If Varro were motivated enough to turn his head, he guessed he would see three men in their clean gray tunics conferencing over some scroll or tablet. They seemed to spend more time reading than tending a patient. But he did not turn and remained staring up.

He wondered if the doctor, being Greek, was eager to defeat the Macedonians. They said King Philip occupied Athens and was a despicable person. Varro knew a smattering of Greek and wished he knew more than cliched phrases. Maybe the doctor could teach him more.

Anything to keep his mind off what he had done to Nonus.

His side still burned and was tight with the stitches he had received. The same for his forearm. That was more painful than getting the wound itself. In fact, the entire treatment hurt worse than all the cuts and blows he had sustained.

"That's because during a fight you are a different man," the doctor had explained. "You do not experience pain as your normal self. But once the battle is done and the normal Varro returns, then you feel everything keenly."

"Is it true that I become someone else?"

The doctor had just smiled. Varro hoped to blame his actions on another, even a fictional version of himself. But there was nowhere to hide from the facts.

He heard a knock on the open doorframe of the hospital. Varro recognized Optio Latro's voice, even if he could not hear what he said. The doctor mumbled with him. Varro heard phrases like "no mortal damage" and "light duty" interspersed with Latro's grunts. He also heard "not now" but couldn't guess at the context.

Then he heard the clop of hobnails on the wooden floor, and a shadow slipped through the low light to slide across Varro laying on his bed.

"No need to stand to attention," Latro said. "I understand you must rest."

Varro tilted his head toward Latro. His round, rugged head hovered against the dim ceiling. His blue eyes seemed to glow. He wore an expression that seemed an attempt at fatherly patience. To Varro, it looked like a wolf struggling to smile. The optio looked over Varro's bandaged side and arm.

"Thank you, sir." He tried to sound weaker than he felt. His head throbbed and his cuts burned, but otherwise he could run a race if the stitches would hold.

"I wanted to visit you. The doctor says you just need another day of rest, then you can resume light duty."

"Thank you, sir. I'm doing well here."

Latro nodded, then folded his hands behind his back. For once, he did not hold his vine cane. If he wanted to whip Varro, he'd have to use his bare hands. He puffed out his cheeks and raised his brows, then rocked on the balls of his feet.

"Wonderful, I'm glad you're doing well."

He looked over his shoulder. The doctor and two assistants watched, but at Latro's glance the two assistants fluttered away. The doctor sat at his desk, but did not leave.

A dark cloud seemed to cross Latro's face, but he returned to Varro with his half-formed smile.

"It's like this, Varro. I have to apologize to you."

"Sir?"

"I should've stopped that fight the moment Nonus stabbed you with his pugio. Only the gladius was authorized for that duel. But I let it carry on and you were seriously hurt. I, well, I blame myself for your condition."

"That is kind of you, sir." Varro was unsure what else he could say. His honest opinion was Latro enjoyed watching him get stabbed.

"Very well, then, I'll see you tomorrow."

"Sir, a moment, please."

Latro stopped in mid-turn, hands still clasped behind his back. He rotated to face Varro again, raising his brow.

"Sir, I was not the only one seriously injured. I fear I gravely wounded Nonus. I know he lost teeth and probably broke his jaw at the very least. But he was not taken to the hospital with me. What happened to him, sir?"

"He was executed."

Varro stared at Latro. A hint of satisfaction flickered across his face.

"Executed? When?"

"After you were taken away. Don't be so surprised. He tried to kill you. That was obvious to everyone, the centurions included. They passed sentence right there. Nonus and his contubernium were executed on the spot. Carried out by the rest of the century."

"His contubernium? Sir, it was just Nonus."

"And who equipped him for the duel?" Latro's authority crept back into his voice and his eyes narrowed. "An example must be made, and something as foul as Nonus's actions require the sternest penalty. You are responsible not only for your own actions, but those of your companions. Remember that well. If one of your fellows ever retreats from the enemy or falls asleep on guard duty, then you all suffer the consequences. That is the way of the army."

Varro's mouth slackened. He did not know Nonus or his contubernium. But now he recalled them cheering and sending him out to fight. Were they complicit in Nonus's actions enough to be executed? Varro doubted it.

Latro was again about to turn, when Varro stopped him.

"Why, sir?"

"Because these rules have been in place for generations, and they work.'"

"No, sir, I mean why did Nonus try to kill me? It makes no sense."

Latro's face seemed to blur, and he blinked before answering.

"I've no idea why he would attempt something so foolish. Maybe there was something between you?"

"Sir, I never met him except in passing. There was no reason—"

"Of course there was a reason, Varro. All madmen have a reason for their actions, just nothing that makes sense to anyone else. Nonus is dead. You've nothing to worry about any longer. Now, get your rest and I expect you to report for duty tomorrow."

Attempts at patience had ended. Latro seemed to grow taller and his eyes flashed with threat. Varro knew better than to say more and shrank into his bed. The optio stared at him a moment longer before stalking out of the hospital.

Varro glanced at the doctor, who grinned and shook his head.

Bed rest was a torment to him, not because he disliked idleness. After the months of ceaseless drilling and labor, rest was a gift of the gods. His thoughts and doubts ravaged him. Alone in the cool room, where only one other patient slept at the far end of the hospital, he had only thoughts for company.

He dozed a short time, before the doctor was again shaking him awake.

"You have a visitor," he said. "Though he shouldn't be here. So make it quick."

The doctor backed away and Varro tried to sit up, anticipating a visit from his father. His stitches pulled hard enough to persuade him to lie flat again. He wanted to be on his feet when his father arrived and not appear defeated as he so often had.

He turned to the sound of hobnails on the floor.

And his heart sank.

"Well, look at you. Looks like you fell on a pile of knives."

Falco stood with arms folded, his fresh muscles bulging in that pose. He wore a plain off-white tunic and sandals, no sword or pectoral.

"What? You look disappointed."

Varro sighed and lowered his head to the soft pillow. He looked back to the ceiling and the shadowy rafters.

"I'm surprised to see you. Are you here to laugh at me? The doctor is an officer and he'll see what you're up to."

"You know, everything you say to me starts with an insult. Then you wonder why I want to break your nose."

Varro waved away the accusation. "The doctor says you shouldn't be here. What do you want?"

"I wanted to see how you are doing. Last I saw, you were a little crazy. Crazier than I'd ever seen you before."

Varro rubbed his face, his stitched forearm generating a burning pain.

"I would give anything to undo yesterday. If I had just controlled myself better. But it was unlike anything I've ever felt. I had no control."

"That's your opinion," Falco said, forcing a spot to sit at the edge of Varro's bed. "But I think you'd be dead if you didn't fight back. Nonus got you good in the side. Let's have a look at it."

"Are you my doctor now?"

"Gods, I just want to look at it." Falco shifted and forced over Varro's arm. He didn't protest, as to resist would only cause pain. His arm bent over his chest as Falco examined him. "Well, it's all wrapped up. Can't see a fucking thing. Are you going to live?"

"Are you going to my funeral if I die?"

"Of course, but you will not die." Falco set his arm down, realizing that he was holding the injured one. He winced at the realization. When had Falco cared what hurt he did?

They sat together in awkward silence. Varro did not know what he could trust to Falco. If he shared all in his mind, would he later blurt it out to Latro or somehow use it against him? Was this some new play by Falco? Since fighting would bring them trouble, maybe now he would try to abuse him in other ways. If that was his ploy, Varro was ready for it. He was stronger in mind and character than Falco. Just let him try to play games.

"I'm glad you're all right," Falco said. "Scared the piss out of me when Nonus stuck you like that. I thought it might've popped your liver. But I don't even know what side that's on."

Varro stifled a laugh. At first Falco seemed confused, but then he chuckled. He still smiled like a brutish animal, but for once it seemed genuine. He and Falco were smiling together.

"Why did he do it?" Varro asked. "Did anyone ask before he was—done away with?"

"That's a civil way of saying it. After they carted away you, Optio Latro and the centurions were quick to deal with Nonus. He wasn't the problem. You about killed him anyway when you bashed him with his own shield."

Varro pressed his eyes shut, but Falco continued in his casual description of the punishment.

"Trouble came from the rest of his contubernium. That lot were surprised to be dragged into it. But Latro got the century after them. Couple of them ran but were caught. Anyway, the centurions screamed at us for about an hour while Nonus just bled away. Then they made him sit up, stripped off his clothes, and did the same for his friends. We were all given clubs. It's like they had them ready for us. Anyway, we lined up in two rows and they all had to run between us as we beat them. I don't think I killed any of them, but I knocked a few teeth out. Sad business all around. They were crying, begging to live. Except Nonus. Latro finished what you started, and just busted his head open in one go. None of the others reached the end of the line."

Varro swallowed hard, trying not to see Nonus's bloodied face staring emptily at the sky.

"What have we gotten into, Falco?"

He shrugged. "Not like we had a choice. But now you see what your little peace plan is going to get you. You've got to fight and kill and be the meanest bastard you can imagine. Or else you're going to be running down a row of former friends who'll beat you to death. Don't make me be one of them, Varro. I'll be fucking angry if you do."

"Seems it won't just be me, either," Varro said.

"That's right. So if you're going to show your belly to the enemy, make sure you die. You can't run away anymore."

"Yes, thanks for cheering me up. Don't know why I expected cheer from you, anyway."

"Just telling it to you straight. Your way of peace is a problem for all of us now, Panthera, Gallio, and the rest."

"I will do my duty. I told you before, I'm not a coward." Varro sighed and shifted on his bed to draw closer to Falco. He lowered his voice, looking toward the other patient across the hospital room.

"Why did Nonus want to kill me? It makes no sense. Have you or any of the others asked yourselves?"

Falco blinked and seemed to think, then he snapped his fingers.

"How about because you cut him first, you idiot? You should've had better control, but you sliced his ribs. That probably got him worked up. Some men just need a little pain and insult to carry them over the line. And since all we do every day is train to kill, does it surprise you Nonus lost control?"

"That's not it," Varro said. He shifted closer, lowering his voice so the doctor and his assistants would not hear if they were close by. For now, it seemed except for the sleeping patient, they were alone.

"Nonus was acting strange before the fight. He looked defeated, like he knew he was going to die. Now that I think of it, he looked guilty more than defeated. He had tears in his eyes when he was trying to kill me. That's not rage, Falco. That's regret, remorse, or something like it."

"You think Latro put him up to it?"

Varro fell back on his bed, eyes wide and mouth open.

"So you think so as well?"

"No, but that's the next obvious thing you'd say. Listen, I know you think I'm a brute. You've told me enough. Everyone thinks that. But I am smart enough to know what's going on under my own nose. I have common sense. I don't hold noble phil-os-o-phies like you."

"Falco, please don't sing it. It's aggravating."

"Rather the point, friend. Anyway, I don't think Latro likes you, but it's a bit much to say he'd force another soldier to murder you in front of everyone."

"Then why else would Nonus do that? He and Latro seemed to have had some understanding. I didn't think much of it then, but now I just keep seeing it over and over. That look between them."

"Varro, you went fucking crazy. I wouldn't trust your memory. Listen, I will not say anything. But you better keep your opinions about Latro deep inside your peaceful heart. Not even a hint to the others, either. After what we saw yesterday, they'll turn you in for treason rather than risk getting their heads pulped. Anyone would."

"But not you?"

"How long have we known each other? You piss me off every time we speak, but that doesn't mean I want to beat you to death."

Varro rubbed his face and let his palms cover it as he spoke.

"In one day my entire world has changed. I've become a killer, and you're acting like we're friends." He dropped his hands and narrowed his eyes at Falco. "Are you acting like this because you're glad to see me break my vow?"

Falco stared at him, his dark eyes searching his face and his heavy brow furrowed.

"Don't break your vow. You'd become someone else if you did. But you can keep it without letting everyone walk over you."

He then looked away toward the door.

"I've got to go. Remember, not a word about Latro."

"All right, but my father said he was trouble even before I joined the army. I believe him."

"Ah, your father, that's right." Falco stood, straightening his tunic. "I heard your father fell ill. I'd actually thought he'd be here with you."

"My father's sick?" Varro sat up, ignoring the tug and burn from his stitches. "When did that happen?"

"Yesterday. I heard he fell, collapsed, and he had to go to the hospital. That's why I expected to find both of you here. But I guess it wasn't that bad after all. Rumors, you know."

Varro stared through Falco. Yesterday, the same day Nonus tried to kill him.

12

Varro found light duty as taxing to his injuries as the regular duties the rest of his fellows carried out. The senior officers had called Optio Latro to spend more time with them. But he had been certain to detail the work of his beloved hastati, particularly Varro. He now stood watch at the northern gate. He discovered how taxing standing guard could be on his feet and knees, and the gash on his side. The weight of his bronze pectoral did not help either. He and Gallio had the early morning shift, and both were now looking forward to ending the day. More than anything, he yearned to remove his bronze helmet. The under-chin thong scratched his neck.

Gallio stood on one side of the gate in the stockade wall, flanking the dusty track that flowed to the center of camp. Varro stood opposite. The gate was open between them to allow traffic to flow unimpeded throughout the day. Various forage teams were out to bring back firewood and game. Some had already filtered back to camp and had to provide passwords even when they were the same Roman soldiers that had left only hours before.

Varro did not question procedures. As the centurions had

drilled into him, procedure makes the army function and turns stupid farmers such as himself into the fist of Rome's might.

He and Gallio stared toward the distant woods. He had never been this far south before. His world had been Rome and the surrounding farmland. Here were fewer hills and more wood-lands, which made him feel hemmed in. Brundisium sat close to the ocean and he could smell the salt on the air. Soon, he would have more of it, as they would embark for Macedonia within the week.

Since exiting the hospital, Varro could not get more information on his father. He had apparently never entered the hospital. But no one could offer him other information. Being stationed at the gates gave him a chance to speak to many people, but not for any length. They were all in transit.

His father should have sent word to him at the least. Was that such an effort? They were in different centuries, but the same legion. He could not find an excuse for his father that did not grate on him.

He leaned on his pilum, the heavy spear he would cast at an enemy before closing for battle. The coincidence of his father's illness with Nonus's attempt on his life seemed connected, however tenuous. He needed to know if his father might have been poisoned. It seemed far-fetched and senseless. Why would anyone want to kill either of them? But Varro had a hunch, and it would not leave him.

"That whole thing with Nonus is still bothering you?" Gallio asked. He leaned against the inside of the gate, long yellow and red painted shield resting against his leg. "You've not said much since getting out of the hospital."

"Of course it bothers me," he said. "The stitches aren't even out yet."

"When will they take them out?"

"Before we leave for Illyria."

Gallio nodded. He blinked uncontrollably, a habit as irritating as the grunting sounds he made when overly excited. But Varro liked him best among all the contubernium.

"Why do you think he did it?" He knew Falco was right in warning him off from mentioning his thoughts about Latro. But he had to know if anyone else agreed with him.

"I've thought about that a little, and I just don't know. You must have offended him somehow. I know you say you never met him, but maybe you don't remember."

"Before the army I lived on a farm. The people I saw on a regular basis couldn't be more than a dozen. I couldn't have offended him or anyone he knew. So why would he try to kill me?"

"I think it's like Falco said. You cut him first and he probably wanted revenge for it, but just got carried away."

Varro nodded. The desire to ask about Latro burned through his teeth. They both stared off at the distance, where a returning foraging party appeared. Neither spoke as they observed the foragers, which seemed as nothing more than white spots from this distance.

"Say, Varro, I know you have this vow about not hurting people."

"Don't worry for it." Varro waved off Gallio's comment. "I'll do my duty when the time comes. I am not a coward."

"Well, actually, I wasn't going to say that. I was going to say that even though you claim to be all about peace, so far you've really been the opposite."

"What do you mean? You think I'm a bully like Falco?"

Gallio held up both hands for peace. "No, no. Everyone likes you well enough. But you have a temper. It seems to take a lot to bring it out, but when it's out...."

Varro waited and Gallio searched the distance as if the right words could be pulled from the trees.

"When you get mad, you get crazy. I've seen it twice from you.

I'm just saying, when we do have to fight, I don't think I'm worried about you not fighting. I'm worried about you not stopping."

"Gods, what has this place done to me?" Varro touched his forehead, bowing his head in shame. "I spent my entire childhood restraining myself from violence of any sort. Even to the point of not fighting back when I was beaten. I used to control myself, but no longer. This army is training me to become an animal."

"It's not a bad thing, for a soldier anyway. But maybe that's why you're finding it hard to control. You're finally allowed to act. You know, if you told me I can't ever eat cheese, then that's all I'd want. The moment I got some, I'd stuff it down without a thought."

There was sense to Gallio's observation, and Varro decided he would mediate on this. For he wanted to keep his vow to his beloved great-grandfather, but not bring himself and others to grief for it. Yet as he pondered this, he noticed something unusual about the forage party. He stood straighter and peered into the late noon sun.

"Gallio, do they look like they're running to you?"

"Yes, and not from being excited to return home."

Foraging parties comprised six men each, and Varro did not count how many had gone out that morning. This party had five men that he could see. They ran at a loping pace in a tight pack.

"Are they running from an attack?" Gallio asked, picking up his shield and spear. Varro did the same. "Should we sound the alarm?"

"If they were fleeing an enemy, some of them should be ahead of the others. Everyone would run for their lives. But they're keeping together."

"Well, that's true. Smart of you, Varro." Gallio shaded his eyes with his right hand. "Say, they're carrying someone."

Varro realized what he had seen as a bulky soldier resolved into one man with another over his shoulder. The rest of the forage team paced him, one keeping his hand on the carried soldier.

"Get an officer here," Varro said. "Whatever this is, it can't be good."

Gallio raced back into the camp while Varro awaited the team's arrival. His heart pounded against his ribs. He hoisted his shield and readied his pilum.

As they drew closer, one of their number pulled ahead of the others. He waved his hands overhead, shouting for attention.

All the foragers went into the field in their armor and helmets, but carried neither pilum nor scutum, as both would be unwieldy for their assigned task. Neither were they in enemy territory to require full gear. But to see the face of the soldier running toward Varro now, he reconsidered the dangers.

"He's been shot! We need a doctor! Hurry!"

Varro's first instinct was to follow instructions. But he realized his duty required otherwise of him. He took his gate and swung it shut, then moved to where Gallio had stood.

"What are you doing?" The lead man's shout was breathless and full of frustration. He slowed his run, as he was now a dozen yards from the gate.

"Password?" Varro knew it was foolish to ask. But what if this were some trick of Latro's getting him in trouble? He could then flog him to death and not have to answer for it. So he clung to procedures.

"What? He's fucking dying!"

Varro began to swing the gate door shut.

"Eagle! Eagle! Now get the doctor, you shit!"

Satisfied that Latro could not hold him responsible for neglect, he swung the gate open again. The wood dragged and stuttered across the track. To his relief, Gallio was arriving with a centurion and two other soldiers. The officer's grumbling complaints rolled ahead of his charge down the track.

At the same time, the forage party staggered through the gates. The lead runner followed behind them. He glared at Varro. As was always his impulse, he wanted to apologize. Yet he had carried out his orders and did nothing wrong. He felt bad for the injured man, but this soldier needed to obey the rules as much as he did. So he returned the glare, and he enjoyed that the red-faced solider looked away.

The team laid out the wounded man on the track. His helmet was missing, but his square pectoral covered his chest. His eyes were closed as if sleeping peacefully and his chin had a fresh cut from shaving. Compared to the flushed and sweaty condition of his teammates, he seemed inspection-ready.

But a white-fletched arrow protruded from his side, just beneath the pectoral. The shaft had sunk to the fletching. It seemed someone might have shot him while extending his arm. His light brown tunic showed only the slightest tinge of blood around the wound.

His companions surrounded him. These were not young velites or hastati. This soldier was one of the triarii, who even with their age and experience still owned the same duties of any other soldier. His peaceful face was framed with short brown hair that had been lightened with considerable gray. The bags and wrinkles around his closed eyes showed his years.

The centurion shoved his way to the man and kneeled beside him. His red-crested helmet caught the sun as he placed his fingers on the wounded man's neck.

"He's dead. Not a surprise," the centurion said. His voice was gruff, lacking any warmth or emotion. His crest fluttered as he shook his head. "Who did this?"

"Sir, a brigand ambushed us."

The centurion rose to his feet. "And you bastards better tell me he's dead."

Varro noticed what the senior officer must have noticed. None of the foragers showed any sign of a fight. Only the one who had carried the body of their companion had a dribble of fresh blood on his shoulder and back. The five soldiers all snapped to attention. The man who had addressed Varro at the gate now answered.

"Sir, we could not determine the shooter's location. Two more arrows were shot, but Tanicus was wounded. We beat the area, but found no trace. We thought to save our companion first, sir."

The centurion's face darkened and he curled his lip at the one who had made the report.

"Five veterans and you come running back here because they shot one of you. We'll have a discussion about this with your centurions later. For now, you take me back to the scene. We're going to find this brigand before the sun goes down."

All five men shouted their acknowledgement.

The centurion began commanding the soldiers who followed him, issuing orders for more soldiers and a stretcher team to carry off the body of the man called Tanicus. Varro watched from his post at the gate. He wondered if Tanicus had any family, and what would happen to them with his passing. Did he have sons serving here just like him and his father?

"You two are finished with your guard shift," the centurion said. "You're with me."

"Yes, sir!"

But both Varro and Gallio shared a suffering glance. Varro did not dare indicate he was restricted to light duty. This centurion had the face of a mad bull, with eyes that bulged to enhance his general demeanor of rage. He would break Varro over his knee before he allowed him off for his wounds.

Until now, Varro had never witnessed his legion mobilize. He was already geared up and ready. However, the scores of other soldiers might not have been, yet they assembled in armor within moments of orders passing through the camp. Optios arrived, shouting at their men to form marching columns. The triarii foragers and the centurion Gallio had fetched were at the lead, and Varro found himself there with Gallio. Optio Latro was nowhere among the assembled force.

Altogether a mixed band of over one hundred men left by the north gate and toward the woods where presumably a brigand hideout would be found.

"Do you suppose after we find the brigand that every man here will be required to stab him?" Gallio asked as they marched across the grass.

"This many men seems much for one brigand, but maybe the centurions expect more in hiding. If they did, they should've taken a more ordered force."

Yet once they arrived at the edge of the line of trees where the foragers were ambushed, Varro realized they were not deploying a battle formation. The centurion who had pulled the force together now stood at the front, along with another centurion.

Varro recognized the newcomer as Centurion Protus. He commanded Varro's century and the maniple, along with Centurion Drusus. He was by far the more lenient and understanding of the two which was not saying much. Drusus seemed perpetually bored and uncaring of anyone other than himself. But Protus could at least bond with the men, and Varro felt he was the better officer. He was glad to see him instead of Optio Latro.

The centurion divided them into teams of ten, each with instructions to search the woods for brigands and capture them dead or alive. Varro wondered why the centurion even offered a live capture, as he would be the only one foolish enough to attempt it. The others would likely kill first, then determine if they had killed the right man.

The centurion counted off teams arbitrarily. But Centurion Protus picked his own men, which included Varro and Gallio.

"How is your wound?" he asked as Varro joined his team.

"I'm recovering, sir." Varro learned the less said to any officer the better.

"Glad to hear it," he said. "What a mess that was. Now, let's get after this brigand."

The way he spoke seemed to indicate doubt of the brigand's existence. Yet someone had to have shot poor Tanicus.

They spread out into the woods, one hundred armored soldiers in hobnailed sandals and bronze helmets. If there were brigands here, they would do well to flee, Varro thought. With a journey to Illyria only days away, and the promise of combat to follow, many were eager to see blood.

Yet as they fanned out, Varro lost sense of direction. Woodlands were unfamiliar to him, and the closeness of the trees and shadows like heavy blue felt filled him with unease. His sandals crunched on twigs and debris. Branches caught in his tunic or else pinged off his helmet. The ten-man unit had spread out wide, with Centurion Protus at the lead.

He suddenly raised his fist to halt all of them. Varro pulled up his scutum and angled his pilum against it. But he saw no enemy.

Protus turned with his finger over his lips for silence, then pointed through the trees to a clearing beyond. Varro searched after the centurion's direction, and spotted a lone farmhouse through the trees and across a cleared field.

To Varro, it did not seem like a brigand's hideout. For one, it was so close to their camp that whoever lived here must know of the army on the other side of the woods. Second, the farmers were doing nothing to conceal their presence. In fact, a thin thread of wooly smoke twirled up over the old farmhouse.

Yet Protus waved them forward at a crouch. Varro followed as indicated, but doubted they could sneak up on even a half-blind old man. They wore an array of tunic colors, mostly cream or white, and carried painted shields, all of which would show through the trees. Centurion Protus's red helmet crest might as well have been a signal fire to anyone looking. Then all wore bronze helmets and armor, which would reflect light.

They drew to the edge of the woods. Behind the house two children played, brother and sister neither older than ten, chasing each other in circles. The front door of the villa hung open and activity fluttered beyond it. The cream plaster had chipped in patches to bare stone and shattered roof tiles scattered shards over rotten wood. Scraggly bushes along the walls were the only attempt at decoration. These were not landowners of any account, and likely weren't wealthy enough to serve in the legion.

Varro and Gallio crept forward to join their centurion, who had gathered the ten soldiers into a cluster. He kneeled behind a tree, staring ahead while his men settled around him. The earthy scents of the woods now gave way to the smokey flavors coming downwind from the villa. The children's screams of joy were thin and distant. A goat brayed beyond the house.

"And there's our culprit," said Protus in a whisper. "Look by the door."

The entire squad leaned forward at the centurion's command. Beside the opened door, an unstrung bow and quiver rested against the wall.

"There's only ten of us," Protus said. "We must cover all the exits. Four will enter the front with me, two on each side and two in back. No one escapes."

Varro's heart thumped against his neck.

"Sir, if I may," Varro said. "The arrow in Tanicus's side had white fletching. The arrows in that quiver are black."

Protus did not look at him but continued to study the farm.

"Are you sure of what you saw, Varro?"

"Sir, yes, it was white fletching."

"Gallio, what did you see?"

The entire squad turned to Gallio, who straightened and

began blinking. He looked from Varro to Protus, then to the others who stared on with flat expressions.

"Sir, I don't know. I went to get an officer and only just glanced at the body. I—I don't remember, sir."

Protus smiled. "Well, then we can't say for certain if Varro's memory is correct. But there is a bow and quiver right by an opened door and near to the ambush. I say we've found our brigand."

"Sir, this is a farm. They're not hiding from anyone. I think—"

"I did not ask what you thought, Varro." Centurion Protus stood. Even angered, he had a warm smile. It was his eyes that flashed with threat. "You'll remember not to offer your opinions until asked, which won't ever be soon. Now, let's move."

They all stood, dropping any pretense of hiding. As they approached in a loose line, shields up for any sudden attack, Protus again repeated the order of attack. He waved two off the left end of the line to circle one side of the house. Toward the end, with Varro, he waved at four of them.

"Two on the side and two in the back," he said. "Make sure no one escapes from the villa."

"Gallio and I will take the back," Varro said. The children's laughter had ceased and he did not see them any longer. He guessed they had spotted soldiers emerging from the woods and fled.

The teams formed up, and Varro dragged Gallio around the back of the farm.

"Why did you have to get me in trouble?" Gallio asked under his breath as they broke off from the other two soldiers.

"This isn't right."

"How would you know that? Maybe the brigand used his last white arrow on Tanicus."

"These are poor farmers who had no reason to shoot a soldier from an army they must know is camped on their doorstep. Protus is mistaken. We're not letting those children become caught up in this mess."

"But that's not our orders," Gallio said. His eyes were blinking so rapidly now, Varro wondered how he could see. "Protus knows there're children here. We can't let them go."

They rounded to the back of the villa. They found a pen where a goat chewed weeds and two chickens scratched the ground. The plaster on the wall here had fallen in piles along its length, and a broken barrel lay rotting at the far end.

"Shut up, Gallio. These are fellow Romans. What if they were your family?"

"But they're not my family."

The two children hid behind a lone fir tree. Their dirty faces were bright with sweat from their play, but each stared like wide-eyed rabbits ready to bolt.

"There they are!" Gallio pointed with his pilum and the younger girl screamed.

At the same moment, a roar of male voices and a woman's shriek echoed in the main villa. A crash followed.

"Let's get them," Gallio stalked ahead, and the two children burst from their hiding spot.

Varro swept Gallio's feet with his pilum. The point caught on his skin and he skipped back, which caused him to fall atop his shield. Varro dropped his own shield, then tore Gallio's pilum away.

"Stay down," he said. "I'll help you cast."

The two children ran screaming into the field behind their home. To Varro's relief, a long line of dark fir trees seemed their likely destination.

"Run," he shouted. "Don't come back." He hurled Gallio's pilum as if he had never practiced with one before. It arced and thumped into the earth short of the two fleeing children. Their young, pale legs carried them far out of reach.

"What are you doing?" Gallio shouted, as he struggled to regain his footing.

"Following orders," he said, then heaved his pilum with the skill of all his training. He knew the children were out of effective range. He essentially was disarming himself. It sailed ahead and landed true, even with a contrary wind fighting the cast. But it stuck into the ground, useless.

Gallio now recovered, then started to chase the children until realizing they were fleeing beyond reach. The two were already at the edge of the deeper forest and soon vanished into the darkness. He glared back at Varro.

"What have you done?" He breathed hard, grunting and flexing his hand for his gladius.

Varro raised his brow at the motion.

"You want to kill me instead?" Varro stood motionless. "We saved those two children. Protus can eat shit if he thinks I'll bring more innocents into this disaster."

The ruckus from the farmhouse ended with a strangled scream. The long, mournful cry of a woman followed.

Varro smiled without humor. "Tanicus's killer," he mocked the word, "is dead now. His wife will follow, and those children are orphaned. Would you like to see any more justice done today?"

Gallio's hands relaxed and he instead wiped the sweat from his face.

"You explain this. But I will not be flogged for your conscience."

Varro retrieved his scutum, wiped the grass stains from the white paint, and sighed.

"Do what you must, Gallio."

13

Varro and Gallio stood at attention before Centurions Protus and Drusus. Optio Latro stood to the side, with arms folded and a disgusted frown. His blue eyes pierced Varro throughout the entire proceeding. He did not even seem to blink. The centurions sat on field chairs made from cloth and wooden trestles. Two clay lamps lit the tent, oily black smoke rolling away toward the center tent pole.

Centurion Protus was the older of the two. Coarse wavy hair the color of faded planks covered his wide head. He looked like a staggered boar as he rubbed his chin. Drusus sat beside him, shaking his head and rubbing his scarred arm. Why he was present confused Varro, as he commanded a different century. He decided it was at Latro's request, so that Drusus the disciplinarian would push for a flogging.

"My orders were not to allow anyone to escape," Protus said. "There were two children behind the farmhouse, and you fools let them go."

"Sir, as I stated," Varro said, his back straight and eyes at the rear of the tent. A rack with Protus's muscled breastplate stood in the corner, like another soldier at his trail. "The children were already fleeing us. I understood our orders were not to allow anyone to flee the villa. I assumed that the children were already noted and considered of no account. If we chased them, then we might fail in your direct order to prevent anyone from escaping the villa."

"Sir, let me make an example of them," Optio Latro said. "I don't care for Varro's attitude."

Drusus at last emerged from his ponderous thinking. It seemed to have taxed the limit of his endurance from the perspiration shimmering on his forehead. He cleared a nostril with a thick finger. Varro hoped the man was not as coarse in his thinking as he was in his mannerisms.

"Thank you, Optio. I know you take great pride in your command. But these men did follow orders. Protus, you told them not to let anyone escape from the villa. All the others confirmed no one escaped it. These two did not fail in that regard, and Varro has a point."

"They why throw your pilums after the children?" Protus asked.

"A bit of sport, sir." Varro said, forcing a smile. "We heard the end of the fight in the villa. So we just thought to have a laugh."

Protus again shook his head. Latro rubbed his face. But Drusus chuckled.

"We're already down eight men," he said. "And we're sailing the day after tomorrow. You brought the brigand to justice. I don't see the need to belabor this point."

"Very well," Protus said. He gave both Gallio and Varro a skeptical grin. "I suppose it's too much for you two to work out what I intended. I'll grant my order could've been clearer. We'll set this aside for now. But I don't want to have a discussion like this again. Varro, your name is coming to my attention far more often than it should, and not for the right reasons. Let's hope that changes."

"Yes, sir!"

Latro followed them out of the tent, sticking close to Varro.

"You better be more careful how you address your betters." The scent of wine was heavy on Latro's breath. "Both of them are too easy on you young ones. They're not doing you any favors by it. If it were me in Protus's chair, I'd have you collecting your teeth off the ground."

"Yes, sir!" For there was nothing else Varro could say. He stood at rigid attention, staring across the field toward his row of barracks. Gallio also stood beside him.

With a sniff, Latro dismissed them.

Gallio leaned on his knees as if he had finished a race. "Don't bring me before the officers again. I don't want to be flogged."

"You weren't flogged," Varro said, raising his friend. "And we did what was right. Those children might be orphaned now, but it's better than being dead. Or at least I hope it is. Anyway, feel good about that much."

They both arrived at their barracks, where the rest of the contubernium awaited them outside. All along the row of barracks soldiers squatted around campfires and cooking pots. Most ignored them as they passed. Others gave them knowing smiles, having seen them exiting the command tent. First among their own, Falco greeted them.

"Varro, you can't even stand at a gate without causing trouble. Are you certain you can survive army life?"

"It wasn't my fault," Varro said, pushing past Falco to enter the tiny front room of their quarters. He wanted to rack his weapons and armor, and feel free of their oppressive weight. Gallio remained outside, laughing with the others. But Falco followed him into the stuffy gloom of their quarters.

"I heard you gave Centurion Protus some trouble in the field. Not obeying orders?" His brutish face was bright with glee. Varro set his shield against the wall with the others, all painted different colors that faded to gray in the dim light.

"I obeyed his orders to watch the villa."

"Don't be like that with me, Varro. I already know better secrets about you."

Varro snapped his head back to look beyond the door where Falco's bulk crowded the view.

"Be careful," he whispered, checking that no one else heard. "I would not help kill children. It's bad enough I couldn't do anything to stop the murder of their parents."

"Murder? I heard they were the ones who killed that Tanicus fellow. Seems he was quite a friend to many people. The whole camp just about fucking cried at the news. If you stopped Protus, I'd say half this camp would put you in that farmer's place."

"Well, it's over now. Better to forget the whole thing. I only hope I did what was right."

Falco slipped in behind Varro as he unbuckled his pectoral.

"Well, the children will live. The boy will probably become a real brigand and the girl a prostitute. Or maybe they'll just find their way to Rome and join the army of beggars there. I'm sure it's better than death."

The pectoral thumped to the floor, and Varro stared at Falco. He smiled wolfishly, then slapped Varro's shoulder. The meaty whack sent vibrations through his injured forearm.

"Your arm looks fine," Falco said. "But how's the side? Saving children from evil soldiers isn't light duty."

"It pulled open when I cast my pilum. Not serious, I think. Just a bit of blood leaked and it still burns."

He lifted his arms to reveal the brown stains on his tunic. Falco hissed through his teeth.

Retrieving his pectoral, he set it beneath the peg where his sword hung.

"Did you see where Optio Latro was all day?"

"No, I wasn't feeling much like a flogging today. So I attended my duties rather than spying on my officer."

Varro nodded and pursed his lips.

"Gods, don't go off on that business again." Falco pulled him into the crowded bunk room and lowered his voice. "You think he was behind this?"

"I didn't say that. Do you think he is?"

"No!" Falco stepped back, his dark eyes glinting in the low light. "No, Latro is a bastard and he hates us. But he hates everyone. He hates us for being less than he is. He hates the centurions for being above him. He probably hates his mother, too. But this complete fantasy about him killing soldiers has got to stop. Listen to me, Varro. You're getting that stubborn face you get whenever you won't fight back but want to. I'm serious about this. You'll get yourself executed."

"What are you talking about? What face? Anyway, don't you think it's strange that Latro, who has to be in the middle of everything, was nowhere all afternoon?"

Falco folded his arms.

"I'm going to find out where he was, if I can."

"See? That's the face. Gods, I just want to pound it right off your head. But we'll both be up for a flogging if I do."

Varro raised his hands and shook his head.

"Let's just forget it. I'm hungry."

They both stood in awkward silence until Falco lowered his eyes and joined the rest of the contubernium. Varro followed and accepted a bowl of steaming puls from Panthera.

"Extra beans in it," he said. "To help you recover."

They both looked to his bandaged side, and Varro inclined his head in gratitude.

"And I think you did the right thing," Panthera said. "I'm not sure I could've done the same. I've got a little brother and sister at home, too."

Varro looked to Gallio and then to the others gathered around. They all wore soft smiles, and Varro felt a warmth spread through his chest. Falco shoved him playfully from behind.

"Come on, lily, eat up."

The following day Latro summoned the century for an early morning march. Varro's so-called light duty was deemed to have ended, even though clear fluid still wept between his stitches. In deference to this, Latro granted him a visit to the hospital for a quick cleaning and redressing of his wound. The doctor proclaimed he would survive without issue.

Upon returning from the march, they were to pack up and prepare to board ships leaving for Illyria the next morning. While the camp buzzed with excitement, Varro felt a sickening dread. After seeing what his officers could do to fellow Romans, he imagined the horrors they were about to inflict on Macedonia and her allies. That night he dreamed of sacking a village where the only inhabitants were children who were hacked into bloody bits by crazed Roman soldiers. He awakened to a cold sweat in the predawn hours to prepare for boarding.

The entire summer had passed in the Brundisium camp. While it was a lonesome place far from his home, Varro now felt a strange affection for it. He admired its uniform efficiency and organization. It had sprung up at the army's command, and would vanish after it fulfilled its purpose.

That morning, all the legions were arrayed to hear the address by the newly arrived Consul Publius Sulpicius Galba. The speech seemed rousing to those who could hear it. But Varro and the others were too junior to be placed close enough to the podium. Snippets of Galba's speech floated into the rear ranks, all cliches about glory, Roman power, and saving Greek culture. None of it seemed important to Varro. But Consul Galba gestured like Jupiter wielding thunderbolts.

He wore full battle gear more ostentatious than even the

tribunes who flanked him. His bronze cuirass was fashioned into rippling muscle and blazed with fire in the morning light. His magnificent crest was brilliant red, flowing off a bronze helmet that reflected the clouds overhead. A sword in an ornate leather scabbard hung at his right hip. Yet the man himself was paunchy and gray. Varro doubted he lifted anything heavier than a wine goblet in his daily life.

Once the speech ended, centurions ordered their soldiers to the shore, where Varro witnessed the Roman navy for the first time. Both he and Falco gasped, as did every other of the hastati with him.

Scores of triremes had docked or else dropped anchor offshore. They were magnificently tall ships with rows of oar banks stacked atop each other. Some oars hung limp and others were shipped. The soldiers were all ordered onto rowboats to reach their assigned vessel, then climbed rope ladders with all their gear piled on their backs. At last Varro understood how much a summer of constant training had strengthened him. He scaled the rope ladder onto the trireme in full armor, two pilums, sword, heavy scutum, and a sack of his supplies. Yet he leaped aboard without losing his breath. Last spring, he might have collapsed to the deck from such exertions.

He joined his fellows. Optio Latro was too busy with the centurions to pay much attention to him. So he found an open place on deck to set his gear. Falco and the others were still clambering aboard. While he enjoyed the company of his fellows, even Falco to a degree, he was eager to get away from them even for so short of a journey.

Resting against the side, feeling the gentle sway of the ship, smelling the salt air, and listening to gulls cry above, he scanned the deck.

This was one of the First Legion ships, mixing with men from various centuries. He did not recognize them all, but his eyes landed on one familiar face.

His father.

He leaned on the rails, chatting with another of his fellow triarii. Varro's heart leaped with joy. He wanted to show his father how strong he had become, and that he was now a proper soldier.

Varro waved and caught his father's eye.

His father looked at him.

It was the gaze of a stranger. But Varro had not changed so much that his father would not recognize him. His father stared at him long enough that even if at first he had overlooked his son, he would recognize him now. Yet as Varro waved, his father shifted so his back turned to him and continued speaking to his companion as if his son did not exist.

14

The flotilla of triremes sailed in formation, with Varro's ship on the right of it. He had nothing better to do than stand on the deck and remain out of the way of the sailors. For once, he had no duties. The salt air offered a refreshing and surprising taste to Varro, who had never left his farm. The simple rock and creak of the deck left him grinning. Falco too, leaning on the rails beside him to watch the oars of the other triremes beat the waves, smiled. Deep within the hull of their own ship, a drum sounded a ponderous cadence for the rowers. Varro had only been below deck once, and not deep enough to the find the banks of oars stretching to the water below.

He scanned the lead-colored waves, a match to the sky above, and thought he saw forms in the water following. But the white wake and the oars stroking the water made it impossible to see. He wondered if these were sea creatures or agents of Neptune. It seemed more probable that the gods would watch with interest. The entire world was at war in the west and east. Surely the gods had an interest in a gathering of Roman triremes speeding for Illyria.

"Shame this won't last longer," Falco said. "I could stand another day of rest and fresh sea air."

"One sailor was talking to us about storms last night," Varro said, recalling depictions of vast waves and scouring winds. "Sounded horrible. As fun as this is, I'll be glad to reach land."

"You should've stayed below deck and played dice with the rest of us." Falco spit over the side, then leaned to watch it fall. "Serves you right. These sailors just want to scare us."

"My father warned me not to gamble on campaign."

Falco grunted, still leaning to stare down the side of the ship.

"Your father's a good man. Better than mine."

Varro did not know what to say, since it was the plain truth. Sextus Falco was a drunk with a mad wife and no surviving children but for Falco. He did not seem to care for any of it, least of all Falco. All he ever seemed to want was his wine. Varro could not imagine how he was faring in the army without it. If he were drunk on duty, he'd be executed for it.

"Why do you think he ignored me?"

Falco spit again, once more observing its fall. "Your father? Don't know. Probably doesn't want you to look like a little boy in front of us. Plenty of others have cousins, brothers, and fathers here. But they're not holding tearful reunions. It'd be embarrassing."

"It wouldn't be like that. He could've waved back, at least. Surely he saw my arm bandaged. Wouldn't he want to know what happened?"

"I think he knows what happened. That was big news," Falco said. "Maybe he's still sick and doesn't want you to catch it. Who knows, Varro? Just stop thinking about it. We're going to have more to worry about by tomorrow. What do you think is waiting for us over there?"

"A war," Varro said.

They fell silent and Varro continued to watch the dark shapes speeding alongside the ships. There were more triremes in the formation than he expected. But he learned only this morning that veterans from the Punic War had joined them. It gladdened him to know these veterans would offer support and were fresh from victory. Yet he despaired for his own situation. He thought they excused these veterans from this campaign since they had already served in a hard-won war. So either he had heard wrong or else the tribunes had not been honest, which seemed the likely case. Nor were these men being relieved from the trials of war. Varro could not imagine going from battle to battle year after year. How would Rome have any men left under this system? Would he survive such a system?

"Well, seems like you'll have your answer," Falco said, standing back from the rails. "I'll leave you two alone."

Varro raised his brow to Falco, who glanced past him before turning away.

"How is your wound?"

He whirled behind to find his father leaning on the rails next to him, squinting into the dull glare of the sea.

"Father," he backed away, his face suddenly warm. "I—it's healing."

Quintius flashed a quick smile at him, then stared back out to sea. Words fled him, and he unconsciously rubbed his side. But his father seemed relaxed. The long thin scar on his face was slack. Dressed only in a tunic and sandals, he seemed just like he had back home.

"You look well for all you've been through," Quintius said.

"Father, I heard you were sick. What happened?"

"It was nothing. Nothing for you to worry about. You had a far worse day than I."

"I'm still trying to understand it," Varro said. He relaxed his stance, but when his father said nothing more, he leaned on the rails with him. For a moment, without armor or weapons or officers shouting at him, he imagined he was on a sea voyage with his father. His mother and sister were elsewhere, and soon they would all gather on deck to enjoy the ocean air. But such fantasies were as fleeting as the foam of the ship's wake.

"Optio Latro has a special interest in you," Quintius said. "That concerns me."

Varro lowered his voice and sidled closer to his father. "So you do know what he's doing. I think he somehow put Nonus up to killing me. I just can't prove it."

His father hissed him to silence.

"That kind of talk will get you killed. Never say as much again about an officer without proof and half the army in your favor."

"Father, I know I'm right. The more I think about that day, the more certain I am about it. Somehow, Nonus and Latro had an arrangement. But it didn't work out, and so Latro killed him. But why try to kill me at all?"

"Don't give the officers cause to notice you," Quintius said. He pushed back from the rails, yet remained leaning on his palms. "Do your duty and follow orders. Sleep with one eye open always. This campaign will end eventually. They always do. You will come out of it fine. Let everything else develop as it will. You can do nothing more."

"What do you mean? You think I'm imagining this? What about Tanicus? Who really shot him, and why? It wasn't those farmers, I can assure you."

His father stepped away from the rail and smiled to his son.

"Forget those worries. Even if you were right, you could do nothing. You have become a fine soldier, Marcus, and I'm proud of you. I wanted to tell you before we make landfall tomorrow. For after that, we cannot count on what the next day will bring."

His father left him by the rails, his hobnailed sandals clanking on the deck. Varro watched him retreat to the hatch leading to the lower decks, never turning back. Something in his posture was wrong. He had seemed so normal leaning on the rails, but now he seemed frailer and even defeated. Was he still sick? Varro wondered.

For the rest of the voyage, he did not see his father again. He also stayed away from his contubernium, including Falco. If he was going to cram into a tent with them while on campaign for the next year, he would relish the time apart.

Once the lookouts called land ahead, the decks filled with the younger soldiers all eager for a first glimpse of the distant land they were about to invade. Varro could not resist, for he had a special interest in Greece and its noble traditions. Rome had refined and improved on these, but Varro still had to tribute the ancient civilization for its contributions. For now it was a faded purple stripe of jagged land. But as they drew closer, it resolved into cliffs and rocky hills.

Also, his idle days ended with an abrupt shout to prepare for landfall. They headed to a place called Apollonia, which to Varro could have been anywhere. It was near to Brundisium, as they had only been at sea for two days in fair weather.

A tumult of military procedures flowed from landfall, leaving Varro no time to consider anything other than where he needed to point his feet next. They disembarked, unloaded a baggage train, scouted inland, then established a place for a temporary camp. Varro hauled supplies, chopped wood, hunted game, carted water, and aided camp construction, all while maintaining his gear and the discipline of sword drills.

Weeks were fleeting past him, and each night he collapsed into his tent with seven other men. Sleep claimed him before he even set his sweaty head down. Even Optio Latro was so busy he could spare no time to torment Varro. In fact, he seemed to forget Varro's existence. In their few interactions, he spoke evenly and without condescension.

Perhaps he had been mistaken about the optio. He was glad he had not spread his suspicions beyond Falco and his father.

"Probably because we're soldiers now, not recruits," Falco offered during a private moment while loading water into barrels at a nearby stream. "He's got to have our respect if we're going to fight. Can't be shitting on us for no reason like raw recruits. Those days are gone now."

It made sense to Varro. Nonus had been a madman. Though Tanicus had been felled by someone, even if not those farmers, it had probably been an accident. The officers were covering up for a favored soldier. That was more likely than the conspiracy Varro had dreamed out of nothing.

He was freed of worry from within, and could focus on the real danger of the war ahead.

Weeks into their establishing a temporary camp—which with its protective ditch and palisades along with latrines, communal mess, training grounds, stables, and forges seemed even more permanent to Varro than Brundisium—he had been lulled into a routine. Twice daily training with sword drills plus regular rotation on guard duties and foraging parties matched the cadence of farm life with its set patterns. Except this camp housed thousands of soldiers all poised to strike deeper into Illyria for Macedonia. Yet with fall now halfway ended, rumor was they would settle into winter quarters and begin a real campaign in the spring. Such news was a relief, for it cut into Varro's service time with no threat of real danger.

This day, after sword drills, the officers had detailed Varro and all his contubernium to a forage party for firewood. His team was one of a dozen others. Unlike the foragers at Brundisium, four did the scavenging while four others remained on watch around the area. They rotated the duty, and it was now Varro's turn.

Falco had wandered from his position to where Varro stood watch.

"You heard about the fleet going to aid Athens?" Like Varro, he wore helmet and armor and held his scutum readied. He had painted his black. Given the confines of the woods, they had left their pilums in camp.

"You're supposed to be keeping the north watch," Varro said. Falco shrugged and looked over his shoulder back through the gray, leafless trees.

"Looks clear to me," he said. "So you heard? My father's going with them. They're taking a bunch of us, including all the Fourth. Lucky we didn't get picked. Father's the lucky one."

"I'm sorry to hear that," Varro said. He was ill at ease in these forests. He heard too many noises like crunching dead leaves, snapping twigs, rustling branches, and none had any source he could perceive. All the uncontrolled vegetation and dim light made him feel separated from the real world. This was a place of spirits, and he doubted they were friendly.

"Don't be sorry," Falco said. "Good riddance to him. I don't want to hear about it when they flog him for being drunk on duty. Better he's far from me."

"This is not his first time serving. He must have figured out how to get by already."

Falco shrugged, then turned back to face north.

He inhaled to speak, but froze.

Varro's hands went cold. He saw nothing, but knew Falco had.

In the center perimeter, four of his companions gathered wood suitable for kindling or firewood. He heard Panthera's cheerful banter, as he could never abide silence for too long. Other voices answered him as needed. Varro glimpsed their dark shapes moving through the trees. He also saw their pack mule, which seemed bored as it flicked its ears. If it had not aroused the animal, then there was no danger.

But Falco whispered. "See them, Varro. That line of bushes

and that fallen tree. That's where they're hiding. You can just see their eyes."

He stared into the flat, dull light but saw nothing. The forest floor was all brown, yellow, and gray. Rocks spattered with pale green lichen sprouted between trees. Ferns and bushes hid everything else from view. He blinked harder, but saw nothing.

Until something moved.

It was fleeting and he did not catch what had changed. But without a doubt, the branches of a dark green bush quivered.

"They're coming," Falco said. "What do we do?"

Varro scanned wide eyed around, but saw nothing else.

"Are you sure you saw people?"

"Varro, I know what human eyes look like. They have brows over them and hair over that. I'm sure at least three were watching from those bushes."

"I don't see—"

Then a whistle blew from Gallio's eastern position, directly across from them.

A man burst out of a clump of bushes only three yards from Varro.

He was tall but thin. Varro caught a flash of a raw wool tunic and a mass of black curly hair. Otherwise, he saw only the sparkle of a spear point thrusting for his head.

More roars came from all around. The mule brayed. Latin curses mixed with whatever foreign war cries echoed around them.

"We're surrounded!" Falco shouted.

But Varro could see nothing but the spearpoint. Endless drilling had trained him to pull the heavy green and white scutum in front of the striking spear. His legs braced as his right hand tore his gladius from the sheath with practiced ease. He moved as if controlled by another force.

The spear point jammed into the shield, carving across the

144

wood and thumping off the iron boss. A shudder ran through his hand.

Covered from the attacker, he could not see his enemy. The scutum was a bulwark, but left him blind. He heard the man's grunt of effort and his feet sweeping over the dead litter covering the dirt.

Varro lowered his shield enough to see. Thus far he had practiced only against opponents also armed with short swords. But this man was not only tall with lanky arms to match, but also wielded a spear. His clenched teeth flashed bright and his eyes were wide with hateful madness. His spear dominated the space between them.

"Drop your spear," Varro shouted. But if the man understood Latin, he did not obey. Instead, he charged again.

Rather than fall back, Varro stepped into the strike. If he remained at bay, the spear would overcome him. Trust your shield and you'll win a hundred battles, one of his veteran trainers had advised. So he did. He stepped into the strike, punching the spear as if it were an enemy's head.

The force of the collision rocked through his arm. But he had grown strong over the long summer. Rather than crumple from the force, he pushed against it. The spear tip broke through the wood.

He had trapped the enemy's weapon.

With a shout of triumph, he twisted his shield to yank the spear out of place. The enemy did not want to surrender it and held on. This wrenched him forward, pulling his arms up and exposing his ribs.

Varro had trained hours for this moment twice a day every day since the start of summer. He had just drilled the move this morning.

He did not want to kill the man.

But his short sword glided forward without conscious thought.

Its point stabbed through the wool of the tunic, then slithered between the man's ribs. The force of the strike and the keen edge of the blade carried it through, destroying the enemy's innards as it plunged deeper.

The black-haired enemy appeared belatedly to realize his fatal error. His eyes bulged and he opened his mouth to scream. Nothing but a raspy belch of air escaped.

Varro tore his sword back from the wound. A long string of blood followed and the man rolled away, releasing his spear, which snapped and fell atop his body. Blood spouted from the deep puncture in his ribs as he slammed to the ground. His eyes rolled back.

"Dear gods," Varro whispered, stepping back from the blood that flowed out of the body toward his feet. "I killed him."

Behind, he heard iron clangs and wooden thumps. Someone in the far distance screamed, and another shrill wooden whistle sounded through the trees.

Whirling around, shield ready, his back tingled with the possibility of having been run through.

He found one enemy slumped against a tree. He was a stout man in a chain shirt who held his neck as blood pumped between his fingers. A bronze helmet unlike any design Varro knew slipped forward over his face. He wept as he slid to one side.

Falco lay sprawled on the ground. His black shield rocked in the grass out of reach and his sword, covered in blood, quivered upright in the ground. A burly man also in a chain shirt straddled Falco, pinning him. In two hands he gripped a long dagger that he drove toward Falco's throat. Falco, pinned beneath his muscular opponent, had clamped his hands over his enemy's. Both were red-faced and grunting in their struggle.

But the enemy was prevailing, and the dagger point jerked closer to Falco's throat.

Varro screamed in rage. Lifting his shield and fitting his shoulder into its curve, he charged.

The iron boss cracked against the enemy's skull. Varro's feet collided with Falco's shoulders. Both friend and foe shouted in shock and pain. But Varro drove the attacker off of Falco, flopping him onto his side.

He wasted no time. He was young and fast and his vision red. Hot breath hissed through Varro's teeth. Snapping to his feet, he towered over the muscular man who stared dazedly up at him. His beard was thick and dark, unkempt and heavy around his neck.

The gladius sliced through the beard, punched into the throat, and jabbed into the earth beneath.

The enemy spasmed but did not cry out. Varro had nearly beheaded him. A spray of scarlet blood from the sliced artery rained hot over his arms and salty across his lips. But Varro howled with victory. As he withdrew his sword, he inflicted a slash across the dead man's eyes, spinning his head aside to remain attached only by a flap of skin.

Falco coughed and wheezed as he climbed to his feet.

"Two on one," he muttered. "Not fucking fair. But got one."

Varro blinked. Seeing Falco with blood splashed across his red, sweaty face somehow brought him to his senses.

"Are you hurt?"

"He kneed me in the balls. I'll live though." Falco frowned, swept his sword out of the ground, then retrieved his scutum.

Whistles sounded all over. The fearsome battle cries that had filled the dead forest were now wails of retreat. Varro heard the familiar calls from officers to order their men. One was close by.

"You saved my life," Falco said, out of breath. "Can't fucking believe it. Thank you."

Again Varro blinked. When he realized the salty blood he tasted was not his, his stomach clenched and he thought he might vomit. But he shook his head.

"Gallio and the others," he said. "I hear nothing. They better be all right."

He and Falco rushed to the clearing they had been using to store their gathered firewood. The battle had ended. Their mule had fled, leaving a trail of firewood that had fallen from its packs. Panthera and Gallio stood together with the others, hovering over a body. Four men in plain tunics with only leather harnesses for armor lay sprawled through the area. Two were slathered in blood, but two looked as if they were napping.

Varro pushed into the circle of his companions.

One of his contubernales, Titus Novellius, lay on his back. A spear jutted from his gut just below his bronze pectoral. His pale eyes stared up at the tree limbs laced above them. He wore an expression of wonder, as if he had seen the gods just before death. A thin line of blood dribbled from the corner of his mouth.

"What are you bastards doing?"

An optio from another century tramped into the small clearing. His frowning face swept over the enemy dead, then stopped on Novellius's corpse.

"All right, we're clear now. But what kind of fools are you? Never turn your back to the enemy, even if he's in retreat. Pick him up and we'll gather the dead and wounded to camp. Then we'll be back to make them pay for this."

The optio pointed his bloodied gladius at Novellius's body.

Varro looked between Falco and the others.

He had never wanted to kill more than he did at this moment. These enemies, Macedonians or whoever they were, would pay.

Vows did not matter now.

15

At the edge of the forest of dead trees, with leafless branches clattering overhead and brown litter crunching under sandaled feet, Varro realized his left hip was lighter than it should be. He slid his scutum aside and revealed the empty scabbard that held the pugio his mother had gifted him.

A wave of icy dread swept through his guts. While his feet kept pace with the loose line of soldiers marching out of the forest, his mind raced back to his room and his mother's gentle smile as she presented the pugio. His uncle had carried it through all a lifetime of campaigns. Now he lost it in his very first skirmish.

The sun had crossed the zenith and pushed against thick clouds that threatened rain. A light breeze rolled the grassland between the forest and camp. Fifty soldiers were emerging from the trees at once, their mules now bearing stretchers of the dead. The mule that Gallio found wandering by the edge of the battleground carried Novellius's body.

"Shit," he hissed while patting the empty scabbard with his

right hand. He looked to Falco, striding beside him. "I lost my pugio."

"Good thing you don't gamble," Falco said. "You at least have money to replace it. I'm as poor as a one-eyed prostitute."

"It's a family heirloom from my uncle. It must have fallen out when I charged that brute that had you pinned."

"Maybe," Falco said with a shrug. "Or maybe since it wasn't sheathed properly you dropped it elsewhere and never noticed. Anyway, not much for it now."

"I had it when we left this morning." Varro let his hand drop from the vacant scabbard. His worries did not elicit more comment from Falco, who still seemed pale from having evaded his death.

Searching down the line of his companions, each one seemed lost in thought. It had been their first experience of combat. Veterans had warned them it would differ from what they imagined. For Varro's part, he had not overthought the fight as much as he had feared he would. In fact, of all the contubernium he judged himself the least rattled. Novellius was closer to the others than him, but Varro had still lived elbow to elbow with the man for more than half a year. His death was a keen reminder of how quick the end could come. Any of them might be the victim of an enemy's good fortune.

"I can't wait to see camp," Falco said. "There's got to be extra rations for this, don't you think? Maybe a little more wine would be nice. Just something to settle the nerves."

Falco's reaction was the most surprising to Varro, given how he loved violence since he could make a fist. Yet the blood and death seemed to have put Falco on his back foot, or maybe it was because he had stared at a dagger point hovering inches from his throat. In either case, Varro had assumed Falco would dance in the blood of his enemies and scream for more. Now he wanted to get back to camp and drink away the memories.

The empty scabbard slapped his thigh as if asking for attention. He could not leave the pugio behind, nor could he leave to search for it. Woodlands were mazes of confusing paths and strange sounds. With the sun setting soon, he imagined it would be a dead black tangle from which he would never again emerge. Camp was still more than a mile off. They would send him back to fight tomorrow, but no guarantee to the same place as today. He wouldn't even recognize the location tomorrow.

If he were ever to reclaim his pugio, he had to do it now.

Leaving the others would be grounds for punishment. Yet this was a forage team and only had the duty to return a mule piled with as much suitable wood as they could find. He could slip away while he still vaguely remembered the path and the enemy dead still marked the location. He dared not ask anyone else to follow. They would try to prevent him from going, since his punishment would be shared among everyone else. It was an insidious system that at once bonded them together and pitted them against each other.

That pugio had been blessed at the Temple of Mars for him. It seemed a greater sin to leave it lost in the dirt than to risk angering his officers.

"Ah, my sandal!" Varro pretended to stumble, then went to his knee. He set his scutum down to cover his lower half.

Falco and Panthera paused, both frowning after him.

"The lacing," Varro said with an embarrassed smile. "Go on. I'll be right behind."

"Hurry up," Falco said. Then he turned with the others as they left the tree line. The mule and the last of his companions passed him as he pretended to adjust his sandal. Novellius's corpse bounced past, tied to the makeshift stretcher the mule dragged.

He stood up, and Gallio glanced over his shoulder at him. Varro smiled back, and Gallio continued on his defeated march. All along the grassland, clusters of soldiers dragged their dead or injured behind them, heads down and trudging for the camp. It did not seem like a defeat to Varro, but as most of these soldiers were first-time hastati like himself, they were likely just as shocked at what had happened.

Now he turned back into the trees. His heart raced at the first step in the opposite direction, for he knew he defied orders to return to camp. But he would return, and just claim he had become separated. For the same reason Falco and the others would prevent him from breaking rank, they would also support his lie. They did not want to share in punishment. Varro could hardly be blamed for becoming lost in a forest, especially during an ambush.

A dozen strides back into the forest and the light already dimmed to a spectral glaze. Each footfall crunched on dead branches and leaves. He tried not to think of what might emerge from the onset of night, everything from wolves to evil spirits. The gray and brown landscape seemed to lean in on him as he threaded a path into its depths.

At first following the ruts and footprints of his companions into the woods was simple enough. The mule and Novellius's stretcher left obvious marks in the dark earth. But soon the path crossed with others who had either come before or after their passing.

He crouched by these prints and touched the ground as if it might yield some clue. But he had no sense of where to proceed. All paths led into the deeper woods, making one much the same as another. Nothing else about the surroundings suggested anything familiar. Until he had discovered the missing pugio, he had never assumed to return to this place. He had marked nothing about their route toward camp. He had been content to let others show him the way.

"There's a lesson here, Marcus," he said, imitating his father's voice. "Rely on yourself and don't place your safety in the hands of another. Yes, Father."

But mimicking a dialog between himself and his father did not solve his dilemma. So he picked a trail that felt hopeful and followed it.

The trail led to the scene of a battle, but it was not his. The enemy dead remained where they had fallen. Black flies hopped in the dark puddles of their blood. One landed on Varro's face, causing him to shrink away in disgust. He wiped at his cheek until it burned, then retraced his steps. But the more he followed paths, the more confused he became.

Then a thought chilled him to a standstill.

"What if I'm following the enemy's trail?"

The whispered words were like a shout in the quiet forest. He had been so determined to find the pugio, and so certain he could just walk back to the same place, that he never considered some of these trails might lead him to danger.

His scutum now weighed on his arm, and he shifted it off to his back. Sweat accumulated under his helmet and dribbled into his eyes. He blinked the stinging wetness away.

He was lost.

Now he would be glad to find any way out of the forest. But every path around him led to gloom. The light above was nothing more than shards the color of straw. It flickered and flashed with the sway of branches. He considered climbing a tree to learn which direction to go. Forget the pugio and just get back to camp. But no tree seemed taller than another, and he had not been much of a tree climber as a boy.

He raced along trails, desperate for any to lead toward the light. There could be less than an hour left of it, and it would first flee the forest before fleeing the plains. He had to escape ahead of the darkness if he ever hoped to return to camp this night.

As he ran, he found himself in the small clearing where Novellius had died. Seeing it now, even in this low light, it sprang back to memory. He let out a small shout of joy. He had somehow passed the spot and returned to it from the opposite end. The faces of the dead were familiar to him. How could he forget them? They still stared skyward, flesh gray and eyes dry.

He picked a way back to where he and Falco had fought. All the corpses remained where they had died. Varro's assailant lay sprawled out with a deep puncture in his ribs. His eyes were still wide in the shock of his final moments. Falco's first enemy sat against a tree, slumped to the left with his hand still pressed to his neck. His blood had thickened over his hand and arm, and his hair hung over his face to conceal his death mask.

The corpse of the biggest attacker lay crumpled on the ground where Varro had slain him. His head lay at a ninety-degree angle to his shoulders, attached only by sinew on one side. His black beard had been shorn away. A massive puddle of blood had shot from the neck and sprayed the surrounding dirt in black gore. Varro did not even remember that happening. Yet the evidence was splattered everywhere.

His pugio lay in the dirt, weakly reflecting the wan light falling on the scene. It had been ejected from its sheath when Varro had charged this final enemy, then landed just above him with its point facing the dead man as if poised to strike. He lifted it to his eyes and examined its razor-sharp edge.

"Well, if I die out here, at least I have this back."

Varro wiped it against his tunic, then slipped it into its sheath. He pressed it shut until he heard iron click against the wood.

He might still find the trail out with the little sunlight available. The air was already cooling and to be outside all night without a cloak would be misery. At least he was not in some high mountain place where snow and ice killed men as surely as enemy swords. He wondered if the fallen enemies had anything that might serve.

His opponent had nothing to offer that Varro did not already carry. The corpse against the tree was too slathered with gore for Varro to even want to examine it. He turned to the big man he had beheaded.

A chain shirt was a valuable thing, and Varro wished he had the presence of mind to claim it when they had a mule to bear it away. None of them had thought to scavenge from the enemy. The links of this corpse's mail had clotted with blood around the neck, but it was otherwise in good condition. It could be resized to Varro's proportions. He would be the only hastati in his century with a mail coat.

But something else caught his eye. Something sparkled beneath the hank of black beard Varro had sliced away.

He flicked it back, careful not to meet the dead eyes of the victim he was robbing. A heavy gold chain lay in the thickened blood puddle. His sword had broken a link when it plunged through the man's neck. Varro whistled through his teeth.

"Sorry, friend, but I can't turn away from this. You don't know how little I'm paid for this job."

He crouched down, then fished the thick links out of the gore. His nose curled at the bloodied golden chain that dangled between thumb and forefinger. A smile came to his face. He wiped the chain on the hem of the slain main's tunic. He imagined wearing armor to make the tribunes jealous. He would be rich with this much gold. The man must have been a leader to bear such treasures to battle.

Yet while he vacillated between admiring his prize and worrying about the excuse he could make for returning to camp, he realized the background sounds of breaking twigs were not natural.

He shot up from crouching beside the corpse. Without hesitation, he stuffed the chain into his tunic so that his belt held it against his flesh. Then he fumbled for his scutum, still slung across his back.

A shout came close to his left and others answered.

Swinging the shield into position, he felt the relief of its bulk.

But the voices came from all around and were not Roman.

He drew his gladius and faced left.

A spearman with a round green shield broke through the underbrush. He did not charge Varro, but crouched behind the shield and readied the spear against it. He wore no helmet, presenting a crown of thick auburn hair just above his shield. He called out to others.

Varro could not study him more, as all around answers shouted back. A dozen men converged on this spot, and within the space of three heartbeats he was surrounded by men armed the same as the one who had found him.

They edged forward, speaking in Greek that he did not understand. Falco had teased him for knowing basic phrases, calling him a philosopher. Whatever these men growled at him were garbled and angry words. But even without knowing their language, he understood they were calling for his surrender.

There was no surrender for a Roman soldier. Varro had not even received a suggestion of what to do when surrounded by enemies. Every veteran and officer had assumed he would just die in line with his companions and never retreat. For they would only kill him for cowardice in battle. Better to die facing the enemy. But he was the only Roman here.

Spear tips glinted as they closed like the fangs of a giant shark. Varro circled with his gladius held at the ready. Some of the enemy laughed. They looked just like him, well-built men in plain tunics. Their shields were round and they carried spears rather than swords. He had not guessed what to expect from an enemy. The officers dehumanized the Macedonians and their allies. Varro envisioned men more like satyrs than humans. But these were just ordinary men.

"Roman, put down your sword. Your fight is over."

The heavily accented voice came from behind. It was deep and commanding, but tinged with humor. Varro wheeled to face it.

A man like a Greek statue faced him. He rested on a spear, with his shield held against his thigh. His face was bright in the darkness, framed by oiled hair and curly beard, both midnight black. He wore a wry smile and tucked his bronze helmet under a muscular left arm.

"The sword, Roman. On the ground. Do it nicely, and you will be my guest. Be a fool, and you'll join my brother."

Of course! He looked just like the big man Varro had defeated earlier. He couldn't help but glance to the body at his feet.

"That's right," he said, staring at Varro. "I cannot bear to look at him for it is to see myself in death. I loved my brother as I love myself, and your companions have slain him. No easy feat, for he was a great warrior. Though, I doubt a young one like you could have ever bested him. I vow to find his killer and have revenge."

Varro swallowed hard. His hand tingled on the grip of his sword. A voice deep in his heart whispered that he could best this man and all the fools surrounding him. But that rabid voice had no sway on his rational mind. A half-dozen spears were poised to run him through from behind if he even jerked his shoulder.

He slowly replaced his sword to the sheath and set his shield to the ground. No other choice remained. The statuesque leader nodded to his recovered pugio. Varro surrendered it, then loosened his chin strap and set his helmet aside.

"These were expensive," he said. "I expect them to be cared for and returned in good condition."

The boldness of his words surprised even himself. The leader's eyes widened then he bent back in laughter.

"Such are the men of Rome that even their basest children think themselves kings." He then swept his hand at Varro's equipment while speaking in what might have been Greek to his followers. Two set their spears aside to collect Varro's gear.

In the same instant, someone grabbed Varro by the sword arm and wretched it behind his back. He called out and struggled, but another set of powerful hands held him.

"We will bind you, Roman. You are the only captive we have today. So you are lucky. I will keep you alive for questioning. Prove useful, and you might live a few more days."

Again Varro swallowed. A burning desire to lash out swept across him. All thoughts of peace and nonviolence evaporated from his heart. A hateful lust to see this man dead overwhelmed him.

But his captors jerked him backward, causing him to stumble between them. Some chuckled at him, but the others jumped to the orders shouted by their leader.

As Varro turned to be led away, he glimpsed three white faces staring out at him from a thick row of dead bushes.

Falco, Gallio, and Panthera were such a contrast to the dark, leafless branches framing them that Varro wondered how no one had seen them. Yet they stared in horror as Varro was tugged forward, arms bound with heavy rope. He tried to shake his head at them, to warn them away. But his captors shoved him with such violence he could only yelp and fall ahead.

After recovering, he looked back. All three faces had vanished.

16

Though a prisoner, Varro had not yet suffered any mistreatment beyond imprisonment in a ditch. The earthy scent clogged his nose and the air was stale. If rain fell, he would likely sit in ankle-deep mud. But for now his sandaled feet were on hard ground. His neck had grown sore from staring up at the night sky. The moon had sat just outside of his small view of the world, broken into squares by a rusted iron grate. He did not think the brigands locked it, but just set it over the hole. Even if he reached the top by some boon of the gods, he would need their magic to lift away the grate. He could never generate the leverage himself.

Being a captive alone in a pit led him to strange thoughts, though he had only passed a single night in his enemy's camp. He fretted for his equipment. How would he pay for replacement gear? The richer men would lend him money, but he had heard the loans were impossible to repay. Would he be flogged for becoming a captive? It seemed like something the centurions would do, though he had never been warned against it. Again, because they expected him to die fighting.

All night he had heard his enemies shouting, singing, and wailing. There were women here, and they joined their voices to each. They were especially keen while wailing. Varro imagined his own mother and sister receiving news of his death. He did not wish to torment himself with such imaginings, but felt powerless to stop. His overwhelmed mother would collapse on the hallway mosaic floor, Arria hugging her shoulders as both cried hysterically. The scene repeated all night.

For he must die, he decided. The leader of his captives only wanted to dangle hope before him so he might betray whatever information they believed he held. Without hope of survival, he would have no reason to endanger his companions. But once he became useless, they would kill him.

"Then I guess I've no worries for new gear and loans. There's positive news." Even hearing his own voice in the dull silence of the pit was a comfort.

They would probably let him starve. Despite the rampant terror of his situation, Varro still had an appetite. He had spent a hard day foraging, followed by a harrowing battle, and a run through a dark forest. He was exhausted and hungry.

Time alone also calmed the killing lusts that emerged in him. Had such feelings always been there, or were they born from a relentless summer of military training? Falco had beat him for years after taking his vow of nonviolence. He had never once acted on any impulse to strike back. But today, had he the chance, he would plunge his gladius to the hilt into the first enemy he found.

What kind of person was Marcus Varro really? he wondered. Not the man he thought he was.

The evening of misplaced introspection passed into the dull stain of dawn. The grate squares above shined broken light on Varro's face. He now sat against the earthen pit wall. The cold and wet has seeped into his bones, fixing him in place like rusted metal. His stomach gurgled. He might have slept, for time seemed to have sped by unaccounted. But he was not rested.

Roosters called in the distance. Dogs barked. If he closed his eyes, he could imagine life at home. He had a dog when he was a boy, but she wandered off and never returned. She would bark alongside the roosters every morning. But a flicker of shadows over the pit interrupted the happy memory.

The grate lifted aside and thumped to the ground. Varro felt a shudder through the dirt wall at his back. Two people muttered to each other, and a frail wood ladder descended into the pit. A man shouted commands Varro did not understand, but guessed well enough. He put his feet to the rungs and scaled out of the pit.

Two spear points touched him immediately. He had to smile. What threat was he without a weapon or shield? Yet they did not judge him lightly. One appeared a year younger than him, with a serious face and beautiful brown eyes. Had he been a woman, Varro might have been smitten.

The other man, older and pox-scarred, jabbed him with the spear. Sharp pain pricked the back of his left arm, and Varro walked in the direction the jab indicated.

The camp was like his own, without the severe organization. They built it on a hill, he remembered that much from the prior night, and surrounded it with wooden stakes that formed a man-high wall. It would hinder an infantry charge. But any Roman war machine would destroy it in one shot. The buildings were a hodgepodge of wood or hide tents. All had some pens for live-stock. Everywhere white smoke puffed up as this village woke to the new day.

His two guards herded him to the most extravagant tent. This reminded him of the tribune quarters, though more barbaric. Two more spearmen stood guard outside the tent and spoke to Varro's escorts. After a brief exchange, they entered first with Varro shoved behind them. He was in a box of guards now. Did they think this much of his fighting ability? They must have had other experiences with more capable Roman soldiers, he thought.

Light spilled through the open tent flap. Also, the tent had been constructed to allow light in from the top, much like the atrium in his own home. The handsome leader from the night before now sat on a wooden chair. He had changed into a light blue tunic. Lazing on his chair, his heroically proportioned muscles left no doubt to Varro that this man could snap him like an old branch. If he was a twin to the man Varro had slain, he counted his luck.

"Roman, I hope you slept well."

"Well enough. I'm hungry, though."

The leader's brow raised and his mouth rounded in surprise. But he again leaned back in laughter. The four guards with him only seemed to understand Varro had been disrespectful. The young one with beautiful eyes butted Varro's chest with his spear.

The force staggered him back, but did not knock him over. Varro narrowed his eyes at the boy. If he tried that again, he would teach the fool a lesson.

The leader shouted something that chastened his men, and all stepped back. The leader now leaned on his knees. His oiled hair shimmered with the light falling from above.

"Roman, my name is Artas. You are in my humble home, and will be treated well enough given the nature of our meeting. But do not presume too much, or I will teach you respect. Yes?"

While Artas's Latin was accented, he spoke with sophistication surprising for his barbaric company.

"Yes, sir." Varro had become a soldier, for the words came easily.

Artas smiled and sat back. He stared at Varro with hooded eyes.

"You are less impressive without your armor and helmet. Don't worry, Roman. They are well cared for." Artas stretched his powerful arm to indicate the corner of his tent. Varro's gear had been dumped into a pile there. "And you are one of the young ones. I am wondering if my investment in you was misplaced."

"I'm not going to tell you anything, if that's what you mean. I know you will just kill me. So why not get to it? I'm sure your men would enjoy the sport."

Varro hoped Artas would disagree. But he could not roll over like a dog. Beside his own pride as a Roman, he did not want to endanger his friends.

Artas smiled placidly.

"Roman, you overestimate yourself. If I want you dead, I will cut your throat and fling your corpse over the walls."

"Walls, sir? Is that what you are calling those pile of sticks surrounding us? Go to Rome, sir. You will see real walls there."

Artas sat back in astonishment. He ran his hand over his curly beard, then barked a sharp command to one of his men.

The blow to the back of Varro's head was sharp and sudden. He collapsed to hands and knees, his vision hazy and ears ringing. But he endured. Falco, true to his word, had trained him for worse beatings than this.

"We don't share the same sense of humor, Roman," Artas said from his chair. Varro raised his head to see sandaled feet.

With another growl from Artas, two guards hauled Varro from the ground. He wobbled on his feet, and rubbed the back of his head. Artas smirked at him.

"We are Illyrian, Roman. We are not barbarians. I have been to Athens and seen all that Rome has claimed as her own. Yet I admire your people. That is why I speak your language."

Varro considered he might have more practical reasons for learning Latin, but declined to voice his thoughts. His head was still spinning. If army life had trained him for one thing it was to admit to as few of his own thoughts as possible. Artas shifted on his chair, looking into his imagination as he spoke.

"I had once imagined myself visiting Rome as you have suggested. But my fortunes have changed since those days. And I fear they will soon change again. Your arrival here is proof of that."

"I will not tell you anything," Varro repeated. "I'd rather die."

Artas laughed, dry and humorless.

"So quick to throw your life away. Ah, but that is what makes you Romans so fierce in battle. You are young. You do not understand how well I am treating you, as you've no comparison. But I will educate you."

Varro raised his chin. His knees quivered, his heart raced, but he would never show the terror coursing through him.

"How many others are there of you? Is it true you come to punish Macedonia? See, these are simple details I want to confirm. I could have asked you in the forest, but instead I made you my guest."

"Your hospitality is interesting, sir. My pit was especially luxurious and the lack of food and water is a delightful surprise."

Artas folded his hands and gave a soft smile.

"The tribes have not all decided what to do about Rome. Do we stand with Macedonia, who are at our backs, or do we side with the Romans, who the gods favor with victory? I am no more than a brigand, an outcast with no voice. But if I were granted one, perhaps I would choose Macedonia."

"Then you would have chosen poorly." Varro again lifted his head with pride for Rome. But his stomach flipped with his own audacity. He had just violated his principle of keeping his thoughts silent. From Artas's swiftly reddening face, he realized he had at last gone too far.

"Roman, you have wasted enough of my morning. I want to confirm your numbers and location. You can either answer now and live your life as a slave, or you can defy me. If you defy me, I will still have my answers though you will not have an unbroken bone remaining, and then I will let your death last a week."

"Sir, I am ordered to reveal nothing to an enemy which you have plainly stated you are. Besides, you attacked us while we were no threat to you. You will never make an ally of Rome now."

Artas stared at him, his face red and expression flat. The four guards looked between their leader and Varro. They gripped their spears as if ready to join a battle line. At last, Artas spoke low and threatening.

"That attack was ill-advised. My brother, who must still be buried, has paid for that foolishness. We wanted a few captives only. I am well aware of what that attack will cost us. So I've no time to waste learning more about who might come searching for revenge."

"A Roman army, sir. What else do you suppose? We are here to crush Philip of Macedonia and free Athens. This much should be known even to your grandmother."

Artas lowered his head. "I have been a fool. We are done here."

He leaned back and shouted clipped orders to his guards. They smiled with delight at Varro. Three were before him, but one remained directly behind to prevent his escape.

This time the blow to the back of his head turned his vision white. He collapsed once more to the packed dirt floor of the tent. Blow after blow hammered down on his back. Each strike was fire, crashing against his spine, shoulder blades, and ribs. He curled up to protect the back of his head, which they seemed to avoid. Was this how Nonus and his contubernium had died? The thought rose through the numbing pain. It was as if he were outside his own body, able to see himself surrounded by four men clubbing him with their spear shafts.

Varro, his head tucked to the ground, heard Artas lean forward on his chair and his voice sounded close as if he leaned forward.

"This is how Roman soldiers die, is it not? Beaten to death. Once all your bones are broken, we will break your head. It will be a mercy."

The beating stopped when he spoke. Varro only realized this when he ordered his men to start once more.

Curled up, helpless against four men battering him into the ground, Varro's desperate mind flashed with inspiration.

"Stop! I know something you want! Something important!"

Artas laughed. "Of course you do. Anything to stop the beating, yes? But we've only just begun. A little longer, Roman."

Varro dared lift his head. A blow slammed against his shoulder, rocking him with sharp agony.

"Your brother's gold chain! I know what happened to it!"

Artas shouted and the beating stopped.

Varro lay panting, curled up on the dirt. He felt the chain pressing against his belly. It had warmed to the temperature of his own flesh, and he had forgotten it in his terror. But now, as the blows drove him against the gold, he realized he had a means to escape.

Artas kicked him over with his foot. Varro flopped to his aching back and felt the chain shift against his skin. His pulse surged from fear it might slip from his tunic. But it remained tucked into his belt. He stared up at Artas's angry face. The four guards, including the beautiful boy, hovered over him. From this angle, he saw a resemblance in that boy to Artas. Perhaps they were relatives.

"That chain was missing from my brother's neck," he said. "Whoever killed him must have claimed it for himself. But if that were true, how would you know he wore the chain?"

"Because I was there, sir. I know who killed your brother. When it was over we fought over who should claim the chain. It was as thick as a man's finger."

Varro's mind raced along with his heart. Lying was not his strength, but then his life had never depended upon it. Artas stood with his muscled arms folded over his chest.

"So it was. But tell me, Roman, how did he die? He and his bodyguard could not have been slain by young ones like you."

"We're not all young, sir. Plenty of veterans were with us. It all happened so fast. I didn't know which way to look."

Varro decided he had better make the brother's death sound heroic.

"Your brother had thrown off two of our men. I had my own attacker to deal with. When that finished, your brother and his bodyguard had killed his attackers. If others hadn't arrived, he'd have killed me next. But my contubernium and some veterans surrounded him. They got lucky and killed your brother and his guard."

Artas turned to his guards and spoke in a low voice. Varro collected himself, being sure that the chain did not shift from beneath his belt as he sat up. His ribs hurt and he felt like vomiting. But as all the blows had landed on his torso, he could stand and move his arms.

"So what happened to his chain?" Artas asked.

"The veteran who killed him claimed it. But we all thought it should be broken into pieces and shared equally. There were only two veterans but almost eight of us. I think they were considering killing us, to be honest."

Artas chuckled. "It was a thick chain and worth much to soldiers like you. But to me it is a memory and a mark of rank. You did not break that chain?"

"No, sir. The veterans knew they couldn't take on all of us. Plus, your men were still all around. An officer was nearby, and if he saw that chain then none of us would ever see it again. We agreed to settle later. No one could be trusted to hold it. So we buried it nearby, next to a tree and under a round stone that was covered in moss. We agreed to return to the spot and decide who should claim it."

Artas stroked his beard.

"So you had a part in killing my brother, then?"

"In a manner of speaking, sir. I was there and part of the distraction that led to a vulnerable moment. But I never raised a sword to him. I had my own fight. It was our best soldier that killed him, and only then because he had help."

"And so while leaving the forest, you slipped your companions and returned to the battleground?"

Varro nodded. "But I got lost, sir. I'm no woodsman. When I found your brother once more, I could not mark the spot where we buried the chain. It was close but off the clearing somewhere. I was trying to retrace all that had happened from the moment your brother fell. Then you arrived."

Artas stepped back to his chair, his hand patting his beard as he thought. His guards looked expectantly after him. Varro shifted again. A sharp pain tore through his stomach as he tried to follow Artas's steps. A short gasp escaped him.

Now that he had created this lie, he had to figure out how to make his escape. He knew Falco and the others had seen his capture. They could not do anything other than report what had happened and risk punishment. He and Falco had formed a nascent friendship, but was it strong enough to risk punishment? Varro had also just saved his life. Of course, he might not have come for him at all, and rather Gallio or Panthera forced him. Still, despite their history, he believed Falco would try to aid him.

The question remained if the tribune would be motivated to do anything in retaliation for the attack on the foragers. If they did, Varro guessed they would not delay. Then Falco and the others might stand a chance of rescuing him. The tribune would ask them to show where the Illyrian forces had last been spotted and follow the trail from there.

At the least, Varro had to return Artas and his men to that spot to have any chance of encountering help. Even if the army did not arrive, he had a better chance to escape in the forest than he did as a prisoner in this camp. He might die in any attempt to run. But he would definitely die if he remained on Artas's tent floor.

Artas conferred in a low voice with his men. They all cast sideways glances to Varro still kneeling on the floor. He wondered if he should try to convince them. Yet if he seemed too eager, it might raise suspicion. He lowered his eyes whenever they looked to him.

"You can't have been the only one to sneak away," Artas said, sitting on his chair once more. His arms remained folded over his chest. "The chain may be gone by now."

"That is possible, sir. But I was in the rear and able to slip away. The others were in front with the optio. It's less likely they got away. Foragers go out all the time, sir. We figured to wait until our next rotation, then go out together. Though probably everyone would be trying to get back alone before then. Eventually one of us will get it, and soon. Today might be your best chance."

Artas's nose twitched as he thought. Varro looked to his guards. The young one seemed eager, as if he were ready to run. Perhaps he wanted the chain as well. Artas waved him away like shooing a fly.

"It is tempting. For that chain represents the true leader of our people. With my brother dead, it would strengthen my leadership after him. People need symbols of authority, Roman. I'm sure you're aware."

"I can show you where we hid it, sir. With better light and no pressure from my companions, it will be easy to find."

"That may be true, but I cannot leave my village before I know your army's response."

Varro inclined his head. "Of course, sir. You can keep me in the pit until you are ready."

"A few blows and your attitude has changed, Roman." Artas unfolded his arms and leaned forward with a smile.

"Sir, if I may ask, have you or your men ever fought against Rome?"

Artas's smile vanished. "Never, and we've no mind to. At least now that I am ruler."

"Well, sir, in fairness you probably have the wrong idea of how the Roman army works. The army does not act in haste, nor does it ever act for revenge alone. Everything it does has a greater purpose. If Illyria has yet to join Rome, then our consul will not jeopardize that possible alliance. We need Illyria, sir. We have to go through it to reach Macedonia. I'm sure the consul wants allies in our rear rather than enemies."

"You know what your consul wants?" Artas again folded his arms.

"Sir, it only makes sense. If I had to fight you, I would not want your armed guards behind me. If I wanted your friendship, would I earn it by killing your guards? I don't think an attack will come. At least the consul will send an emissary first. But I think some of my companions will get to your brother's chain within days. It's worth too much to a common soldier to ignore the temptation."

Varro hoped he sounded convincing. Artas stared past steepled fingers, eyes unfocused. The young boy whispered to him at his side. Varro hoped he whispered encouragement.

For he had stated the opposite of what he believed would happen. Defeat is not tolerated, and any perceived humiliation would be avenged in blood. So he had checked first if Artas had any experience with Rome. For if he had, he would realize to flee now.

"Very well, Roman," Artas said with a shrug. "It is not far to travel. Take me back to claim my brother's chain. If you do this, then I will return you to your men with a message of peace. Perhaps we can prevent any more violence."

17

Varro trudged across the sun-drenched fields toward the forest where he hoped freedom awaited. The homely scents of cooking vanished behind him, as the Illyrian brigand village faded behind a gentle rise. Soon he could no longer hear the barking dogs.

He felt like a dog himself, being bound with hands behind his back and a rope around his neck. The beautiful young boy led Varro like his pet hound. He also tugged unnecessarily, sending jolts of pain along Varro's back. An intense burning with bouts of sharp pain in his ribs indicated broken bones. After such a brief but vicious beating, he was glad to be alive. So he staggered forward, his will to survive pumping strength into his body. In any other circumstance, he doubted he could move.

Having been provided water from the largest of Artas's kitchens, they had denied him food. His limbs were weak and his legs quivered. With each feeble step forward, he realized he was at Artas's mercy. He had promised Varro freedom upon finding the chain. But he was not a man of honor. Varro had a sense for these things, and Artas's eyes were full of deceit.

Artas led ten of his warriors with them. All carried round shields of various faded colors, and all slung long spears across their shoulders. They wore bronze helmets, but otherwise were garbed only in their plain tunics. Artas alone wore a mail shirt and bronze helmet. His shield was freshly painted black. He seemed prepared for a fight. Varro mused that the rest of these men would make good dummies for sword drills.

If Rome came, they would be cut down like a barley harvest.

If Rome came. That fear repeated as Varro tried to keep pace with the tugging rope. Perhaps with enough fear powering him, he could run a short distance. But he had been honest with Artas in that he was no woodsman. These men, however poorly trained, would run him down among the trees.

Falco, you better be bringing me help, he thought.

To further enforce his fears that Artas would cross him, he had not only been denied his gear but his mother's pugio now slapped at the hip of the boy yanking him along to the forest. He had seen Varro staring after it and somehow guessed this mattered more to him than anything. So he claimed it for himself, triumphantly snatching it out of the pile of gear in Artas's tent. He had waved it before Varro, who tried to act as if he did not care. The pretty boy then shoved it into his belt. The fool wasn't even wearing it correctly, Varro thought.

All his other gear, bronze helmet and pectoral, gladius, and scutum, remained in the tent.

"I need some compensation for your time here," Artas had said.

And to Varro, that meant he was not sincere in making peace with Rome and his promises of freedom meant nothing. To send him back unharmed and in shame would be a provocation, not an offer of peace. Not that anyone cared about him, Varro understood, but Roman pride was already bruised after that ambush. Beating and humiliating a soldier and sending him back would inflame the tribunes who were already likely planning revenge. Even Artas, who claimed inexperience with Rome, must understand this.

At last they were at the tree line. Artas called a halt and his men gathered around him. Varro wanted to flop to the grass, but knew he would struggle to rise again. He hung like a dying sunflower, the brilliance of the sun warming the top of his head. Pretty boy yanked his neck, giggling like the girl he appeared to be. Varro stared at his pugio. To plunge that into his tormentor's heart would be a joy.

He offered a thought of apology to his great-grandfather. Violence was going to be the answer to everything while he was in the army. He had been a naïve fool to think otherwise.

"Roman, we are going to take you back to the spot of my brother's death."

Varro nodded. What else are we doing out here, you shit? But he held that thought to himself.

"I will untie your arms so you can search," he continued. "But you will remain tied by the neck. Do not think to run."

"I can't fucking run. You've broken my back and I haven't eaten in a day."

Artas roared with laughter, but the pretty boy hauled on the rope. Varro splayed out on his face. A shudder of pain tore through his back, radiating around to his stomach. But he bit down on any sign of pain. Instead, he felt a cold flicker of fear.

The gold chain shifted, popping up from his belt.

His heart thudded as another man wrestled him back to his feet. He felt the warm links shifting around his belt. All the beating and stumbling had dislodged it. The only luck here was that it had dislodged above the belt rather than beneath it. Otherwise, it would have fallen to the ground. It might still worm out from his tunic. He had to be careful not to reveal it before time.

They threaded paths between the trees that Varro could not

see. The pretty boy dragged him along, giggling. He struggled against his avowed nonviolence and an intense desire to saw off both arms of his skinny, foolish tormentor. The shadows of the trees cooled the air within three paces of entering its dim confines. Varro's hobnailed sandals dug into the dirt and provided traction. Otherwise, in his weakened state he might slip and fall.

He did not recognize the place where he and Falco had fought for their lives. Yet Artas and his companions halted. The boy let the rope slacken, providing relief to the chaffing at the back of his neck. It was a small clearing that looked like any other to Varro— forest debris littering the floor, bare fall trees and bushes, mossy stones. What separated one from the other? he wondered.

"Here we are, Roman," Artas said, spreading his arms wide. "Does it look familiar?"

Varro blinked, looked around, and answered honestly.

"Are you sure this is the place?"

Artas frowned and pointed to the ground. "The marks of battle are still upon the earth, Roman. My brother fell here. His body-guard's blood dried on that tree and the branches near it. Now, where is the rock where you buried the necklace?"

The pulse in his neck raced and he forgot all about his pain. Artas and his men surrounded him. The pretty boy still held the rope, fidgeting with the pugio dangling at his hip.

"I've got to search for the spot," he said, fearing the crack in his voice betrayed his fear. "I was trying to retrace my steps when you captured me. I should do the same again. But do I need this rope on my neck still?"

"Of course you do, Roman. You are not free until I have that chain."

"I don't even know where I am. Where would I escape to that you couldn't catch me?"

Artas shook his head and again pointed to where he claimed his brother had fallen.

Varro sighed and stood on the spot. His plan was vanishing with every moment. Falco and the others were not coming, or were coming too late to be of any help. He had to save himself.

If he could lead off the boy, then he might wrestle his pugio away. It was already loose in the sheath, or else he wouldn't have lost it in the first place. So snatching it away was possible. Then if he could drop the boy, he might escape. From there, he had to count on the gods for mercy. He would run and evade Artas. If not, he would die. But he would certainly die if he didn't try.

"What are you doing?" Artas asked. "Stop staring at the ground and search. Don't waste time, Roman."

Varro leaned over the spot, then scanned around. He wanted to lead the boy out of the circle of guards. Artas, now satisfied that Varro had started to work, leaned against the tree and mumbled something to his men. They relaxed and set their shields against their legs. Some sat on the ground as Varro parted bushes, pretending to search.

His motions awakened the pretty boy's foul temper, and he tugged hard on Varro's rope. He stumbled back and screamed with a sharp pain that jolted through his back. The boy giggled again. But Varro whirled and shouted to Artas.

"Tell your boy to leave some slack in the rope or we'll be here all day."

Artas barked something that sounded chiding. The boy lowered his head and let the rope slacken. Varro glared at him, glanced at the pugio, then pretended to sort through bushes. He feigned exclamations of excitement, claiming he was getting nearer. Each time he slipped farther beyond the line of bored guards. They were confident Varro could not escape. Their confidence was Varro's only weapon against them now. They were letting him creep forward with only the boy holding the rope to follow. Patient step by patient step, he had gone beyond them and moved just far enough that he would have a head start.

"I remember this tree," Varro said. "Let me see."

He bounded forward. His heart pumped up into his throat and his temples throbbed. But he also tingled with excitement and fear. He felt light enough to float out of the forest as he had led the boy along.

"I think this is it," he said, looking down at nothing. With his back to the boy, he fit his fingers between the rope at his throat so it could not tighten against his windpipe.

He snapped around. The boy held the rope with both hands, but had grown bored in the few moments Artas had forbidden him to torment Varro. His large eyes widened in shock.

Varro hauled on the rope and as expected the boy did not let go. Instead, he sought to retain his grip. Weakened and beaten though he may be, relentless training had hardened his muscles far beyond this mere boy. His pull sent the boy flying toward him with a squeal.

Artas called from the clearing. "What's going on, Roman?"

The boy lurched forward as Varro pulled his hand out of the now-slackened rope around his neck. He balled a fist and slammed it into the boy's temple.

He screeched and crumpled with foreign curses following him down. The boy bounced against a dead bush that deflected him back to Varro's feet.

Without thought, he dropped on his knee into the boy's upturned stomach. The wind flew out of his lungs and his eyes rolled back. Varro thought to punch him once more, but that would be foolish. Instead, he snatched the pugio from the sheath at the boy's side.

In the next instant, he slashed the razor-honed edge through the rope now dangling at his chest. The loop remained, but only a nub of cord hung from it. He was freed.

"Roman?"

Varro could not see his enemies. They were behind him and

obscured by bushes. But he imagined them gathering their shields and snatching up spears. He heard the jingle of Artas's chain shirt.

"If I had time to repay you," Varro said, glaring down at the boy. "I would. I hope to never see you again."

He shoved down on the boy's soft stomach as he popped up to his feet. The boy had recovered and his eyes were wide with hate. As Varro regained his feet, so did he.

They faced each other now, but Varro held his pugio between them. He smiled, then turned to run.

But the boy leapt at him, clawing for his face.

Even with his injured back, Varro was still stronger. He sloughed the boy aside, then slashed with his dagger. To stab would be to kill, but to slash would hopefully injure the boy enough to delay pursuit.

The boy was fast and skirted back from the worst of the slash. The honed blade instead sliced across the chest of his tunic, cutting the plain wool open and drawing a line of red blood.

And revealing female breasts.

Varro stared in amazement as the boy fell away screaming, stumbling over a bush and out of sight.

The astonished delay had spent half of Varro's advantage. For now, Artas and the others were alerted to the danger.

"Roman! Stop or your death will be hard!"

He did not heed Artas's words. Instead, he leaped like a scared doe into the trees.

Fear of death, he discovered, was a potent motivator. Not only did all pain in his back vanish, but he ran faster than he ever had before. He felt as if he were running across air instead of uneven forest floor.

The Illyrian brigands shouted curses. The boy, or girl as now revealed, howled with pain and indignation. But all of it was vanishing behind Varro as he sped through the forest.

Toward something.

His headlong rush was glorious, and his plan had proven flawless. But he had no notion of direction. His feet chose paths that seemed to lead away from obstacles. He had to leap one fallen log. But otherwise he sped forward with no direction other than to keep distant from the Illyrians. For a short time it seemed he could continue indefinitely. Yet as he covered ground, his strength ebbed and the pain in his back returned.

And the echoes behind him did not vanish.

In fact, where they had been fading, they were now strengthening.

His legs pumped. Gray, brown, and faded green sped past him in blurs. Branches tore cuts and scratches into his face. Sweat stung his brow and his breath dragged hot through his chest.

He was slowing. His fear-born strength was ebbing.

And in that moment, he heard familiar Roman voices.

"This way!" Varro shouted. "Falco! I'm over here!"

Whether he called to Falco or some total stranger, he did not know. But he heard Latin commands and soon he saw to his left the flickering flashes of bronze helmets and oblong, colorful shields.

The army, never to be humiliated by brigands, was returning for revenge and starting from the spot the enemy had last been spotted.

Varro stumbled ahead, slowing as if his race had ended.

But the Romans he spotted moved in formation, deliberately pushing deeper into the forest and bypassing him. His shouts, he realized, had not been heard.

And he was out of strength to continue. He rested on his knees, heaving his breaths which sent waves of pain along his back. Sweat dripped from his face to patter on the dirt beneath him. The rope loop still around his neck hung before his eyes, reminding him he had not yet escaped.

"Roman! What have you done? It's a trap!"

Varro turned to face Artas. He was crashing through bushes and branches had knocked off his helmet, left red scratches on his glistening face, and deposited twigs and dead leaves into the links of his chain shirt. His reddened cheeks puffed with his breathing.

"You better run to your people," Varro said. "Don't underestimate how fast we can march."

But Artas did not take that bait. Instead, he roared and readied his shield. His powerful hand drew a long, slashing sword that gleamed with the dappled light of the forest.

Varro had a dagger and no armor. He turned to flee, knowing he could not count on luck twice to save him.

He ran for the Romans filtering between the trees. He screamed out and thought he saw at least one figure pause at his shout.

Then three thunderous footfalls followed him, and next Varro flew through the air. Something hit his back, exploding his mind into bright lightning strikes of pain. When he crashed on his face, white flashes seared him with agony.

He lay crumpled as Artas flipped him over.

"You fucking dog! I'm going to have your head!"

The white pain left a residual fog over Varro's vision, but he realized he looked up into Artas's rage-contorted face. He had grabbed Varro by the rope still attached to the neck and hauled him to his knees.

"One strike is all I need, Roman," he said with a growl. "Your head will go flying back to your friends."

Varro kneeled before Artas. Through sheer will, he still held the pugio that Artas had either overlooked or did not care about. As his would-be executioner positioned his head with one hand, he shook off his shield from his other arm.

Behind Artas, a figure emerged into the small space where Varro would die. He carried a red oblong shield and wore a bronze helmet. He had a pilum ready in his other hand.

It was Optio Latro.

"Optio! Help me!"

"That's not a trick I will fall for, Roman." Artas stood back, taking his long sword in both hands and raising it over his shoulder.

But Optio Latro stared at Varro.

And smiled.

Cold terror spread through Varro's body. Latro was going to let him die. He had been right, after all. Latro wanted him dead.

"Go to your gods, Roman!"

Artas hauled back for his beheading strike.

Rage gushed from the core of Varro's heart, whisking away all fear and pain. The white clouds in his vision burned away to red mist, but all doubt fled his mind to leave it clear.

"Hold, Artas!"

Varro reached into his tunic and tore out the golden chain that had bounced along his belt line through the entire chase. He dangled it between him and Artas, who slackened his sword arm at the sight of it.

"Your brother's chain," Varro said. Then he flung it into the bushes. It twirled through the air, then a golden spark winked as if bidding farewell before vanishing into the forest.

Artas screamed, watching it fly away.

Varro pounced on the distraction. He sprung from his knees, pugio firmly in hand, then collided with Artas's solid torso. The chain links of his armor crushed against his flesh, but Varro did not err.

He plunged the dagger into Artas's kidney. The sharp, tapered blade snapped the chain links and slid into his torso. Artas arched his back and screamed.

Varro continued to push against him now that he was off balance. This drove Artas onto his back with Varro riding him down. He already twisted the pugio as he tore it out. Hot blood splashed over his hand, and Artas's face twisted with suffering.

Scrambling atop the muscular Illyrian, Varro raised the pugio for a killing strike. He gave a wicked smile.

"I killed your brother, too!"

Something smashed into him from behind. Varro collapsed atop Artas, his sight whirling. The pugio slipped from his hand.

His eyes fluttered, lids too heavy to remain open. Artas wheezed in his ear, trapped beneath Varro. He gave a coughing, bloody laugh.

Then a second blow stole the world from Varro, and he knew nothing but cold blackness.

18

The world bobbed between nothingness and fuzzy gloom. Varro smelled the earthy forest, heard Roman voices, felt hands turning him over. But he could not hold consciousness long enough. It slipped away into cold blackness the moment he thought to awaken.

Falco's white face leaned over him, gazing into his eyes. Never in his life would he have expected to feel joy at seeing him. But even in this shifting consciousness he felt a warm glow. The gods were strange. For seeing Falco meant safety.

The world faded. Then he awakened to someone placing him on a stretcher. Voices spoke in clipped tones. Varro again saw Falco leaning over him.

"You're all right," he said. His expression, however, made Varro believe he was about to die. He felt like it.

Then memory flooded back of the fight with Artas. He snatched out with his arm, grabbing Falco by his gray tunic.

"Mark a tree," he whispered, pulling Falco closer. "Don't forget this spot."

Falco shook his head as if he did not understand. Varro lacked the strength to explain it and tugged on Falco's tunic for emphasis. Then he rose off the ground, and his hand pulled away.

"Get him back to the rally point. If there are more soldiers injured, they'll all return together."

Optio Latro appeared over him. Varro was raised to his waist level and had to look up into those fierce blue eyes and unruly brows. He smiled, but it was the smile of a viper.

"You should get your rest, Varro. You're lucky to be alive. Close your eyes for a while."

Varro just stared at him.

"Sorry, sir," said the stretcher bearer over his head. "But he shouldn't sleep after being hit in the head. Might not wake up again, sir."

"Ah, well, that'd be a pity," Latro said. He smiled down once more, then placed something heavy on Varro's chest. "Your pugio. Looks like it saw good use today."

His view from the stretcher shifted as the two bearers maneuvered him around. He turned to the side and saw Artas's corpse starting up at the trees. He smiled as if he were happy. Perhaps he was happy to be free of this life, Varro thought. Where was there any joy in it?

The young boy, or girl as he now knew her, kneeled over the body and wept. Varro hadn't remembered her being here.

"Your time in this fight is over for now," Latro said. "I'll see you in camp."

The stretcher bearers carried Varro away. His companions were lined up and watching him depart. Falco stood in full dress, scutum resting against his leg and pilum in hand. His bronze helmet now held three long, black feathers. Gallio, Panthera, and the others likewise watched him go, all now with black feathers decorating their helmets. Their faces were pale and inscrutable as Varro was carried past them.

"Lucky us," said the stretcher bearers above Varro's head. His tone said he thought otherwise. "No treasure or slaves today. We got the shit job after all."

"We're not missing anything," said the bearer at Varro's feet. "The bandits will vanish before we even reach them. There won't be anything to grab. Eh, Varro? It'll be fine to miss this one."

But Varro did not answer. His mind was too scrambled from the blow to his head and all else he had witnessed. His pugio rocked on his chest as his bearers carried him out of the trees. He had almost made it out on his own, he realized. Too bad he had to be carried out.

He grabbed the pugio from his chest or else it might fall as they marched him away. His eyes grew heavy even as his stretcher bearers tried to engage him in talk. His hand crushed down on the pugio as he drifted off to sleep.

Sleep was deep and turbulent, something inescapable. Varro felt as if a lead ball had been chained to his ankle and then thrown into a frozen lake. He wrestled against the icy blackness, struggling to breathe and live. But the air in his lungs was fast burning away, bringing him closer to sucking in the dark water enveloping him and drowning. His heart raced and his temples pounded. His chest threatened to burst. This state seemed to ebb, then return worse than before. Each cycle he thought he would drown in darkness. The weights around his legs ensured he would never surface. His screams were muddled in the frigid water and rippled away into blackness.

Then he awakened.

The living world differed from his place of dreams. He experienced warmth again, feeling heat shimmering upon his face. A pungent odor wafted up from his chest. He shook his head in response and felt the softness of a pillow against his face. He was on his stomach, pressed into the feather-stuffed mattress.

He opened his eyes and stared at the dull amber of a plank wall. But sounds came from behind, the scrape of wood on wood.

Turning toward the sound made his head swim. But he settled back into the pillow.

This was the hospital.

The Greek doctor had pushed back on his stool while sitting at his desk. He studied wax-coated wood slates by the light of a clay lamp. Its flame was like staring into the sun, and Varro closed his eyes. He moaned to attract attention.

"Varro?" The doctor spoke his name, then again his wooden stool legs scrapped across the floor. "Are you awake now?"

He opened his eyes to find the doctor crouched down beside him. Indistinct figures drew closer behind him. Rather than speak, he nodded.

"Who am I? Do you know?"

"The doctor," Varro said, wondering at the question.

A smile grew on the doctor's face. He adjusted his crouch to lean in.

"Do you feel well enough to get on your side?"

Again without answering, Varro shifted to his side. His ribs ached and he feel dizzy. But he faced the doctor now. One of his assistants stood behind him, also smiling.

"This is the best you've done in days," the doctor said. "I was worried for you. I was about to let those old healer women have their turn with you."

Varro furrowed his brows. "I just got here."

The doctor smiled and closed his eyes. "What is your last memory?"

"Some men griping about not getting to fight. I was just out of the forest."

"That was a little over two weeks ago."

Varro studied the doctor's smiling face. He seemed honest.

"I really got hurt, didn't I?"

The doctor stood up from his crouch, and his assistant shifted the stool over to allow him to sit by Varro's side.

"Actually, your wounds were not so bad. Your ribs were bruised, but no broken bones."

Varro's heavy eyes widened but swiftly fell half-closed.

"That's impossible. I must have broken my ribs."

"I doubt you could have done any of what you did with broken ribs. The blow to your head was the worst of it. But fortunately your skull seems thicker than the average man's."

"That is what my sister says."

Both he and the doctor chuckled before falling into silence. Varro felt as if he could return to sleep, but feared that dark and cold place. Now that he had surfaced, he had to remain here.

"If I wasn't so hurt, why have I been asleep for so long?"

The doctor shifted and a shadow seemed to flit across his face.

"I have wondered as much too. You remember nothing after being rescued?" Varro shook his head. The doctor studied him before continuing. "After a few days you were recovering fine. Your companions even came to cheer you. But then you suddenly developed a terrible fever. Normally this could be attributed to an infected wound or else sickness. But in my estimation you didn't suffer from either. Still you turned babbling mad before falling unconscious."

"I don't remember that." Varro heard the weakness in his own voice.

"It's not uncommon to forget events that bring us close to death. This is perhaps a mercy from the gods. I don't understand it, yet see it often enough in my work. Varro, you were as close to death as a man can be. Your breath was so shallow it barely fogged my mirror. My assistants would've buried you had I not been here."

"Then I'm glad you were here."

"I placed you alone in this room. In case you carry some plague you picked up from the brigand camp. Many of the people there were sick, including the slaves we took. But you have no signs of illness. Yesterday you awakened, but I've told no one yet. Today is the longest conversation we've had. You seem far more alert. I'll want to examine you, of course, but I might even say you are recovering."

"If I'm not sick, and it was not my head wound, then what was it?"

"I said neither thing." The doctor straightened in his chair and rubbed his nose. "You may be ill with something beyond my knowledge. And being struck in the head causes many strange behaviors in the victims. While a student, I met a man who broke his skull falling from a horse. He forgot how to speak yet could write with ease. So your fever and delirium may all very well be your reaction to the blow to your head."

Varro shifted off his arm, which grew numb, and lay on his back. He felt an intense soreness radiate along his shoulder blades and winced.

"My bones are not broken?"

"Not at all," the doctor said. "But the back can be more sensitive than you think. Pain may last long after the bruises have faded. You are young and strong enough to recover soon. I can mix a medicine to help with the pain, but it may make you sleepy."

"I don't want to sleep again."

"I understand. Let me examine you, and then we can start to get you back to eating solid food. It will take some time to recover your strength and your appetite."

"All this so you can put me back in line to get my head cut off by some Macedonian."

The doctor hissed through his teeth, but said no more. Instead his warm fingers prodded Varro's ribs, pulled up his eyelids, exposed his teeth and gums, then pressed against the base of his neck. The doctor completed another circuit, pressing his hands into Varro's ankles and legs. He concluded his exam with a gentle smile and a pat to Varro's shoulder.

The next two days Varro passed resting on his cot in this small room. Beyond the door he heard the doctor and his assistants treating other patients. Unlike his first visit, the hospital was full of injured or sick men. He heard some cough, others moan, and others complain. To his chagrin, he would have preferred to sleep through all the sounds of suffering.

He knew Falco had come to visit. While half asleep, he heard him arguing with the doctor. But he never made it into the room. If Varro's father had come, he must have been rebuffed when he was asleep.

His father would not ignore him so close to death. He was not so callous as to leave his own son to struggle against death. But the doctor was adamant about Varro's recovery, even to the point of keeping his father away.

Within the week he was sitting up, eating porridge, and walking around for a short time. Every day his strength returned, the pain lessened, and the dizziness abated.

Every day Falco came to visit and was turned away. At the end of the week he was allowed inside.

Varro had been seated on his bed, pressed against the wall, staring at the confines of this tiny room when Falco appeared in the door. He seemed taller and stronger than before. His prominent brow was wrinkled over his serious eyes.

"The doctor says you're not sick, but he's keeping you in here as a precaution. I don't think you're sick, Varro. But you look weak."

"I've been lying on my back for weeks. What else should I look like?"

Varro rubbed his chin, which itched from stubble finally growing there.

"You might even have to shave," Falco said, then leaned against the doorframe. "The army has made a proper man of you."

"When I'm done with my service, I want to grow a flowing

beard like the ancient Greek philosophers." He stroked the imaginary length of it, leading down to the center of his chest. Both he and Falco laughed.

"I recovered all your gear," Falco said. "It was easy enough to find in the camp. Only Roman stuff there. It's back in the barracks house."

Varro thanked him and both fell to silence. At last, Falco looked over his shoulder and then pulled up the stool the doctor used during examinations. He dropped his voice.

"We've been watching this place day and night," he said as he shuffled the stool closer. "One of us is always on duty, so it's easy enough to see if Latro has come back."

Varro shifted on the cot to lean in to Falco. His heart raced.

"Latro? Why are you watching him?"

"Why do you think, you fool?"

Over the last few days, Varro remembered seeing Latro smile at him during his fight with Artas. In his state of confusion he had wondered if he had really seen Latro. But Falco had a look of deadly seriousness.

"When I was fighting for my life, Latro came upon me. I called for his help, but he did nothing. I don't remember what happened after that. I was hit in the head."

Falco again searched over his shoulder before continuing. "You really don't remember when we all came here to drink to your health?"

"Last I remember they were carrying me out of the forest in a stretcher. Now is the first time I've seen you since then."

Falco rubbed his face then let it rest in his hands. "I thought you were full of shit before, but I believe you now. Latro is trying to kill you."

To hear it confirmed from another turned Varro's fingers to ice.

"What convinced you?"

They again drew closer. He could smell wine on Falco's breath and the sweat that stained his tunic. In the room beyond, someone groaned.

"We came to toast your health. You weren't looking great, but the doctor said your wounds were nothing compared to some others that came back with spears through their mouths."

Varro cringed. "Is that real?"

"Of course. Some of our boys got lazy or else just had bad luck. We turned the brigand camp red with their blood, then burned it down. But some still got their revenge before they died."

"Makes me glad I wasn't there for it."

"Well, you lured out their leader and killed him. So there were a lot of fine things being said about you. Except Latro. Before we set out for the brigands, he called you a deserter. When I said you were captured, he called me a liar. But he had to relent when Panthera and Gallio backed me up. We went before the fucking tribune. Can you believe it? I've no idea why he called us. Seems like something the centurions would handle. But he believed our account."

"So Latro came to toast my health after calling me a deserter?"

"We all did. The whole contubernium was so glad you made it out. Though it was pretty fucking stupid to risk your life for that pugio."

"The doctor said you have it now?"

"Don't worry. All your gear is with me, including your pugio. Anyway, Latro pours us all a cup of wine. Really good stuff and not the vinegar we get with our rations. This was officer quality, right from the doctor's desk. So we all drank to your recovery. You looked at your cup funny but didn't say anything. I was going to call you a lily for not appreciating a good cup of wine. But I didn't want to give Latro an excuse to insult you. We talked a short time, then left. Within the hour, we heard that you're dying."

"It's like you're talking about someone else. It's giving me the chills."

"You really can't remember? Gallio found out on his way to a guard shift. He saw Latro going back into the hospital and just had a feeling. He listened at the door and heard the doctor throw Latro out. I guess Gallio got away without being caught, but saw Latro smiling as he left."

"So you think I was poisoned?"

Falco leaned back and pursed his lips. "Of course you were fucking poisoned. If something was wrong with the wine, we'd all be in trouble. But Latro poured your cup. I remember that because he seemed too eager to toast you. He grabbed the doctor's wine decanter without permission, then ordered the assistants to get cups for everyone. But he had a cup ready for you. Isn't that strange? I'm sure it held poison. Just not enough to kill you."

"But wouldn't the doctor know I was poisoned?"

Falco rubbed his face and sighed. "I'm going to forgive your stupidity because you got your brains scrambled. Of course the doctor knows. Why else are you being held here in a special room away from everyone else? You see those men in the main room? They're a lot worse off than you, but they're sent back to duty as soon as they can stand on two feet. One luckless bastard got an arrow through his nuts. He's already been put back on guard duty. But here you are two weeks later, under special watch. Whatever that means."

"Well, this place is starting to feel like a prison. But I'm still weak. Maybe the doctor is just being cautious."

"Varro, an arrow straight through the nuts." Falco mimed an arrow flying into this crotch, then gritted his teeth in mock agony. "That guy is limping around, but he can stand at a gate and ask for passwords. You're still here because the doctor must know Latro wants to kill you. He's protecting you as long as he can."

"But then he should say something to the tribune."

"Knowing and proving aren't the same. He hasn't said anything about his suspicions to us. But he has been kinder to me and the others than he has been to Latro, who checks on you every day. Latro is saying you're well enough to get back to duty now, and will involve the tribune if he keeps holding you. The doctor has to let you out sooner or later. He's probably hoping we'll think of something, but I don't know what to do."

"I still don't understand why Latro would want to kill me. It makes no sense."

Falco shrugged.

"And another thing," he said, snapping his fingers. "After that Illyrian boy nearly broke your head with a branch—"

"Is that what happened? I still haven't found out who hit me, I thought it was her but couldn't be sure."

"Her? Anyway, who cares?" Falco waved his hands in dismissal. "Latro found you first, and when we got there, he had your pugio. The girl which I say was a boy was hugging the brigand you killed. At first it seemed Latro had saved you. But if you think about it, he should've fought with that boy. Instead, the boy was sitting by as if letting Latro have a go at you. We just showed up in time to prevent it from happening."

Varro imagined the scene and his fists tightened in rage.

"But the boy, who was a girl, Falco, I swear it, wanted to kill me too."

"Whatever happened," Falco said. "I think Latro was going to see you dead that instant. I saved your life."

"You did. Thank you, Falco. I owe you."

"We're even now," he said, waving away the issue. "But the bigger problem is what to do next. I don't know why Latro is so bent on killing you, but there's no doubt that he is. He put Nonus up to it at first, then tried to brand you a deserter which is a death sentence. Then he tried to poison you. Not to mention, you say he was ready to let the brigand cut your head off. You're a marked man, Varro."

They sat in defeated silence, both staring at the worn wooden floor. It had been as new when Varro first stayed here after Nonus had wounded him. Now the boards were worn and dirty, just like himself. He shook his head, then released a long sigh.

"This is beyond anything I know to handle," Varro said. "If the doctor won't or can't do anything, I must figure out my own solution. I need to see my father. He'll know what I should do."

Falco's complexion drained to white, and he leaned away as if Varro were a blazing fire that might scorch him.

"What's wrong?"

Falco's dark eyes searched his.

"Varro, I'm sorry. Your father is dead."

19

The autumn wind lifted Varro's wool cloak. He huddled within it, still weak but no longer bone sore. The neat row of graves were marked only with fresh earth and headstones in a small corner of the camp. The wood walls formed one edge of this burial ground. He counted thirty-two total graves, most of which were men who were killed by the brigand ambush or in the resultant destruction of their base. Behind him were the soft echoes of camp life. A throaty officer hollered at his subordinates. A hammer clanged at a forge. The chatter of thousands formed a droning backdrop to it all.

His midday shadow reached the edge of his father's grave. Falco's shadow, standing just behind him, reached the edge of his own. He stared at the headstone, a gray rock with one smooth side. He read his father's last presence in this world.

Quintius Varro, age 47, Triarii First Legion, Second Century, Marcus Varro, heir.

It was a pitiful stone, shaped so that the flat angle was misaligned with the grave. He wished his father had been cremated and sent home to his mother. But the camp was preparing to move farther inland now that talk with Illyria seemed positive. As the tribune had explained upon arrival, the Illyrians were not yet allies but not enemies. They required special care and would soon understand the benefits of siding with Rome against Macedonia. It was all beyond Varro's understanding. He just knew his father's corpse was being left behind to rot in foreign soil while the camp and campaign moved on.

"He's gone to the Elysian Fields," Falco said. "He was the best man I knew. My father loved your father like a brother."

A smile trembled on Varro's mouth. He wondered at the accuracy of Falco's statement, but appreciated the sentiment.

"I can't believe he's dead." The words sounded like someone else speaking them. "I wish I had more time with him. There was so much more I wanted to learn from him. I will miss him."

He felt heat rising in his eyes, but he swore he would not break down. Though he and Falco were alone, the entire contubernium had seen him off. It would not do to return with puffy, red eyes. He was a soldier now, a killer of Rome's enemies and a veteran of combat. His tears had to remain hidden and silent, no matter how much he wanted to throw himself across his father's grave and weep.

His mind must remain clear and focused on what lay ahead. Tears were for later.

Falco cleared his throat.

"My father always said the Varros were the best people in Rome. He wanted to be like your father, but never could. Every time he reached for virtue, he reached for wine instead. Your father spent a lot of time in my house, cleaning up after my father's mistakes, helping my mother when Father was too drunk. Even my father admitted our farm belonged to your family. He just held it together on his good days. Your father kept it making a profit."

Varro turned to him. Falco's brown wool cloak clung to his bulging shoulders as the wind blew across them.

"I never knew that."

"Well, that doesn't make it less true. We owed your family a lot. Why do you think I wanted to pound your face in all the time? It got a bit tiring to hear how much better you were than me."

"What? That's nonsense. I thought your father considered me a weakling?"

"The opposite. My father admired you for keeping such a difficult vow. He does whatever comes to mind, and has no willpower. It's made a wreck of his life. Since he lacked discipline, he wanted me to have it. He'd say, 'Be like the Varro boy.' I wanted to show him you weren't special, that you'd break your vow if pushed. But you never did."

The wind blew between them and Falco seemed much smaller than he ever had.

"I had no idea."

"It wasn't like I was ever going to tell you. But things have changed, Varro. I've changed. You've changed. Your father's dead. My father might as well be. I don't want to die in this fucking war. I don't believe you want to either. So we need each other. And my father is right, Varro, you're a good man. I should stick close to a good man. Maybe I'll learn a few things."

Varro searched Falco's face. His heavy brow shaded his eyes, but there was no trace of dishonesty. A profound guilt overcame him. He had so often cursed Falco as being less than an animal. He was prone to violence and could dominate others with his personality. But he was not as evil as Varro had accused him of being.

"I'm sorry, Falco. I never understood any of that. I thought you a brute."

"You've said as much to my face. And I am a brute. That's what my role in life is."

"No, you're smarter than that. I've always known it, but just wouldn't admit it to myself. I owe you an apology."

Falco sighed. "Let's not worry about me. I'm fine. It's you who has an officer trying to kill him. Focus on that for now."

"Latro killed my father," Varro turned back to the pitiful grave marker and the patch of fresh earth. "I know you've just praised me for my vow of nonviolence. But I am not sure I can hold to it. I want to kill Latro."

Falco chuckled. "Varro, you've been stabbed, abandoned to the enemy, and poisoned all within the space of a few months. Kill him. Your life is in danger."

"It's not for myself. It's for my father. He did not deserve this. He should never have been selected to serve. He had done his six years and would be forty-eight within the year. He died for no purpose to an enemy he couldn't even face."

Falco drew a long breath.

"You don't know for sure Latro was behind your father's death."

"I don't?" Varro turned to frown at Falco. A horse and cart passed behind him. "The first time I was in the hospital, my father fell ill. Next time I was in the hospital he died. He warned me from the start that Latro was trouble. He told me to sleep with one eye open. My father probably knew someone wanted to kill him. Who else but Latro? He wants both of us dead for reasons I may never know. He must have thought his plan succeeded, except I survived the poisoning. My father did not."

He turned back to the grave again. He imagined his father's death. As Falco had explained, his father wanted to organize a rescue party the moment he learned of his son's capture. By that night he fell terribly ill, then died within hours from a delirium-inducing high fever. It was an ignoble end to his proud life. Varro imagined his father sweating and babbling on his cot, then exhaling a final time.

"I agree it's probably tied together," Falco said, breaking Varro out of his imaginings. "But I don't know if Latro ever met up with your father."

"There is no room for coincidence anymore. If we look deep enough, I'm sure we'll find Latro's black hand involved. He makes others do the work for him, like he tried to do with Nonus and Artas. No reason he didn't do the same for my father."

They stood together, wrapping their cloaks against a cold autumn wind. Clouds cast them into shadow. Another cart loaded with crates and casks rolled past. The baggage train was organizing for the camp's departure to permanent winter quarters. The clangs and shouts of men loading goods or dismantling their temporary housing were all dampened and dull to Varro's ears. His head was wooly with anger and confusion.

"What are you going to do?" Falco asked, his voice small.

Varro shrugged. "If I didn't care for my own life, I'd just walk up to Latro and drive my pugio through his heart. But I need to survive for my mother's and sister's sakes. I can't take on an officer alone, even if he's just an optio."

"I've spoken with the others," Falco said, leaning closer. "Gallio, Panthera, and the rest would back you up. They've seen what Latro is about. They don't want to be next, either."

"I appreciate that," Varro said, patting Falco's shoulder. "But they're just hastati like me. We're all new recruits. We've got one battle to our names, and it was just a skirmish. I'll need help from higher up."

"Then what are you thinking? Do you know someone higher up?"

"I wish I did." Varro rubbed his face, then stared into the distance at a work gang loading lumber onto carts. "All I can think of is to go to Centurion Protus. He has been reasonable and might be open enough to listen to me."

Falco sucked his teeth. "Are you sure about that? The officers line up together. Plus, he's the one who picked Latro. You're going to be calling his picked man a murderer."

"I'm not going to name Latro. But maybe I can lead Protus to that conclusion on his own. I've got to convince him that what has been happening to me is not a coincidence."

"Then what? If you can't connect Latro, I'm not sure what you're doing."

"I'm protecting myself, Falco. I'm going on record with an official complaint about my own safety. Maybe Protus will watch more carefully and keep Latro off me."

"Well, if you make noise to the officers, they'll suspect you for anything strange that happens to Latro. You'll face execution."

"Falco, no matter what I just said, I'm not going to walk up and kill Latro. I'm going to report my concerns to an officer. At best, justice will be done and at worst I'll be dismissed as a fool but would've called out Latro before the officers. That might be sufficient to stay his hand long enough to come up with a better plan."

"It seems risky to me. Wouldn't your father have done this if it'd work?"

"Gods, Falco! What do you want me to do? I have no fucking idea how to handle this. I need an officer on my side, or else I have no chance."

His shouts echoed off the camp walls, and nearby laborers turned to him. He tucked his head down, then faced his father's grave again.

"I'm sorry," he mumbled. "I never expected to be involved with something like this. At the beginning of the year, I was running around my home like a carefree child. Now I'm at the center of some mad officer's plot to eliminate my family. I don't see any other way out."

"It's all right," Falco said. "I don't trust officers, even ones like Protus. One day they're your friendly neighbors. Next day they're deciding whether to have you beaten to death for not shining your helmet to regulation brightness. How do you trust that?"

"I suppose you can't," Varro said, sighing. "But I have to try. Without someone higher up to protect me, Latro will have me dead within the week."

"He's been quiet since you were released from the hospital."

Varro smiled without humor. "I'm sure he has another plan. For a man with such a temper, he is patient. Besides, it's only been a few days."

They lingered by the grave a while longer. Varro could not manage the memories that poured into his thoughts. Every memory of his father returned wreathed in fondness, even memories when he had been cross. While his back was turned, Varro let a single tear slide halfway down his cheek before wiping it aside. His eyes stung, but he held his head down as he turned away. Falco followed him.

"I've got gate duty in the next hour," Falco said. "Do you want me to go with you to Centurion Protus?"

"No, you had better not draw attention to yourself. Latro seems to take no interest in you. Better not entangle you in this mess."

Varro did not know where Latro was, and he had completed his duties for the day. He had sword drills beginning the next morning, as the doctor had excused him for a few days after release. So he had no better time than now to find Protus. In fact, it was better he acted without anyone knowing his plans. No one could prevent him or dissuade him from the idea. He was certain Gallio and Panthera would never agree.

He stared at his feet as he worked through the regular lanes of the camp until he arrived at headquarters in the center of camp. Drusus and Protus shared a small office there, along with other centurions. Most were seldom here during the day. What they did when not haranguing the soldiers under their command was a complete mystery to Varro. It seemed they lived to march, drill, and march again. He paused outside the door to the long barracks which seemed much like his own, only more spacious. He glimpsed a flicker of white tunic beyond the opened door and heard the scrape of hobnailed sandals over wooden flooring.

Soldiers and laborers passed him in the road, each preoccupied with their own duties. He waited outside the open door so long he felt like an old stone in a meandering stream. Men and pack animals flowed around him, aware but not noticing him.

Latro might also be present, in which case he would have to improvise an excuse for his intrusion. Whether it was Protus or another officer inside, he couldn't be certain. This was his best moment, and he drew in a deep breath before approaching the door.

He knocked on the frame, peering into the darkened space. By sticking his head inside, he was nearly halfway into the fore room. Centurion Protus sat at a desk just beyond this area, where the centurions kept their armor and weapons racked.

"Sir, it's Marcus Varro. If I may, sir, could I have a private word with you?"

The simple string of sentences flowed easily enough. He was proud to have not let his voice crack or rise. Yet the same string of sentences was an audacious risk. The centurions did not invite the common soldier to discussions. Protus's reply might be beating Varro to the floor.

Instead, his head snapped up from whatever he was reviewing on his desk. His scowl melted to a smile when he recognized Varro in his doorway.

"Well, this is a surprise. I thought you were still in the hospital. Please, Varro, come inside. You've caught me in a good moment. And close the door behind you."

The door thumped softly, barring the exterior drone and emphasizing the quiet of the office. Protus increased the flame of the lamp at his desk, which was strewn with scrolls, wax tablets, styluses. A sheathed dagger sat at one corner, not of Roman design.

Protus dressed informally in a pale blue tunic. His graying hair was messy, as if he had just awakened from a nap. Perhaps he had.

Varro stood at attention before the centurion, who waved him to ease.

"I was quite worried for you, Varro. Twice now you've nearly come to death, and you've not been in a proper battle yet. It seems you are doing much better now."

"I am. Thank you, sir."

"It was quite a trap you set for the brigands. I have been wanting to know how you lured out their leader and his picked men. And to kill both the leader and his successor! That is quite an achievement. I dare say I had you wrong when I first met you. You're becoming quite the soldier."

Protus smiled and folded his arms. He raised his eyebrow as he watched Varro.

"Ah, well, sir, the reason for my intrusion today." He felt his throat closing. If he misspoke, he could bring disaster on himself. If he delayed too long, Latro might show up. Protus held his smile as if it were engraved on his face.

"Sir, I believe my life is in danger."

"Of course it is."

Varro stepped back, his hand rising to his chest. Protus laughed.

"This is a war. You are in the First Legion, Varro. We'll be in the thick of all the fighting and you'll be one of the first to meet the enemy at every engagement. Death is always near."

"Well, no, sir, that's not what I mean. I believe someone is trying to murder me here in camp."

Protus's smile did not falter. If anything, it seemed to widen. The statement stretched out to uncomfortable silence, begging Varro to fill it.

"Sir, I believe Nonus was working with someone to make my death seem like an accident during an out-of-control duel. Most recently while in the hospital, I believe my sickness was brought on by poison."

The centurion's smile and silence continued. The terrible silence of the room was thick around Varro's head. He had expected anything from derision to rage to wholehearted acceptance. He had not expected to twist in silence.

"Sir, my father warned me there might be someone with cause to murder me. I believe he too was murdered by poison, possibly by the same person who provided it to me."

Again Varro awaited a reaction, but Protus's smile seemed to weaken only from the strength required to hold it so long. He gave a subtle nod to acknowledge Varro's statements.

"I am hoping you could offer me protection, sir. At least until I can determine who intends to murder me and why."

"Protection?" The word sounded explosive, given the intense silence engulfing the centurion's office. "From whom?"

"That is the point, sir. I'm not sure who. But I am certain Nonus was put up to killing me, and that I was poisoned while in the hospital."

At last Protus set his elbows on his desk and folded his hands before his mouth. His eyes stared over his knuckles into Varro's. The smile had left him.

"How do you know any of this, Varro?"

"Nonus acted strangely before the duel, sir. He had tears in his eyes during our fight. I know he did not want to kill me, but was compelled. As for the poison in the hospital, the doctor cannot identify any other cause for my illness."

Varro realized without connecting Latro to all of this, his evidence sounded too flimsy for belief. He had omitted the battle with Artas altogether. Now he wondered if he should just confess all he knew.

Protus grumbled and began to rub his hands. His eyes lowered in thought. Varro waited, coming to attention out of reflex. The congenial mood vanished from the small office.

"Varro, without saying much you have still managed to make many accusations. First, the graduation matches were under my leadership. It becomes my final responsibility to ensure the matches are fair and no one dies. In all my years, I've seen some serious wounds but never a death. In all cases, these were accidental. Now you say I selected a murderer to attack you."

"Not you, sir." He slammed his mouth shut, hoping Protus would name Latro.

"Well, who else? It was Drusus and I who organized that event. But that aside, you now accuse your doctor of poisoning you."

"Sir, I did not say it was the doctor. Someone also poisoned my father. I believe the same man did it to both of us."

"But if not your doctor, then once again I must ask who else? He is the final responsible person for anyone in the hospital."

Sweat beaded on Varro's brow and heat rippled over his face. Protus stared at him, his hands still folded. But Varro noticed his knuckles had whitened.

"Sir, I realize it may seem coincidental to you. But it is not."

"How so? And Varro, why? Murdering you in such a way that your death could be attributed to another cause seems far-fetched. You are nothing but a young man from a small farm. If one of the men disliked you enough to kill you, they'd just do it in the night or find you on the battlefield. There'd be no need for the elaborate scheme you describe."

"Sir, I cannot say why. It is as confusing to me. But I know I am a target, sir."

He paused, drew a long breath, then held it. Protus again raised his brow, leaning back expectantly.

"Sir, Optio Latro is behind it. He selected Nonus to fight me. He handed me a cup of wine while in the hospital, and I nearly died after drinking it. And there is one detail I did not share, sir. While fighting Artas in the forest, I was almost killed. Optio Latro came upon me, and rather than aid me he laughed and left me to be killed by Artas."

The words clanked to the floor like iron balls. Protus's face shaded red. He set his hands on the desk, but each was balled into white-knuckled fists. Gone was the patient smile, replaced with a deep frown.

"You are accusing an officer without a shred of evidence. You've had two coincidences that place Optio Latro close to your misfortunes. Nonus was mad. The doctor has ruled your condition as the effects of your head wound. And as far as what you saw in the forest, it is my understanding you remember little of what happened there."

"Sir, I—"

"Silence!" Centurion Protus shot up from his seat, fists balled at his side. "I'll indulge you this one time, Varro. You've been under much stress for a young man, with your wounds and your father's unexpected death. But I will not hear this again, nor will you speak of it to anyone. You are to return to your contubernium and prepare to leave for winter quarters like everyone else."

"Yes, sir!" Varro stomped his foot and stood to rigid attention, eyes set to the dark back wall.

"See that you don't forget yourself," Protus said, lowering his voice. "And never bring an accusation against anyone without solid proof. Now you're dismissed."

Varro again saluted, then opened the door and stepped back out into the camp. The sunlight dazzled him and men weaved to avoid his sudden appearance in the road.

He staggered along the path to the barracks as if he had been beaten over the head. Thoughts flooded through his mind in a jumble of images and feelings, all bound with fear.

Then he stopped in the middle of the path.

It was as if the clouds over his head broke apart to allow the brilliance of the sun to flood him with understanding.

He could not fight Latro without help from higher up.

But neither could Latro act so boldly without the same.

Varro realized Latro had accomplices in the officer ranks.

And the only officers that made sense were Centurions Protus and Drusus.

20

Varro looked between Falco, Gallio, and Panthera. They stood together in the cold night behind their barracks. The other half of the contubernium slept, or at least acted as if sleeping. All were eager to learn what Varro had to tell them, but he felt these three should be the first to know since they had risked their lives to come back for him in the forest. Thin moonlight draped them in a gauzy silver light. Falco's heavy brow furrowed and filled his face with shadow. Gallio growled like a dog ready to bite, and Panthera simply shook his head.

"It makes sense now," Falco said. "Of course the centurions would be lined up with Latro. Why didn't we see this before?"

"We didn't know about it before," Panthera said. "Until we saw what happened with the brigands and then Varro getting so sick after the wine, how would we know?"

"It's not right," Gallio said. "We've got to do something about it. Maybe go to the tribune."

Varro raised his hand for silence. He lowered his voice again to emphasize they should do the same. "I don't know what to do. I didn't even want to tell you. Now you're all in trouble with me."

"We were already in trouble for being in the same barracks," Falco said. "Latro is going to assume we talked even if we did not. If anything, he can't kill all of us. So you still did good to let Centurion Protus know you're onto their plans."

"Are you sure?" Varro rubbed the back of his neck. "It feels like at any time they could arrange for our executions. They'll find a way."

The four of them fell to silence. At last Gallio patted Varro's shoulder.

"We'll figure out something. Let's all just stay close. I'll bring the others out for you to tell them."

"Not tonight," Varro said. "It has been an exhausting day and I'm tired."

They broke up, each searching over their shoulders as if concluding a deal in Rome's alleys. They could not linger outside before a watchman spotted them. Varro welcomed the humid warmth of body heat in the crowded barracks. Those pretending to sleep had actually done so, filling the darkness with their snores.

The next morning Varro explained his thoughts to the others, who sat on their bunks and exchanged worried glances. Yet the all agreed to watch out for each other and that something had to be done about Latro.

The optio visited them as part of his morning rounds and seemed disinterested in any of them. He oversaw their sword drills in the morning, then assigned them to their tasks for the day. When it came to Varro, he gave him no more than a glance. "Night watch at the northern gate. Get your sleep before duty starts. Password will be shared when you relieve your predecessor."

It seemed so commonplace that Varro wondered if he had been wrong about Protus. But during a break in sword drills, Falco dissuaded him from the idea.

"Of course they're going to act like nothing's going on. They'll get you while on the march to winter quarters or else figure out something better. They've got time."

"But they were in such a hurry before," Varro asked. "Why ease up now?"

"You're hard to kill, Varro. They've got to think about how to do it while keeping their hands clean. Told you my beatings trained you good."

Varro shared a laugh with Falco, amazed at the truth of it. He had long taken such punishment and suffered such pain that he endured it better than most. At one time he might have cursed Falco, but now it seemed he should thank him.

A quiet day passed, until Latro returned to the barracks just before Varro was preparing to rest in advance of his night shift. Gallio and Gaius Senna, another of the contubernium, were also resting.

"Outside, you three," Latro said. "I've got news."

Varro's hands chilled. Something in Latro's voice sounded foreboding. The others must have heard the same note, for they too slid from their bunks with worried glances. Outside in the cold gray light, Latro stood with a young man at his side. He was small, and next to Latro seemed like a child. But his hazel eyes were bright with curiosity and an easy smile revealed straight, yellow teeth.

"There's been some reorganization after losses," Latro said, looking at none of them. "You're down a man after Nonius. So this one is promoted from the Velites to join you. He did well against the brigands. So, here he is."

The former Velite stepped forward, smiling brightly. "Camillus Curio," he said. "Glad to join you."

Latro waved him off, then walked off in silence. Varro watched him go, wondering what he planned next. Hatred smoldered in the pit of Varro's stomach, for he was convinced he stared after his father's murderer.

"A velite?" Gallio folded his arms, looking the new arrival from head to toe. "You look like a puppy."

"Well, I bite like a wolf," Curio said. "So don't try to pet me."

"And Gallio growls like one," Senna said. "So you two ought to be fast friends."

Yet it did not seem as if Gallio and Curio were headed for friendship. Nonius had been Gallio's close friend, and his scowl made it seem he did not welcome a replacement for him. He let Curio pass as Senna led him into the barracks.

"I don't trust him," Gallio said, stopping Varro before he followed them inside. "What if he's Latro's man?"

Varro narrowed his eyes. "Seems a weak choice for a killer. But I guess he only has to get me when I'm unaware."

"I'm going to watch that bastard," Gallio said. "I won't let him cook. Doesn't take a strong man to slip poison into our meals."

They both entered the dim barracks. Curio had claimed Nonius's bunk, which was topside and next to Gallio's. Varro let the three others mumble and mutter about the changes. He had to sleep, or else he would during his night shift. He listened to Curio recount his heroic battle against the brigands as he drifted off to sleep. It seemed the small man had courage, but was more likely a good storyteller. Varro regretted being unable to trust him, for he seemed likable. Of course, that would make him an excellent killer.

Varro awakened later to a reset landscape in the tiny barracks. Falco was snoring below him, as well as Gallio across the small room. Curio was on his side, asleep. It was Panthera's cold hand that woke him.

"Time for your shift," he said. "Will you be all right?"

Varro scratched his head. "I'm feeling much better. Back is still a bit sore but nothing serious."

"It's quiet out there," Panthera said. "All the work of packing is done. We'll be moving out soon."

So Varro equipped himself and left to guard a gate that would be dismantled after their leaving. It all seemed wasteful to him, for this temporary camp was better built than most villas he had seen. He crossed the nighttime camp, passing no one. He expected an attacker at every step until he realized he was probably safest out in the open and in full battle gear. His step grew lighter and more confident.

Varro found the guard commander, the tesserarius, at headquarters and received his gate assignment and watch word. He then hurried off to relieve his predecessor at the north gate, who could not leave until he arrived.

When he arrived, he found the guard glaring down at him from the wall.

"You're late."

"Wolf brother." Varro provided the password to confirm his assignment. "Has it been busy?"

The guard clambered down from the parapet and leapt the final distance to the ground.

"Not a fucking thing. No Macedonians here, friend. Good luck staying awake."

Varro climbed the ladder to his position overlooking the gate. He stared ahead into the gloom. If anyone approached, he doubted they'd be Roman. Still, he lit a new torch and set it in place to begin his watch. Across the gate, another guard stood at his post. In the light of his own guttering torch, he seemed like a statue of a Roman legionnaire. The shadow sculpted the muscles of his arms and the clean-shaven ridges of his jawline and face. His nose was like an eagle's beak and a slanting, stern mouth was tightly closed beneath it. He stared ahead, massive hand on a pilum, and ignored Varro.

"No conversation tonight," he mumbled to himself. He had been paired with one of the veterans, and they were not known to chat with untested newcomers like him.

Varro wrapped his cloak tight and set his shield against the wood wall. An owl hooted in the distant clump of trees. He stared at the silver grass and indigo trees that shaded into the thick night. Dawn could not break soon enough, he thought. Even with sleep he would struggle against tedium all night. It seemed that after full-gear marching, the soldier's next most important training was standing for hours. Marching and standing were not what he expected a soldier's life to be, but had thus far been the majority of his experience, punctuated with the raw terror of fighting for his life at unexpected moments.

He cast hopeful glances at the rocklike visage of his partner. But the man was immobile. Even his expression seemed to have not changed after an hour. Varro imagined pigeons settling on him like they did on the statues in Rome. Eventually he abandoned hope and blinked ahead into the blue gloom.

By the middle of the night, he heard a creak on the ladder behind him. At first he was unsure, but then realized he heard hobnails on the wooden rungs. His heart flipped, and he grabbed his pilum.

"Hold on, Varro. Wolf Brother."

"Wolf brother," Varro repeated. But he stepped back with pilum in hand. His station would not allow more than one man to stand here, and certainly no room to fight. But if he slid back, at least his visitor could join him.

He realized the statue of the legionnaire had vanished. His eyes widened in astonishment as the statue climbed the ladder to join him on his side of the gate.

"Been waiting for the right time," he said. His voice was as a deep mountain valley and just as rocky. The boards underfoot creaked from his weight as he mounted the top. He did not carry his shield or pilum. He would need neither, for he wore a full chain shirt. His bronze helmet reflected the moonlight, and three black feathers stood straight atop it. Varro envied this, for he had not added the feathers to his own helmet yet. He felt like covering the empty knob at the top of his helmet with his hand.

"You surprised me," Varro said. "I thought you might be someone else."

"I'm sure you're jumping at every shadow. Rough business with your father. I'm sorry about it. He didn't deserve to die like that."

Varro blinked. "What do you mean? They say he never recovered from the illness earlier this summer and died from it."

"Is that what you believe?"

The statuesque soldier leaned on the parapet wall and stared out into the night. His jaw muscles twitched and his eyes were like black slits in the shadowy light.

Then Varro wondered if he were one of Latro's men sent to throw him off the parapet and make it seem he broke his neck in a strange accident. His hand slipped toward his pugio.

"Stop that. I'm not your enemy. Obviously, you don't believe what you just said. Neither do I."

Varro's hand pulled back and his heart raced. The man had a naturally commanding voice, and Varro worried he might respond out of his training rather than rational thought. He could trust no one now, no matter how authoritative.

The soldier twisted to face him, then smiled. His eyes were naturally squinting, as if the pitiful torchlight fluttering around them was a bonfire. Face and head were square, like the capstone of the massive fortress that formed his body. His bronze cheek plates obscured most of his clean-shaven face, but Varro noted deep wrinkles at the corners of his eyes.

"Decius Oceanus," he said in his bass voice, then extended his arm. "I was a friend of your father's. In his contubernium."

Varro looked at the extended arm, an offer of greeting and friendship. But he could just as easily pull Varro into a hidden knife or else fling him from the wall.

"Cautious," Oceanus said. "That's good. You should be. But you weren't the least interested in why no one relieved me from my watch."

"I was late. I thought maybe you arrived ahead of me."

Oceanus shook his head. "This is my second shift. I paid off the man who was supposed to be here tonight because I wanted to meet with you in private. This is a perfect time and place for a long talk. Now, my arm is tiring. I'm your ally, Varro, and you need one now."

Gripping Oceanus's arm sent a lurch of terror through him, and he nearly fell from the parapet as he imagined Oceanus hurling him down. But the strong man steadied him.

"All right, boy, don't kill yourself for them."

Varro released his grip and pushed back against the wall. Oceanus laughed, dry and rough like the stone he resembled.

"You're not high enough to die from the fall unless you landed on your head. Look, Varro, take a breath. It's the middle of the night, and while you're with me nothing is going to happen. Your father and I go way back. I'm sure he must have told you stories about us."

"Well, no, sir, he didn't."

Oceanus's tiny eyes widened to almost normal size. "What? And don't call me sir. I'm not an officer. Your father never mentioned me?"

Varro shook his head. "I met his old Centurion Titus once. He's the one who summoned us to the dilectus. But Father never spoke much of his time in the army. None of my family ever did."

Oceanus put his hand to his forehead then chuckled.

"Titus, that old bastard. He's still making life miserable for others, I see. Anyway, I guess they're not stories you'd tell your son. But I wouldn't know. All my children died too young. The gods are cruel. I'd be a great father, as I'm sure yours was."

"He was." Varro paused, clipping off the word sir. Oceanus's natural command made him seem a perfect officer. "And you believe he was poisoned?"

"I not only believe it, I know it."

The questions flooded through his mind and flowed out of his mouth in a garbled rush. "Who did it? Why did they do it? Will I be able to have revenge? How did you know? Am I still in danger? What will happen next?"

The flurry set Oceanus back with both hands raised.

"Boy, calm yourself. I'll explain what I know and what I suspect. Just let me say my piece, then you can ask questions if you still have them."

Varro nodded, stepping back after realizing he had nearly drawn his face up to the veteran. He checked over his shoulder, seeing nothing but orange torchlight and darkness beyond.

"We're alone," Oceanus said. "Now, I heard you went to Centurion Protus and accused Optio Latro of trying to kill you."

"And was I wrong?"

"You're not wrong about Latro. But you were stupid for spilling it all to Protus without any solid proof."

Varro, not even realizing he stood on his toes anticipating his answer, rocked back on his heels and lowered his head in shame. Heat rose to his face. But Oceanus clicked his tongue.

"All right, I was hard on you there. You look a lot like your father did on his first campaign. I forget who I'm talking to. You're just seventeen and getting your first taste of the world. You've got much to learn, but you have to learn it fast."

"I didn't guess Centurions Protus and Drusus were involved."

"Drusus isn't. He's a bore and an ass. But he's a fine centurion, and mostly ignorant of anything not about gutting an enemy army. He'll lead you to victory every battle, and you'll be sure Protus will claim the glory for it. He and Latro are old friends, and they work together on all sorts of shady things."

"But he seemed so reasonable."

"It's what makes him a perfect pair with Latro. Not many suspect Protus of being anything more than a fine citizen. But most of the veterans are wise to Latro. Your father was, and I believe he warned you."

"He did!" Varro made to grab Oceanus's cloak, but thought better of putting hands on the noble veteran. "From the first day he said Latro was trouble. But why didn't he tell me how much trouble he'd be?"

"The trouble he expected was for himself, and you only as a second thought. But that turned out otherwise, too late for anyone to do much. We've kept you as safe as we could. There's only so many of us. But Latro and Protus are two persistent snakes, and they got your father eventually. We didn't think they'd try the same thing twice."

Varro's eyes stung as he imagined his father suffering the delirium and madness of his final moments.

"I just don't understand why?"

"So that's where your father could've done better," Oceanus said. "Not to speak ill of the dead, of course. Varro, your farm is in trouble. As your father's heir, he should've been preparing you for it. I don't know why he didn't. I expect your mother will be able to give you details, but the farm is in debt and barely making a profit."

"Wait, you're saying Latro wants to kill us because our farm is not profitable? That makes no sense."

Oceanus shook his head, closing his tiny eyes.

"It makes complete sense. Varro, Latro and Protus are working to free up small farms like yours to be purchased by larger ones. The large farms get larger, and they have the money and size to turn a failing farm back into a profitable one. So with all the male heirs eliminated and the farm in trouble, your mother will have no choice but to sell. And Latro and Protus's patron will be first to know it is available. He'll snap it up for a fraction of its value. And he'll do it again and again for as many failing farms as he can find."

"That bastard!" Varro punched his fist into his palm. "Who is he? I swear he'll pay!"

Oceanus put his hand on Varro's chest. "Easy. I said we're alone, but won't be if you keep shouting like that. Now, who is it? That's a good question. None of us really knows. But he's high up, high enough to be hidden by clouds."

"Well, whoever buys my father's farm is the one."

"The farm is yours now, Varro. And the buyer will be a representative, not the actual person at the root of this. The real villain will remain distanced from all the dirty business. If I had to name anyone, I'd pick a senator. That seems to be the right size."

Varro's mouth hung agape.

"Latro's working for a senator? How do I even fight something like that? I'm as good as dead."

Oceanus grumbled and turned back to the darkness beyond the camp.

"You don't fight it alone. That's for certain."

He and Oceanus fell into silence. Varro's mind swam with the revelation that he was a trifling problem to a wealthy and powerful senator who wanted his family farm.

"But this is more than just me," Varro said. "The Falcos' farm should be in trouble too."

"It is," Oceanus said. "But you own that too. So you and your father are the lucky targets."

"What?" Again Varro's voice echoed through the darkness, drawing a sharp hiss from Oceanus.

"Your father really kept you in the dark, didn't he? Again, I don't have the details, just what your father told me. He said he loaned Sextus Falco a lot of money. He staked his farm as collateral. When your father's bills came due and Falco had pissed away his money, I guess he gave over his farm as repayment. Anyway, you'll inherit that mess too."

Varro fell against the wall, his vision filled with Falco's angry face. What would he say if he found out? They would be back to their old antagonism again, and Varro needed all the friends he could muster.

"I don't know what I'm going to do. This just gets worse every minute."

Oceanus laughed.

"It's a bit to take in. I really thought your father would've told you more. You know how Nonus tried to kill you, right? He was in the same situation. I think Latro made him a deal. If he killed you, he would make sure his family was untouched. After all, you bring in two farms and Nonus barely makes enough income to be hastati. The poor fool probably knew he would be executed for doing it, but believed Latro could help his family. Actually, I bet Protus convinced him. Seems more like his touch. Probably said he'd get it ruled as an accident and have Nonus forgiven, then take care of his family. No matter, you see how you recruits bring in lots of opportunities for predators like Latro and Protus. It's dark business, but you're not alone."

"What does that mean?"

"What it sounds like. I'm going to help you, Varro. I owe it to your father, and besides, you seem to be a likable fellow. Got yourself out of a scramble with the brigands and killed both their leaders. I admire that."

"It was mostly luck."

"And you're modest," Oceanus said. "It's a fine trait but won't get you far in life. Most men your age would've pissed themselves and just waited for someone to rescue them. But you led their leader out of camp, making our jobs a lot easier. There were hundreds of brigands set up there, and probably more camps farther north. But without a leader present, they fell apart. That's your work. Don't underestimate it. Your father would've been proud of you."

"Thank you." Varro rubbed at his eye, fearing the tears that lingered there for his father's memory. "I'm glad to have your help. Falco and the others are watching out for me, too. But I'm not sure we're enough to take on a senator."

"We're not. But I'm just one of a few others who knows what's happening in the First Legion and in your century especially. You remember Tanicus?"

Varro's eyes widened. "Of course! He was killed foraging, and Protus blamed those farmers for it."

"Of course he did, as I expect Protus either shot Tanicus himself or hired someone to do it. Tanicus was our leader. Not an officer or anything like that. A number of us veterans have learned to stay close through all our campaigns. We watch out for each other and shared news. Just an informal thing, really. Your father was part of it. Tanicus was getting close to something, I suspect. I don't know what, but it alarmed Protus enough to remove him directly."

"So he shot him," Varro repeated, remembering the arrow and the tiny splotch of blood. "Why didn't he just do the same for me and my father?"

"Well, how many foraging accidents can happen before everyone knows something is wrong? If Nonus had finished you and your father later collapsed, who would call it anything other than an unfortunate coincidence? They'd say your father was so grief-stricken he died from it. Truth was, your father was distraught after he learned of the attempt on your life. He requisitioned some wine to steady himself. Latro paid the servant who delivered the wine skin to take his instead. A bold move, but if your father had died, then what would it matter? Protus would help cover for Latro's clumsy ploy. Anyway, you and your father ruined their plans by being so hardy."

"Now I'm going to be shot like Tanicus."

"Probably," Oceanus said. "But not if we act soon."

Varro shook his head. "Act how?"

"Varro, your father told me you had this vow of peace or something like it. He was fearful it could lead to you a bad end. If you want to survive, you're going to have to amend this vow of yours."

"Well, I've already killed three men. I'd say my vow is ruined."

"All part of a battle where you had no choice. Look, you helped those children escape the farm. Yes, I know about it. Don't look so surprised. So you've got a soft heart. What you did for the children was not bad, but it was against orders and probably could've got you and your fellows in serious trouble. Disobey an order to kill even an old grandmother if that's what your officer wants and you'll be taking her place. But I'm not talking about that."

Oceanus paused, his squinty eyes searching him. Varro tilted his head back, drawing a taut smile from the veteran.

"We can't stop these powerful men from playing with the lives of poor bastards like us. But we can send them a message and force them to look for easier prey. We do that by killing Latro and Protus. Their patrons won't miss that message. If enough of us know about their schemes, we'll be too much trouble for them. They'll go elsewhere."

"Murder?" Varro asked.

Oceanus nodded. "It's the only way."

Varro peered into the dark night. The owl hunting in the distant trees called again. He studied the blackness, his mind buzzing, then turned back to Oceanus.

"I'll do it."

21

Varro marched with his life strapped to his back.
Between his armor, scutum, weapons, and all the
supporting gear, he hunched over with the effort. But
his legs were like iron and the army had built his strength over
ceaseless marches around the old camp in just the same gear.
Dead grass swished under his hobnailed sandals. The long
column of men was mounting a steep rise and Varro felt it in his
legs with every step forward.

"So you know nothing about this Decius Oceanus fellow?"
Falco marched next to him in the column. Gallio and Panthera
were behind, followed by the newcomer, Curio.

"Nothing more than what I told you." He looked over his
shoulder. Gallio and Panthera both had their heads down with the
effort of mounting the rise. But Curio trotted along behind them
with the others. He looked like an overeager puppy. Could he
really be working for Latro?

"And he hasn't contacted you since your shift?"

"He said he'd contact me with a plan, but if an opportunity
presented itself that I should not hesitate. It has only been a few

days. Besides, today is the easiest day we've had since orders to break camp."

"Marching top speed in full gear is what you call easy?"

"This is not even close to top speed. Falco, you've gotten soft."

Falco chuckled and blew sweat off his lip.

They continued to climb, and Varro admitted to himself that the march was harder than he portrayed. They were in the rear-guard to the baggage train, and scores of draft horses and their creaking carts had just topped the rise. Most of the legion had already crossed over ahead of them.

Optio Latro was in the lead of his column with the two centurions Drusus and Protus. Varro struggled not to look at them, but their presences made the side of his head tingle with the desire to stare. Neither officer had made any move at him since his visit with Protus. But he knew they plotted something and had the luxury of patience.

His desire for revenge and his vow to his great-grandfather were at odds. As he dug his feet into the grass and struggled ahead, his mind kept turning to a day that felt as if it had happened in another life.

Promise me, Marcus, swear to it before all the gods and all our ancestors. You will not live the life of violence that I have lived. You must not, cannot, become what I was.

He wished his father had stopped him then. But he made the oath alone with his great-grandfather as witness. He died in peace, knowing he had saved his descendant from something he dreaded.

But now it seemed the only way to honor that promise was to offer his throat to Latro and Protus.

"I know what you're thinking," Falco said, huffing beside him.

"That this ridge is going on forever."

"No, you've got that face again. You're getting stubborn about that oath you made."

"It was a solemn promise, Falco. It's not something I can break easily."

"Well, you're not breaking it. You're defending yourself. Isn't that the difference? I know you're calling it murder—"

"By Juno, Falco, shut up!" He glanced over his shoulder. Panthera and Gallio still had their heads down while Curio chatted with anyone patient enough to listen. The line of soldiers behind them were stringing out from exertion.

"Nobody knows what I'm talking about. Not even the beast and nanny."

Falco had a derisive name for everyone, with Gallio named for his grunting and bullish attitude and Panthera for his tendency to soothe even the slightest arguments. As far as Varro knew, he was still a lily to Falco's mind.

"Just make sure it stays that way. I shouldn't have told you anything."

"I'm your best friend, Varro. If you can't tell me, then who else?"

"Best friend?"

"See anyone else around who has known you since birth? Practically shares the same farm with you?"

Varro shuddered at the mention of the farm. What would he do when he found out the truth?

"See? So I may not be the best friend you want, but I'm the one you've got. Now listen to me. You've got to survive this. If you don't want to do it for yourself, then the rest of us are still involved. We'll all be targets sooner or later. So think of it as protecting others. You can do that, I'm sure."

"I never knew you were such a positive person. What do you think of Curio? Gallio says he's Latro's man."

"Gallio likes even fewer people than I do. So his opinion isn't worth much. I think Curio lied about his age, and is not even old enough to be here. But I can't say. I've tried to get more out of him, but he gets quiet about himself if you ask too much. He could be trouble."

Varro again looked behind. Curio continued chatting away, unhampered by his paucity of gear. Being a new promotion, he claimed he would acquire his hastati gear upon reaching the new winter camp.

Then Varro noticed something else far behind Curio and the others.

A throng of horsemen emerged from the trees at the base of the ridge, followed by hundreds of wild men.

"An ambush!" Varro shouted the words just as the rearmost soldiers sounded alarm horns. The sharp notes echoed up the slope, turning everyone to where Varro looked.

The attackers charged as hundreds of dark shapes in tunics of every hue. Their bronze helmets gleamed and their colorful round shields bobbed as they raced across the grassland. The horse-mounted enemies swept up the side of the column with javelins in hand.

"How did the scouts miss that?" Falco said, whirling around.

"Drop your packs! Form up!" Centurion Drusus shouted commands, moving to the front where the maniple would form. Being the senior of the two centurions, he commanded the maniple in battle.

Alarm horns sounded to the top of the rise and beyond, or so Varro hoped. The mighty legion was stretched like a snake so long that it could not double back to its own tail. The canny ambushers realized the sharp incline would space out the marching soldiers, and so had set their ambush to nip the tail. Varro had no more time to admire the enemy's tactics. The centurions were shouting orders and directing men.

"Come on," Falco said. "A real battle this time."

Being up the slope, he and Falco along with his maniple were shielded from the fast approaching riders. Their thundering hooves and battle cries echoed across the grass as they closed.

The enemy riders galloped within javelin distance, and with practiced grace the lithe riders let their shafts fly. The javelins arced and flexed through the air. Their wooden shafts shimmered with the sun, then crashed among the Romans as they assumed their formations.

Most thudded off raised scutum shields. Men in the midst of formation did not have the benefits of closing together to block out all the missiles landing among them. Rows of men toppled over with javelins protruding from their torsos. Their screams were drowned out by thundering hooves and the wild cries of the riders, who now turned back toward their companions.

Varro's heart raced. He clutched his pilum and pulled up his shield. As he hustled into line with Falco at his side, he worried his chin strap had loosened from constantly itching beneath it. But he had no free hands to tighten it.

The shock of the horse charge left the Romans wheeling about in disorder. To Varro's inexperienced eye, it seemed the ambushers would be among them before his side formed a sensible defense. Yet Centurion Drusus and Centurion Protus strode to the fore of the maniple, shouting commands and showing no sign of worry. Their calm eased his own fears.

Varro formed the front line of defense, and would normally expect the Velites to be present. But they had been given no time, and the Velites were sent to the rear where Optio Latro would oversee the century.

A score of dead or dying legionaries lay on the ground between Varro and the approaching enemy.

"Hold!" Drusus shouted. "Don't yield high ground."

Falco stood to his right and Gallio was to his left. None of them made a sound, a stark contrast to the screaming and whooping men that lowered their spears and ran at them. Their cheeks were flushed and their eyes wide. They were dirty and bearded, their hair greasy and unkempt.

These were the rest of Artas's bandits, he realized. They had come for revenge.

"Throw!"

Out of reflex, Varro raised his pilum and hurled it at the closing enemy. The spear flew across the gap, but Varro could not mark where it had landed. Instead, he saw a line of the grubby brigands skid and pull up shields. The pilums thrown with skill and force from short range devastated their charge. Brigands screamed and crashed to the ground, tripping men behind them. Exposed, these men also fell prey to the rain of spears stitching death through their ranks.

Varro's fear turned to jubilation as the knot of men headed for him stumbled into bloody piles. Less disciplined men might have shouted in triumph. But he and his companions held their cheers. They needed to listen for the orders of the centurion.

"Shields up, swords ready," Drusus shouted. "And do not move an inch back. Kill these scum!"

The comforting bulk of Varro's shield weighed on his arm. He drew his gladius in one fluid motion, the scrape of metal singing out across the line as the rest of the hastati prepared for battle.

Varro glanced to Falco, whose face had turned white as he stared ahead. He did not have time to look to Gallio at his left. As he turned, the enemy had recovered and brought their charge home.

The brigands roared their foul curses, screamed for blood, and stabbed in with their spears.

The snap and thump of spear on shield cracked out across the line, like a giant tree breaking in a storm. Varro sighted his man, copper-haired and red-faced with a white shield. He vanished behind Varro's scutum and shouted a war cry. The enemy blow clanged on his shield and sent a shuddering force into his hand. But he had turned the spear aside.

Training took over. His guts roiled and sweat flowed from his helmet down his face. Still, he did not yield to the force of the blow. He stepped into it, punching with his shield to batter the enemy's shield aside. In the same motion, his sword stabbed forward and plunged into flesh.

The enemy gasped and spasmed. But Varro pulled back a bloodied blade as his foe collapsed into the madness of his companions.

The battle became a boiling sea of rage-contorted faces and blood. The sickly-sweet scent of it filled the air. His sword hand burned hot with it. He repeated his defense and attack like the steps in a dance. Block, punch, stab. If the first stab failed, he repeated until the gladius found flesh.

For wherever the sword found flesh, it delivered ruin.

To his left and right, Gallio and Falco fought alongside him. They grimaced with the strain of holding against waves of madmen just as he did. They were splattered with blood. Varro's feet began to slip in it. A horrific odor reached his nose, like spoiled meat. He did not understand what it was.

The clangor of iron and wood beat against his eardrums. The screams of men from both sides filled his ears. Someone sobbed underfoot. He could not be sure enemy or ally. His hands had gone numb from the constant battering.

"Is there no fucking end?" Falco shouted.

"I can't see." Varro dared to move his shield aside for a better look. A moment's respite offered a glimpse at a renewing wave of attackers. Bodies were piled like a tide mark between them. Their struggles had churned the grass into bloody mud.

Someone jumped on his shield, wrapping both arms around it. They were thin and white arms and pulled the shield forward. In his wearied state, Varro fell forward.

He felt the cool air brush against his face.

He was exposed and the enemy rushed at him with a ready spear.

"Look out!"

To his left, he found Curio and not Gallio. The former velite had nothing more than a plain sword and round shield for defense. Yet he stood in the front line. He plunged his sword at whoever clung to Varro's shield.

The attacker gurgled and fell away. Varro's shield snapped up in time to block the spear thrust that would have struck his neck.

Curio stabbed again, finishing whomever he had hacked from Varro's shield.

"Hold the line!" Centurion Drusus shouted. "Do not chase them."

Varro looked up. The wall of brigands was melting away. Hundreds of them lay dead and disemboweled on the grass. The horrid stench, Varro realized, wafted up from the entrails spilled in the battle. His eyes watered at its strength, realizing one such enemy had spooled out his intestines only a few feet away. He felt like vomiting.

A cry of victory rose from the Romans. On both sides of his position, Varro saw ordered formations closing down on the brigands. The snake had turned to reach its tail, he realized, and much faster than he would have thought possible.

"Hold or I'll have you flogged raw!"

Some Romans had run forward, swords raised in challenge. But none of Varro's contubernium had. He looked to Falco, who stood panting with his shield and sword lowered. His sword hand glistened with red and blood-splatter shined on his face.

"Are you hurt?"

Falco shook his head, then frowned at him.

"And you? Looks like a thousand pomegranates exploded in your face."

"I'm fine, thanks to Curio."

He turned behind to find Curio hunched over Gallio, who lay sprawled on his side. His cream-colored tunic sopped with blood.

"I think he's alive," Curio said, as he pressed a cloth onto his hip.

Varro kneeled beside him, leaning down to where he heard Gallio grunting and panting.

"Can you hear me?"

Gallio grunted harder and slowly nodded in response.

"A spear slipped under his shield," Curio said. "I saw him fall and I jumped into his place."

"Thanks for releasing my shield," Varro said. "We need to get Gallio help."

But when Varro stood up, he wondered what help was forthcoming. They had won the field with the troops on the flanks sweeping up any brigand stragglers. The brigands would never defeat this army. They just wanted to take a bite out of its haunch, and from the scattered Roman bodies, Varro judged they had done as much. Even in victory, there were casualties and too few to help all the wounded.

"There should be someone detailed for casualty collection," Falco said, leaning over Varro's shoulder. Panthera joined as well, but he was rubbing his face in worry.

"He can't wait for whenever that will be," he said. "Didn't anyone pay attention when Optio Latro was showing us how to treat wounds?"

"It's his hip," Varro said. "All we can do is put pressure there. Nothing to tie off." He leaned in on Gallio, who was still grunting, and whispered to him. "I'll see if I can get help. Hold on."

Again he merely grunted louder and barely nodded his head.

"I'll need a new bandage," Curio said. "This is getting too wet."

Varro left Curio and the others to crowd around Gallio. He

would not allow his friend to bleed to death because of some brigand scum's lucky spear thrust. He would demand help.

He raced across the line, where the men were recovering their wits and realizing how close they had come to death. Varro looked at each of their pale, blood-stained faces and was met with wide, staring eyes.

"My friend is hurt. Who can help?"

But soldier after soldier did not answer. Some had wounds of their own and not even realized it. One had a hunk of flesh missing from his shin, but he leaned on his shield and stared after the brigands as if he felt nothing.

At last, he came to Centurion Drusus. But one withering look from the squat centurion in his mail shirt and he knew what would happen.

"Don't move from this spot," he shouted to his men. "Let the cavalry finish up. Get the casualties in order."

Other than not moving, no one obeyed the second part of his order. A dark cloud of fury passed over Drusus's face. He saw Varro, then pointed.

"You! Get to work on the casualties. Don't stare at my like I'm your fucking lover!"

"Sir, I—"

"And you help him." Drusus pulled an equally hapless soldier from his century and shoved him at Varro. He then stalked off and ordered more men to the casualty detail.

Varro looked to his new partner, who just blinked at him.

"Come on, my friend needs help. Do you know what to do?"

The soldier's sword hung in his hand, dripping blood. He shook his head. Varro cursed and left him standing in confusion.

At last, he found Drusus assigning competent men who were neither bloodied nor confused. He rushed to these as soon as the centurion passed and secured them for Gallio. Two rushed after him as he led them back.

Yet halfway to Gallio he saw Centurion Protus. He stood downslope at the front of the line where corpses had piled to his front. He wore a chain shirt, but his shield rested against his side. He surveyed the battlefield carnage, seemingly absorbed in the conclusion of the brigand route unfolding in the distance.

"Gallio is just over there," Varro said. Falco's tall silhouette marked the place where they crowded around their fallen companion. He pointed the men toward him. "I've got to help others, but you've got to help my friend. Please, it is his first battle. He has to live."

The two soldiers sped off toward the group. Confident he had done what he could for Gallio, Varro turned to Protus.

The centurion was uncharacteristically alone. Optio Latro was stationed to the rear, and Varro could not see him. With the brigand's sudden break and the arrival of the main legion, attention was scattered.

Decius Oceanus, his father's friend and Varro's new ally, had told him to wait for his sign to act. But also said if an opportunity presented itself, he should also take advantage of it.

This moment seemed that opportunity. Protus was distracted and alone. A stab through his back would be suspicious, but Varro could stab him again from the front if he acted fast enough. The chain shirt protected from slashes but could be broken with a direct thrust from a strong blade. He had discovered as much fighting the brigand chiefs.

But could he murder Protus here? Surely someone would see him, even though he was off to the side of the action. One quick thrust through his kidney would collapse Protus.

He found himself inching forward, his bloody hand tightening on his gladius.

Was he really going to attempt murder in front of the legion? This question hovered about him, and he felt as if he were watching himself advancing through a dream.

This was not the time. He would be caught. He could not be certain of killing Protus in one stroke.

Yet his feet slid across the bloody ground.

Was there any better cover than the battlefield? He imagined Protus's knees flexing as the blade slithered into his side, then him collapsing to the ground. He envisioned covering Protus's collapse and finishing him with a quick cut, all while never releasing more than a grunt.

It seemed easy. It seemed right.

A smile flickered on his face. He felt a gauzy sense of distance from himself, as if another man were stalking forward, drawing ever closer to Protus, who still studied the destruction of the brigands attempting to reach the safety of the trees.

And his gladius now pointed straight ahead rather than at the ground.

It pointed to Protus.

His pulse slammed in his temples and he swallowed hard. His feet picked up speed and his hand clamped onto the hilt of his sword.

Protus stared ahead at the distant blur of combatants.

He was a dozen strides away.

Sweat rolled into Varro's eyes.

A half-dozen strides remained.

Then a spear skimmed across his right shoulder.

A hot line of fire scored his flesh. The shaft angled down and slammed into the ground between him and Protus.

Varro drew up short, nearly colliding with the enemy spear shaft quivering in the grass. He whirled to look back up the slope.

Optio Latro stood in plain view up the slope. The line of soldiers had drifted closer to Centurion Drusus's shouted orders, leaving only a trail of dead and spent spears to mark their path. The clustered shadows of his companions, marked by Falco's height, were a small island.

This was the perfect place to ambush Protus, he decided.

But he realized too late.

And now he had stepped into Latro and Protus's ambush.

Behind him, Centurion Protus cleared his throat. Varro did not turn back.

"How good of you to find me, Varro."

Latro shook his round head, apparently dissatisfied with his cast, then started down the slope. As he did, he fetched up another enemy spear.

He heard Protus approach from the rear.

"Here should be as good a place as any."

22

Optio Latro drew closer. He also wore a chain shirt and carried scutum painted red. Varro, trapped between two chain-armored veterans, had no chance of surviving a fight. Latro's ready spear would eviscerate him and make it seem he died to an enemy hiding among his fallen friends.

His back tingled. The more immediate threat was Centurion Protus drawing in from behind. His feet swished across the grass.

Varro whirled to face him, ready to shout for his life. If he could get Falco and the other's attention, the officers might stop.

His gladius swept out, but Protus halted before it, his eyes wide with shock. His own sword remained pointed at the ground.

"What are you doing, man?"

Varro stepped back at the rage he saw in Protus's face. His heart slammed against his ribs.

Then he heard Latro's feet crunching over the grass and spun to face him.

But Latro had stopped, spear lowered but drawing no closer. His blue eyes burned like fire from beneath his wild brows.

"Put your sword down, soldier," Protus ordered. "Or I'll have Optio Latro pull your guts out in front of all your friends. Do it!"

Varro's mind raced. Sandwiched between both optio and centurion, men who wanted to kill him, he had no other choice. He lowered his gladius.

"Put it on the ground," Latro said, not shifting. "You looked like you were about to put it in Centurion Protus's back. We'll not have any tricks now."

"You can't kill me here," Varro said, slowly lowering his gladius until it rested in the grass. "Everyone will see."

"Let them watch," Latro said. "It'll be a good fucking lesson for them."

"Enough, Optio," Protus said. "He's confused. This isn't the best moment for this discussion, but since we've not had any other chance we'll make the most of it."

"I thought we'd wait until arriving at camp, sir," Latro said. "Less chance of interruptions."

"Seeing how you just stopped him from attempting to assassinate me, Optio, I'd say we haven't the luxury of time."

Varro finally acknowledged the burn at his shoulder. He looked to where the spear had glanced him, but it left nothing worse than a stuttering line of thin blood in its wake.

"Sir, there should be some punishment, even if he's mistaken."

"Optio, please keep an eye out for others." Protus emphasized his last word. "Varro needs a quick education."

"Yes, sir." But Latro gave Varro a scowl before turning to watch others up-slope.

"Are you going to kill me here?" Varro turned back to Protus, whose rage had ebbed into what seemed patient understanding.

"Varro, you've met with Decius Oceanus since you stated your concerns about Optio Latro."

Latro snorted at the mention. "What a heaping pile of bullshit.

I ought to have your back lashed to the bone for talking like that about me."

Varro, still caught between the two officers, looked back. But Protus clicked his tongue, causing Latro to fall to silence, then guided Varro to where he could see both of them.

"Here, you don't have to keep looking over your shoulder now. Decius Oceanus met with you during your watch shift several nights ago. I fear he has filled your head with lies and twisted you into a tool for his own ambitions."

Varro's first impulse was to deny it. Of course, any officer could easily learn the watch shift schedule. But rather than say more, he pressed his mouth shut.

"I don't know the details of what he told you, but I have a guess based on what you just attempted to do to me. I can assure you all he said were lies. I know what I'm about to tell you will be hard to hear, Varro. But you must know that I'm telling you as much truth as I can. Your life depends on trusting me in this."

Protus paused as if expecting an answer, and Varro offered a slow nod. Sweat rolled from beneath his helmet, cold and fearful. But the centurion smiled before continuing.

"I can understand your hesitance. Decius Oceanus is a skilled liar and commands a great deal of respect from all who know him. His easy manner is disarming, and he is a hundred times cleverer than he seems. He would make a fine senator, if he were but born in better circumstances. He could deceive anyone, particularly a young and inexperienced man such as you."

"I have only met him once, sir," Varro said. "He seemed to be a genuine man."

Latro, still monitoring the activity up the slope, again snorted.

"Optio, please do not interfere."

"Sorry, sir."

"Decius Oceanus is in a ring of men seeking to increase their fortunes at any cost. Wherever he finds a weak farm or one where the soldier is the sole inheritor of the property, he and his circle ensure those soldiers die. They arrange for accidents, or else help them fall in battle. Then Oceanus's patron sweeps in to purchase the farm at a severely reduced rate. It's an old story, really, but one that is quite successful for those willing to stoop to such ends. Oceanus receives payment for his work, like a bounty paid for a common criminal."

Varro blinked, staring between Protus and Latro, who now looked back at him with something like sympathy.

"That's what he said you and Optio Latro are doing, sir."

"I said so, sir." Latro flung the enemy spear down in disgust. "Thinks to blame me for his crimes? I'll have his tongue."

Protus held up his hand for silence, then peered at Varro.

"And you believed him? Well, of course you did, as you just tried to kill me. Do you know who my chief competitor was for the rank of centurion?"

"Decius Oceanus," Varro said, lowering his head. His hands trembled.

"Correct. If I am killed, the vote will be held again. Oceanus would succeed this time. Optio Latro here is not much liked by anyone, despite being an excellent officer, and wouldn't be promoted. Drusus loves Oceanus and would rather have him than me in his maniple. Though Drusus would never seek to have me killed for the opportunity. He may be a bore but is an honorable soldier."

Varro put his hands to his temples, trying to discern the truth.

Protus dropped his voice. "From your behavior after that shift, plus knowing your opinions on Optio Latro, I guessed Oceanus put you up to killing me on his behalf. He would not only vacate my position early in this campaign, he'd stop one of the few men who knew his other crimes."

"Sir, I can't understand this." Varro pressed his hands harder against his temples. "If you know Oceanus is killing men in the ranks, why can't you just charge him with the crime? You're an officer and he's just a regular soldier."

Protus smiled. "You are not listening, Varro. I said he is in a ring of men doing this. His patrons, whoever they are, are high over my position. Perhaps as high as the senate."

Varro groaned and squeezed his eyes shut.

"He said the same thing about you and Latro, sir."

Protus laughed. "Well, he told a half-truth then. He probably works for a senator and is increasing his wealth in the process. Everyone wins, except of course those he kills or else leads to their deaths. The battlefield is of course the perfect cover for this sort of treachery, as I'm sure you were just imagining a moment ago."

"Sir, I—there are too many questions yet."

Latro turned from watching the ridge. "You'd believe a man you met once on watch but not your officers who live and fight at your side? Do you have rocks for brains?"

"You tried to kill me. You left me to die at Artas's hands!" Varro's shout echoed over the fields, but were lost to the general background chaos of the battle concluding in the distance.

"What a little shit!" Latro stalked closer. "I had nothing to do with killing you before. But I will flog you to death now!"

"Optio, hold!" Protus stepped before Latro, exposing his mailed back to Varro. "By the gods, it's better we did this here than in camp. With the two of you shouting, they'll hear you back in Rome."

"Sir, he picked Nonus to fight me, then tried to poison my father, and tried to do the same to me. I called to Optio Latro in the forest and he was going to let Artas behead me. Falco said it looked like he was going to stab me with my own pugio when they found us after that fight."

"What did that brute say about me?" Latro stepped back, blue eyes wide with hate.

"And my father told me to watch out for you!" Varro could not stop now that he had opened the vein. He would bleed out all his fears and rage. If he died now, it would not matter anyway. "He told me to sleep with one eye open. Because you wanted to kill me."

"You overestimate your worth, Varro!" Latro spit on the ground. "I'd sooner kill a rat."

"Silence!" Centurion Protus shouted.

Varro's pulse set his eyes throbbing. The world fell aside as he glared at Latro, imagining him fallen among the scattered corpses on the ridge. The two glared at each other until Protus turned back to Varro.

"You've got it all wrong," he said. "If anyone will help you, it is Optio Latro and me. Nonus was under Oceanus's thumb. His family had fallen prey to one of Oceanus's schemes. We've no time for details, but their very lives were at his mercy. Nonus was trading his own life for the guarantee of his family. Of course, he was a fool to do so."

Varro stared at Protus in silence. At last, when he found his voice, it was hoarse and cracked.

"You knew this and still executed him and his contubernium? How—"

"That is the law," Protus said, holding up his hand to silence further questions. "Nonus attempted murder, and his entire contubernium was part of that plan to one degree or another. What you were considering for me a moment ago would have led to the same end for all your friends. But you did not seem to care for that risk. Do not be so quick to judge, Varro."

His jaw moved, but he could not say more. Protus was right. However he might think Nonus a fool, he was about to follow the same path.

"As for your poisoning," Latro said. "I've no conclusive proof Oceanus was behind it. But he was in the hospital with you the first time. He might have prepared something then, or else was waiting for the chance to finish you there. For your father had been poisoned the same day Nonus tried to kill you. Only your father's illness was very light. Oceanus was the man with him when he collapsed. I think he pretended to have the same illness to cover any suspicion and get himself sent to the hospital with you."

"Wait, Oceanus was in the hospital with me after Nonus tried to kill me?"

Protus nodded.

Varro thought back to that first stay in the hospital. There had been one other man with him, who rested facing the wall. That had been Oceanus, and he never realized it.

"How he succeeded in poisoning so much later is a trick known only to him. But it was true that Optio Latro poured your poisoned wine. That was an unfortunate coincidence."

"But he tried to call me a deserter and have me executed for it."

Latro rubbed the back of his neck. "What else are you when you don't come back with the others and didn't die in battle?"

Protus cleared his throat, anticipating the sparks between Latro and Varro. "The optio is strict on discipline, as I'm sure you know. He was not incorrect to name you thus. Though I understand you were returning to fetch your pugio, which must be of great value to you to take such a foolish risk."

"It was my uncle's, and a gift from my mother. Blessed at the Temple of Mars, sir. I couldn't leave it behind."

The centurion nodded, then continued.

"After you cunningly led their leaders out of camp, I decided to forgive what you did. For you were simply on a foraging team and not in a battle formation. But don't think to be so liberal with discipline in the future. And one day I'll have to learn how you led those brigands out."

Varro looked to Latro, whose rage seemed to melt away. He glanced aside and stepped back. In that instant, he realized

Latro had found the gold chain he had tossed aside to distract Artas.

"What happened in the forest, sir?" Varro asked with forced calm, though he addressed Latro rather than Protus. His eyes fluttered wider and for an instant he seemed to grow pale. But then his bluster returned.

"I found you on your knees in front of the brigand leader."

"Sir, I begged you for help when Artas planned to cut off my head. You were happy to see me killed, instead."

Latro sighed and pinched the bridge of his nose.

"In the same breath the brigand was about to swipe your head off. But you distracted him. I approached from behind and then suddenly you two were wrestling on the ground. Varro, I doubt you've ever tried to get in between two men wrestling with drawn blades. You don't jump into it even in full armor. I was looking for a chance to help you, but you had it well in hand. I circled around to get a better angle on him."

"I was still struck unconscious from behind."

"That slave girl leapt out and hit you clean in the back of the head. She grabbed your pugio when you dropped it and was going to finish you. But I got that away from her and knocked her aside. That's when the others found me, holding your pugio. You owe me your life, Varro. I never once held that over you. And what is my thanks for letting you go on living without any obligation to me? You accuse me of trying to murder you!"

His raging blue eyes locked with Varro's. It seemed impossible that Latro should rescue him. Why had he smiled when asked for help? Yet, Varro never saw Latro after that first glance. Falco's account of what he found was only the aftermath, and open to interpretation. Latro possibly told the truth. Varro's stare faltered.

"Thank you for saving my life, sir."

Latro's nostrils flared. "Don't make it a waste of my time."

"Sir, you said I distracted the brigand. How did I do it?"

Varro looked back into Latro's eyes and saw them widen. It was a fleeting motion, vanished beneath a snarl.

"You showed him something that got his attention. How would I know what it was? I was coming up behind him, you fool."

"And you weren't curious about what could've distracted him?"

Latro snorted and folded his arms. "You forget who your officers are, soldier."

"All right," Protus interrupted. "This is enough. The battle is concluded and I have a century to command, even if Drusus is running things. Now, Varro, I've told you enough that I believe you can see the truth of the matter. Oceanus has been your real enemy all along. He is behind the attempts on your life and is manipulating you to carry out his crimes. He is also the one who poisoned your father."

Varro blinked hard. He had nearly become a fool for the man who had murdered his father. The taste of blood on his lips enhanced his desire to see more of it from Oceanus's corpse.

"Sir, what can be done? Is there a formal process to follow?"

"If I could prove what I just said, certainly. Unfortunately, Oceanus is talented in these underhanded arts. Also, there is more complexity to all of this than I am willing share with you, particularly while standing in a battlefield in front of my century. You can fulfill a useful role, Varro. I am certain revenge must be top of mind. You are now prepared to handle him when he inevitably attempts to poison you or eliminate you in the confusion of battle. It would send a strong message to his masters were you to eliminate him yourself."

"Sir, you're asking me to kill him?"

"I'm telling you to defend yourself," Protus said, smiling. "No one would blame you. Optio Latro will stay close by to help you if needed. But as long as I am still alive, Oceanus will keep working you until that is no longer true. You have a margin of safety. He is not watching us now. I'm certain he planned to be as noticeably far from me as possible while he hoped you would kill me. He is confident in your being impressionable and blinded with a desire for revenge. He simply confirms your beliefs and you will follow along. But I know you for a thinking man, Varro. Just like your father. It is unfortunate he fell victim to Oceanus."

Varro looked between his centurion and optio. Both men stared grimly, awaiting a response. But he could not be sure how much to trust them. Latro seemed to read his thoughts and hissed through his teeth.

"If you don't believe my story about the forest, at least we took the girl as a slave. She'll tell you the same thing I just did."

Varro believed she could lie just as easily as Latro. His doubt still simmered.

"Why did my father warn me about you? Why did you hate each other at first sight?"

Latro folded his arms while Protus rubbed the back of his neck.

"We've known each other from prior campaigns, and we never got along. Some people aren't meant to be friends, and that's true for me and your father."

"But why did he call you trouble?" Latro recalled their first meeting at the dilectus. It seemed to have happened in another life.

For the first time, something like fear crossed Latro's face. He looked wide-eyed to Centurion Protus, who had stiffened and now stared into the distance.

"Well, of course, it's obvious," Latro said, stumbling through his words. "He knew what I was about. So, of course he'd have nothing good to say."

Varro nodded. Latro was crude and abusive, and his father would never have tolerated such a man.

But Protus cleared his throat. "You're not being clear, Optio. I can see Varro still doesn't understand."

He and Latro shared a long stare, and then at last the optio shrugged.

"All right, Varro. I was hoping you'd let this go until we made camp. But if you're going to push, then here it is. Your father knew I was on to Oceanus. The centurion and I were going to stop him this time. But I guess it wasn't me your father should've hated. Oceanus is the one that did him in. Bad business all around."

Varro cocked his head. "I don't understand."

Centurion Protus broke in, speaking with unmistakable clarity.

"Your father was not only Oceanus's victim. He was his partner, Varro. Your father worked with him."

23

Winter quarters were no different from the last two fortified camps Varro had inhabited. Apparently, this location represented a more strategic position closer to Macedonia. He wasn't hearing much these days. His head was full of noise.

He stood outside their barracks house, fresh sweat from a vigorous sword drill still trickling down his face. It cooled his hot skin when the wind blew across it. After drills, he had an hour of rest before joining another construction crew. Though the basics of the camp had been established ahead of their arrival, refinements were still needed. Hammering of construction teams echoed everywhere from dawn till sunset.

"Gallio will be released after two days." Panthera arrived from the hospital, announcing the news to the contubernium. Everyone except Curio, the recent velite promotion, smiled.

"He made it seem like his guts were falling out," Falco said. He leaned against the barracks, arms folded. "Now he's doing better after two days. Look at Varro. He's been to the River Styx yet he never cried as much as Gallio. What an actor."

"Everyone is different," Panthera said. "I'm glad he'll come through."

They fell into silence and eventually drifted off to their duties. Falco remained resting against the wall, arms folded. He stared at Varro until he caught his eye.

"You've got an hour before construction duty. Come help carry my gear." Falco had lost his shield and helmet in the confusion after the battle with the brigands, and was due to receive replacements today.

"I was hoping to sleep."

"I was hoping to get fucked, but looks like that will not be a thing while we're barricading ourselves in the mountains of Illyria. So none of us gets what we want. Come on, lily."

They left along the main path where soldiers and slaves hurried while shouldering lumber to the numerous construction projects. Falco stared after one dark-skinned man who was short enough to stand in a barrel and remain unseen.

"I hear now that we're on campaign we'll be getting our own servants for the contubernium," he said. "About time we don't have to worry for menial chores. Let some slave bastard handle it. Good times, eh, Varro?"

Varro shrugged. His feet shuffled as if too heavy to lift over the fresh dirt track.

"Say, I'm actually a bit early. Why don't we wait in the shade a bit," Falco said, then halted. "And you and I can, you know, just talk. It's better than sleeping."

"Talking to you is not better than sleeping." But Varro followed him off the track to a shaded spot between two buildings spotlighted in the late morning light. The fresh lumber smell settled over them as Falco pulled up a barrel. He gestured Varro to sit on it, which he did without thinking. Falco sat on the grass and leaned his back against the building wall.

They observed the frenetic activity of the camp. If an officer discovered them seated here, Varro guessed he would be kicked off the barrel and beaten with a vine cane before being put to labor. Free time was rarer than fine jewels, and worth far more. Yet he and Falco sat as if all time was at their command.

"So, you believe them?"

Falco's question seemed like a scream into the silence between them. Varro shifted on the barrel, picking at the loose thread in the hem of his tunic.

"I don't know what to believe anymore, Falco. I've not seen Oceanus since guard duty that night."

"It wasn't that long ago."

"Why does it feel like months ago? Everything is changing too fast. Anyway, I cannot accept my father was working with Oceanus."

Varro had shared all his news to Falco alone, within hours of leaving Protus. The whole march to camp he poured out all his doubts and Falco had listened without comment. After arriving at camp, they had no time until today to speak in private.

"And Tanicus, too," Falco said. "If you're going to believe Latro and Protus."

"That's what Protus claimed, after I calmed down. Oceanus was getting rid of his partners, starting with Tanicus and then my father. I could've killed Protus in that moment."

Falco laughed. "We saw you going mad with Latro holding you down. Were you really going to kill the both of them?"

"If I wasn't so tired from the battle and if they weren't wearing mail, I might have. I'm learning I have a terrible temper and the strength to match it. You should be glad I never let it loose on you."

Falco snorted and waved his hand in dismissal.

"Whatever, lily. But I guess if Latro and Protus wanted to kill you, they had the perfect excuse right then. We all saw it. Latro covered by telling us you were battle mad and to just forget it. But they could've stuck you right there in front of the whole century and no one would've questioned them. You were out of your mind. Instead they lied on your behalf and let you rejoin the ranks like nothing happened."

Varro shrugged.

"I suppose you're right, which is strangely worse than if you were wrong. It means they were honest about my father too."

Falco shook his head. "There has to be more to it. My father swears your father is the greatest man he ever met. I admired your father. Old Man Pius loved him like a son. I can't imagine your father murdering his friends to claim their property. It's just too much."

"Maybe he didn't do the murdering," Varro said. "I've been thinking about it, and even if my father led a hidden life, he was not a violent man. I believe he managed the business end of things for Oceanus. That's why he never brought me into it. I knew nothing of my father's business dealing and records. He was often away in Rome on business. But now I wonder why he was. This just gets worse every moment."

"Actually, that's better than remembering your father as a bloody-handed killer of his friends. Maybe he worked some deals for Oceanus. Still not great, but not outright evil. Everyone makes mistakes, and your father probably made one he couldn't escape."

Varro rubbed his head. "I don't know. It makes me wonder how much my mother knows. Was she part of his dealing?"

"By Jupiter, Varro, stop driving yourself mad. If we're going to accept that Latro and Protus are with us, then we have to accept Oceanus is going to figure that out and make us his next victims. By the gods, now every time I drink wine I wonder if I'm going to fall over dead."

"You keep saying us, Falco. This isn't your problem. It's mine."

Falco rolled his eyes. "Oceanus is no pushover. You're going to need my prodigious muscle to handle him. Besides, you'll want to be merciful or some other such nonsense. I'll do the job if you can't."

"No, I can kill him. I want to kill him." Varro tried to remember Oceanus's face. While he couldn't summon a clear image of the veteran, he imagined him clutching his bleeding throat as he died. "He murdered my father, and that cannot go unanswered. Never mind my vow. I am done with it."

Falco clucked his tongue. "You won't be the Varro I know if you do. Just amend it a bit for army life."

Varro summoned a smile he did not feel.

"Thank you, Falco. You've turned into a better friend than I ever imagined."

"You'll owe me," Falco said. "Don't be too fast to be grateful. But what a surprise, eh? The two of us are going to make it through this war and live to go farm barley together. What a tale. Too bad it doesn't involve vast riches and wanton women."

Varro slipped off the barrel and stretched.

"Falco, I've meant to ask you, did you mark that spot where you found me and the brigand leader?"

"I did. I hacked an X into a tree." He mimicked the act of carving with an imaginary knife. "But I've no idea why. I figured you'd tell me one day."

"Well, it's too late now. When I went back to find my pugio, I found the corpse of the first brigand leader that attacked you. He wore a gold chain necklace. The links were as thick as my thumb."

He extended his thumb to show Falco, whose eyes widened at the imaginary gold. He then explained how he hid the chain in his tunic and used it to distract Artas by throwing it into the underbrush.

"I was hoping we could return to retrieve it later," Varro said. "But I think Latro saw me toss it away. I can tell he has it now. He must have returned to that spot later, so helpfully marked for him, and found it."

Falco cursed. "Just when I thought I might forgive Latro a little, now I want to kill him again. That chain must be worth more than all we'll make serving in the army for our entire lives."

"It was valuable enough for Artas to risk a search for it when he did." Varro remembered the chain against his skin and imagining what its worth could bring him. "But now Latro has it. I'm certain."

"I guess now he'll buy himself a promotion," Falco said.

Varro shrugged. "Good for him. Maybe he'll go high enough to never meet me again. That'd suit me fine."

"Well, that's a lost opportunity. But there's nothing for it now. Say, we better go get my gear before some officer happens by to ruin our day."

They set back onto the road, joining the flow of soldiers and slaves crossing the camp. They had not gone a dozen paces when a young runner approached them. He addressed Varro.

"Marcus Varro, you are to report to headquarters and see Centurion Protus immediately. Please come with me."

Varro's hands went cold. He knew the summons would come, as Protus had promised him something more to prove their claims about Oceanus and his father. He looked to Falco, who shrugged.

"Now I've got to carry my own shield. Things get worse every moment. Go on, Varro. Don't keep the centurion waiting on my account."

He followed the runner back to headquarters at the center of camp. With all the construction combined with an unrelenting training schedule of combat drills and marches, all officers were occupied elsewhere. The runner left Varro at the door, indicating Centurion Protus awaited inside.

The room in this new headquarters could have been the same room they just left miles behind. Centurion Protus sat at the same desk and had the same mess of papyrus sheets, wooden tokens, wax tablets, and a dozen sundries piled there. He seemed besieged behind it, and his brow furrowed as he considered a wax slate.

Varro cleared his throat and stood to attention as he announced himself.

"Come inside," Protus said. Again his hard scowl vanished to a serene smile at seeing Varro. "I heard you had a free moment and wanted to speak to you. Close the door, too. Optio Latro will join us shortly, but in the meantime I want to keep other eyes and ears away from our meeting."

Varro shuffled inside, snapped the door shut, and remained at attention.

"Relax," Protus said. "This is an informal meeting. We will keep it brief."

His eyes fell to a rolled papyrus sitting atop the calamity of his desk. It was tied with a frayed brown string. Varro's stomach clenched as Protus lifted it.

"I mentioned this to you previously as something to prove my assertion about Oceanus. It's a letter from your father. I've read it already. I'm sorry, Varro. But given things, I needed to see it first. These are his final instructions to you. It seems he guessed his end one way or the other. It was well hidden among his possessions, which I of course had to search after his unexpected collapse."

He proffered the rolled papyrus. Varro stared at it, hands trembling yet as heavy as lead. The centurion gestured for him to accept it. He lifted it away in his cold fingers. The dry papyrus was light, yet it weighed with all the potential of anger and pain it might reveal.

"Read it in private," Protus said. "If privacy may be found. I am impressed that you are literate, Varro. Literacy is a requisite for officer ranks and seldom are farmers versed enough in such letters as your father has written. You come from a unique background."

"Thank you, sir. I do not feel special in any way."

"Be assured that you are. Both you and your friend Falco are far smarter than either of you show to others. That is good, for too much cleverness can lead to a poor end. If you survive the coming days, it would be good to explore how to capitalize upon your talents."

Varro nodded, unsure of what Protus intended. He focused on surviving the coming days, which sounded far more important than exercising his intellect.

A rap at the door startled Varro, and Latro's muffled voice followed. Protus called him in. The door creaked open and Latro slipped in to press it closed once more. His bright blue eyes peered out from beneath his unruly brow and appraised Varro, who stood at attention again.

"It's all confirmed, sir," Latro said, ignoring Varro. "The raiding party will leave within two days."

"Two days? They just hung that door yesterday," Protus said, pointing to the office door. "The fort is hardly complete and we're already heading into the field."

"I'm not wrong, sir." Latro tilted back his head, shifting his eyes toward Varro. "But perhaps we shouldn't be discussing all of this before the men, sir."

Protus blinked, then looked to Varro, who still clutched his father's letter like a dagger in his hand.

"Thank you for your advice, Optio. Now, to the matter at hand."

Latro bobbed his round head, sneaking a glance at Varro as he did.

"Of course, sir. Oceanus has been a model solider. As expected, he was a mile away from us during the skirmish with the brigands."

Varro raised his brow at Latro's description of what had been the most horrid display of death and gore he had ever seen. When he closed his eyes to sleep, he still saw disemboweled corpses sprawled in the grass. If that had been a skirmish, what was a battle?

"The better he behaves, the worse I feel about what he's up to," Protus said. "Anything more about the source of his poison?"

"No sir," Latro said. "At least nothing firm. He was in contact with Illyrian traders early on arrival at the temporary camp. He might have secured something from them. I think whatever he has left, he might be saving for our man Varro here."

"Or he has nothing of it remaining. In any case, I worry less for poisoning. He can only use that tactic so many times before suspicion falls on him."

"He could kill half the army with it too, sir." Latro again glanced at Varro. "Or at least a full contubernium."

"Enough about that," Protus said. "You've provided what I needed to know. Now it's time to put our plan into action."

Here Protus shifted in his seat and set both hands on his desk. He looked to Varro with grave eyes.

"By eliminating Oceanus, we're killing one snake from a very large nest. But just like snakes, they slither away if you expose their hiding place. As long as you're standing far back enough, that is. Stand too close, and you'll be bit."

"I've dealt with snake nests before," Varro said, unsure of what else to say given Protus's expectant stare. Latro laughed.

"We're not talking about actual snakes, you fool. Have some sense."

"Optio," Protus said in a cautioning voice. Latro straightened his shoulders and fell silent. The centurion continued. "What I'm going to tell you is confidential, Varro. Share this with no one, not even Falco. In any case, you won't have to remain silent for long. In two days' time, we will be launching punitive raids into nearby cities. The Macedonians aren't coming out to fight, and so we need to offer some incentives. Additionally, we need Illyria to make a firm commitment to us. Our consul and tribunes have decided this expedition will aid their decision-making process."

"They'll shit themselves once we tear up those cities," Latro said. "It won't stretch their imagination to see it could be their fate as well."

Varro swallowed hard. He thought back to the farmer's two children and how Protus called for their deaths, even being fellow Romans. What would this expedition do to the children of the enemy?

"In any case," Protus said. "Our raiding party will be sizable, but not the full strength of our legions. Lucius Apustius will be leading us. I would be too forward to call him a friend of mine, but we are on amicable terms. I will ensure our century is part of that force, as well as Oceanus's."

The simplicity of Protus's plan unfolded in Varro's imagination. He nodded with understanding.

"Sir, you will want me to find an opportunity to kill Oceanus during these raids."

Protus smiled and looked to Latro, who shrugged.

"He's been getting smarter since he's been under my command, sir. He and his fellows just need a firm hand to steer them."

"That is the essence of the plan," Protus said, turning back to Varro. "But of course there is more nuance to it than just finding a moment to slip a pugio between his ribs. It must be done in a way that both conceals your hand in it and sends an unmistakable message to Oceanus's sponsors."

"It sounds difficult, sir," Varro said. "I have no experience with this sort of thing."

"Of course not," Protus said. "We wouldn't be speaking if you did. The game between Oceanus and us will accelerate now that we've settled in camp. He still believes you're seeking revenge on Latro and me. It won't be long before he realizes this is not so. This raid is a fortunate disruption. He will want to use it for the same purpose, to dispose of Latro or me, preferably both. We must not let him dictate this battle. We want to select his target for him. That is how you can help."

Latro now took over at a nod from Protus.

"He'll meet with you before the attack, you can be sure. Since you've been loud about my wanting to kill you, he'll believe it when you tell him you want to go after me first."

"So I'm to tell him I will find a way to kill you in the battle?"

Latro glared at him. "Ever the bright one. And don't get too comfortable with me."

"Of course, sir. Sorry, sir."

"That's better. Yes, tell him that, but also tell him you botched your chance at Protus, which isn't a lie. But make a good story. Tell him you need help, and that he should be near in case you lose your nerve. Don't make a fuss of it if he refuses or he'll suspect you. He hasn't survived this long by luck alone. But if you do well, he'll follow you."

"Follow me, sir? Won't I be in line with the rest?"

"Of course you will," Latro said, recoiling with a hand to his chest. "You'll be in the front line with the others and following orders. Anything less and I will have you all flogged. But this isn't a typical fight, Varro. We'll pull down walls, march into the city, and things will get confused. They always do. That's when you'll make your attempt."

"But Oceanus won't be in my line, sir. He's not even in the same maniple."

"Gods, Varro, I just called you smart and now you're turning me into a fucking liar. You make your attempt on me. Try to kill me."

"Sir?" He stepped back under Latro's sneer, unable to form a better question. "I don't understand."

"Well, that's clear as sunshine. You try to kill me. Try, that's the word to pay attention to. You wouldn't succeed even if you were serious. But we need to play this one however we find ourselves during the battle. In any case, you will fail and I'll go after you. Oceanus will be watching and follow on. I'll give you a chance to hesitate to draw him out. At this point, we'd have led him away from the rest and can finish him together. I'll do the squeamish work of making a message out of his death. Don't turn so pale. You just play the part of an angry young man wanting revenge for his father. It's the truth, isn't it? So it won't be hard. Do your part, and you'll be fine."

Varro thought of a dozen ways this could fail. Others could mistake his attempt on Latro's life as real. Oceanus might not follow. The city might surrender before they attack.

"Your mind is occupied with doubts," Protus said. "I can see it in your expression. The truth is, we are trusting much of our plan to fate. If the plan fails, you will be transferred out. I will send you to join the force relieving Athens. You'll be exposed and endangered here. If you succeed, then the day is won. If we cannot find an opportunity during these raids, we will reassess."

"Sir, this seems complicated," Varro said. "Wouldn't it be easier to prove Oceanus's crimes then punish him, or else frame him for something?"

Protus gave a weak smile.

"Varro, you see our fight with Oceanus unfolding on an enormous battlefield. But in fact it is one tiny clash in the shadows. To drag that shadowed fight into the light of a legal proceeding will invite greater disaster than you know. I beg the gods this will end your involvement in matters like these. It is hard enough to be a recruit without being drawn into lethal intrigues. You've trusted me thus far, so trust me a little further. This is the best way to solve your immediate problems."

Latro faced him now and pointed to the papyrus he still clutched.

"And the best way to prove you're not like your father."

A swift and terrible rage welled up at those words. Latro continued to sneer even as heat rushed to Varro's face. His arms tensed and teeth clenched. But a powerful shout from Protus halted him.

"Peace!" Protus stood from his chair, glaring between Latro and Varro. "Both of you, enough."

"Sorry, sir. Just wanted to get the boy some practice before our little act. He needs to convince Oceanus."

"That'll be sufficient, Optio." Protus stepped around his desk. He patted Varro's shoulder. "We'll leave you a private moment to read that letter. Then be quick to get to your construction duties. Until the day comes to act, you should behave as you normally would."

He and Latro left him in the office, the door closing behind them.

Varro looked around the office. Leaving him alone here was a sign of trust he could not deny. He chewed his lip, then raised the papyrus in his hand. He put thumb and forefinger to the frayed brown tie, then pulled it open.

The letter unrolled, his father's neat script unfurling before him.

24

"Greetings, Marcus. I trust this letter finds you well and in good health. If you are reading this, then much of what I feared has come to pass. I have died. It is strange to write those words, as my hand still trembles with fearful life as I scribe these letters. There is much to tell you, all dictated by the space of a single papyrus sheet. Let me begin with what is most important.

"You have made me proud. You are a principled man, logical and determined in your purpose. You have demonstrated flexibility of thought, but not a total bending or breaking of your intentions. That is key to a fulfilling life. Complete your duties, honor your word, reserve violence as a last defense. But understand you cannot be as rigid as you have been. For then you may be broken, and a broken man is never set upright again. As you mature, I'm certain you will realize this on your own. You will grow into a fine man, one for others to admire and emulate.

"Though I am full of pride for you, by now you may no longer feel the same about your father. I am truly sorry, Marcus. Decius

Oceanus is a charismatic man and I long ago fell in with him thinking we simply dabbled in investments for quick money. He convinced me of a great many untruths. But I cannot blame him in the end. For I know fully his methods, and I have supported him with my knowledge and business contacts. I have never slept a sound night since joining with him. Yet your father is a weak man, Marcus. I have profited a great deal from the misfortunes of others and failed to do what was right.

"The only right thing I have done was to shield you from all of this. I am uncertain of how much you have learned. Doubtless Oceanus has finished me in some manner that removes suspicion from himself. You have likely been approached by Centurion Protus and told the truth. He and his Optio Latro have sworn to undo Oceanus. After all, Latro lost his brother to him. I have written this letter in part to convince Centurion Protus that you have never been involved, and should remain uninvolved. Though he may very well disregard my plea and prosecute you in my stead. I pray this is not so.

"The page is nearly finished, but there are too many words yet to write. I left detailed instructions with your mother. She will tell you more upon your return home. You are my sole heir. I realize you may not want what has been gained at the cost of innocent lives. Do what you will with your inheritance. But remember you mother and sister, who are also innocent and in need of your protection.

"My grandfather extracted a promise from you to not become as he was. I must ask the same for you to me. Do not become what I was. Be yourself. Stay true to your path and seek a life of simple honesty and simple happiness. You will sleep easier and will greet your last days without the dreaded weight of unpaid sin. Remember this much about me, Marcus. I only wished the best for my family. Go now and build a life to be proud of."

~

THE WORDS of his father's letter still filled Varro's thoughts a week later as he pulled up the stakes surrounding the marching camp. With these remembered words came the threat of tears. He had suffered through anger, fear, and sadness in an endless cycle. While he tried to hide this from others, Falco had discerned his stress. He also knew Varro met with Protus, and so wheedled out the story while on the march.

Falco now worked beside him, silently extracting the stakes from the ground. Since meeting with Protus and Latro, Falco never left him unless duty required it. Nor did he speak much, but let Varro initiate talk as he worked through his emotions. Falco's one reaction to his father's letter had been to say, "That explains a lot about Latro's hostility to you. Still doesn't make him a better man, though."

The revelation that Latro's brother had died in a scheme involving Oceanus, and by implication Varro's father, filled him with new dread. Latro claims to have saved his life, but he still doubted it. He was certain Latro was hoping Artas would kill him. This new information only reinforced the idea he sought revenge. Now with Varro's father actually dead, the next best target for revenge would be himself.

He imagined what might happen once they killed Oceanus. Would Latro then turn on him and later claim Oceanus had done it? Varro thought it a certainty.

He looked to Falco. Even in the cool of a late autumn morning, his heavy brow still gleamed with the sweat of his effort. All down the trench he and the contubernium removed stakes lining a narrow ditch surrounding the camp. They had settled on a hill of hoary, leafless trees along a wide river they followed from their main camp. According to rumors flowing through camp, their force was assigned to capture towns on the frontier of Macedonia, starting with a place called Corrhagum. From there they would move on to larger cities and destroy these to prepare for a full invasion of Macedonia.

Throughout, Centurion Protus and Optio Latro had not altered their actions in the least. When either of them looked at Varro, it was as he was only a smudge of air to them. Latro shouted orders in his face and whipped his vine cane at him while on the march. But this was true of any regular Latro contacted. Varro chided himself for acting conspicuously, but other seemed to attribute his moods to his father's recent death.

The former velite, Curio, blathered on to Gallio farther down the line. It seemed he wanted to make a friend of Gallio for having saved his life, yet all Gallio did was groan with each stake he pulled. His wounds had hardly healed. Varro admired his courage and commitment to his fellows.

"Falco," Varro said in a low voice. He shifted to get closer, attacking a new stake as he did. "I've been thinking about what I have to do."

Falco did not look up from his wrestling with the stake, but nodded. Against orders, he had told Falco everything he knew and of the centurion's plans.

"I don't trust Latro still. I'm not sure how it is going to happen, but I want you to follow us. I think he might try something."

He remained vague in case someone else should hear. Falco paused and offered a crooked smile.

"Funny, isn't it? A year ago, I'm sure you spent your nights wishing I was dead."

"I wished for it every day."

Falco chuckled. "Proves that the gods don't listen to crying babies. Good thing, too, or I wouldn't be here to follow. I've got you, Varro. You'll have your time to do the same for me. We're getting through this whole mess alive and with all our legs and arms. And we're doing it together."

They returned to their work, shuffling down the line and pulling stakes as they went. Gallio stepped out of line, holding his wound. Curio followed him out. Blood on Gallio's tunic revealed his wound had reopened. He and Curio fussed over it, with Gallio claiming all was well.

But he was clearly not doing well, and Curio offered to support him. After token resistance, he allowed Curio to take him to a doctor. Their departure created a small island where Varro and Falco were apart from the others.

Varro heard his name called from the edge of nearby trees. He recognized the deep, rocky voice.

Oceanus hid himself well despite his size. His wide shoulders were wrapped in a faded wool cloak that matched the surrounding. He could have passed himself as the trunk of the tree he pressed against.

He waved Varro closer, his tiny, squinting eyes flashing. Falco had turned away. Either he did not hear or else feigned ignorance. Varro searched down the line, finding his companions involved in their work. He set down his uprooted stake, then slid his sandaled feet over the patchy grass to join Oceanus behind the clump of trees.

"How are you holding up?" Oceanus asked. His voice was deep and rocky, but full of concern.

"As well as expected, sir."

Oceanus smiled, his already small eyes nearly vanishing behind the wrinkles.

"I'm not your officer. But on that topic, you know why I'm here?"

Varro nodded and swallowed.

"I don't think I can do it," he said, the quavering in his voice genuine. "I hate Latro for what he did and what he tried to do to me. But I've never murdered a man before."

"It's not murder," Oceanus said, an amiable smile fixed on his blocky face. "It's justice. You'll never get that from the tribune. Like I said, Protus and Latro's sponsors are in high places. There's only one way to deal with this."

Oceanus patted the pugio at his left hip.

"I ruined my chance to get Centurion Protus. I lost my nerve and he turned on me. I swear he realized what I was going to do. He had a strange look. Do you think he knows?"

Oceanus shook his head. "If he did, by now you'd have had an accident on the march or else been sent on a patrol that never returned. In a way, your failure helps us. It proves they are confident where you're at. They've been lulling you, Varro. They don't know we've been in contact, or that you're on to their plan. When this next battle comes, Latro will make his move. But you've got to act ahead of him."

"I do?"

Oceanus laughed. "Of course! Once we're inside Corrhagum, and that won't take long, we'll be sent to round up the population. That's when it will become confusing and Latro can leave your dead body in an alley with none the wiser. But you can do the same to him, if you're ready."

Varro held his arm, trying to look as worried as he felt.

"He wears a chain shirt and has years more experience than me. I'll never defeat him one on one. I need you there, Oceanus. The two of us can do it."

"I'll be handling Protus," he said, shaking his head. "In one battle, we kill the two-headed snake. If you leave one alive, he'll be alerted and you can be sure we'll die for it."

Varro feared his pounding heart would betray him. If Oceanus went for Protus, then he and Latro would waste their time away from the real danger.

"Are you sure about me? I want to kill Latro, but it seems impossible while he's geared up for battle."

"Well, you won't kill him in his bed," Oceanus said. His face grew hard and Varro saw a spark of anger in his small eyes. "You're not that kind of person. He'll have a moment with his shield down and his neck exposed. You won't have to kill him in one go. Just drop him, and then you can finish him on the ground. There'll be plenty of other screaming to cover for it. The women alone will make your head split with their crying. Just find a moment when no one is looking. That is the key."

Varro sighed and stared at his feet.

"Very well. There's no way you can aid me?"

"If I can get to Protus first, then I will find you. But it's a big enough town and rounding up then killing all the men will be chaos. Don't count on me finding you once we're apart."

Oceanus sized him up, one eye widening as he searched him from head to toe. "You look a lot like your father when he had his doubts. I know you're worried, but just remember what Latro did to your father and what he'll do to you the moment you're alone. And Varro, this is going to be a proper battle. These are not brigands but Macedonian warriors. It may only be a walled town, but the Macedonians will fight for it. Keep your wits and stay alive, or else you'll never avenge your father."

Oceanus searched over his shoulder, then patted Varro's with a heavy hand.

"By tomorrow this will all be behind you. You'll be free of fear and you will have avenged your father."

"Thank you for all you've done," Varro said, hoping his smile appeared genuine. "I was lost until I met you."

"Think nothing of it," he said, then pulled back into the trees to leave Varro with his thoughts.

He lingered a moment before returning to Falco, who continued to work at the stakes. He had kept distant from the others, though Panthera saw Varro returning from the trees and gave a slow shake of his head.

"I had to piss," Varro said loud enough for Panthera and the others to hear.

"You talk to yourself while pissing?" Falco asked, not looking up from his work.

"Don't be stupid. I met with Oceanus. He wants me to move on Latro today. But he's going to go after Protus. That ruins the whole plan."

Falco paused as if thinking, then returned to pulling up the stakes. Down the row, Curio returned alone and the other gathered around him for news.

"Are you not going to say anything?" Varro asked. "What am I supposed to do?"

"You're supposed to kill Oceanus without getting caught. So just do that."

"But that's not the plan, and I will not have a chance to speak to Latro or Protus about it before we set out. We're leaving now." Varro put his hand on his forehead. "This is a mess."

"Don't whine, Varro. We'll figure it out. We've got the whole march to Corrhagum to think about it."

"You talk like it's miles away. You can see it from the edge of camp."

"They'll have barred the gates by now. Must have seen us already. So there's time to get in there. We'll come up with something before we're inside."

"When have you become so positive?"

"One of us has to be, Varro. Looks like my responsibility today."

He would have had a retort, but Curio ambled over to them. His bright boyish face gleamed with curiosity. "You two have a lot to say to each other these days."

"Fuck off," Falco said. "Children don't belong with the adults."

"You don't want to hear about Gallio?" Curio acted as if he never heard the curse, and looked expectantly between them. He did not wait for an answer to report. "His wound reopened and looks like he'll be sitting out today and the next few to follow. He was so broken up about it. But he has to heal, right?"

Varro nodded while Falco rolled his eyes.

"Well, we better get ready. At last we're fighting Macedonians today. Are you excited?"

"Fall on your sword, Curio." Falco pushed him aside as he placed the last stake on the neat piles arranged along the trench.

"Falco means to thank you for helping Gallio. We all better get ready before Latro comes around and makes it tenfold harder than it need be."

"I better piss first," Curio said. "I'll just go where you did, Varro. Watch my back, eh?"

Falco seemed unconcerned, but Varro had to force himself not to drag Curio away. Of course he would find no evidence of Varro having relieved himself. Yet what would that mean to Curio? He abandoned his concern and watched out for Latro as requested. Falco had already rejoined the others to head back to their tent.

When Curio returned, he was whistling softly.

"That feels better," he said. "My father told me it's bad luck to piss on another man's puddle. But I always thought that was stupid. Don't you do that in a latrine? My poor father, what kind of stories does he tell? Still, no bad luck for me today. It was very dry back there."

"You're careful about where you piss, aren't you?" Varro squared up to the diminutive soldier. He now wore a bronze pectoral like the other hastati and had a gladius and pugio at the ready. Yet he still seemed like a boy.

"Of course I am. Aren't you? Always watch where you're pissing, Varro."

Curio left him, resuming his soft whistle as he trotted back toward the tent.

But Varro lingered behind, wondering if he had just indulged foolish conversation with a naïve boy or been warned of dangers to come.

25

Corrhagum sat on the Apsus River, protected from the south by its fast-flowing brown water. To Varro's surprise, they had not marched directly to the town but crossed the river at a ford farther north. He worried this warned the inhabitants of the attack, but they would have noticed the Roman camp the day before. The Macedonians were prepared.

He now stood in line with his companions, which to his shock included Gallio. He had rejoined them without a word, offering Varro a curt nod. Curio had assaulted him with a dozen questions, but Gallio ignored him. Like all the other hastati in the maniple, they were focused on the battle ahead.

A stone wall surrounded Corrhagum, ancient rock stained black with decades of rainfall. A single tower stood over the heavy timber gate to the town. It seemed impossible to scale or to breach. This outpost was nothing in comparison to Rome, but it was formidable enough in Varro's inexperienced estimation.

Yet Centurion Drusus commanded from the front of the maniple. The signifier raised their standard beside him, and it cast its shadow to the fore. They approached from the east, out of the morning sun. Drusus snorted at the town.

"It's like breaking a turtle shell. Hard on the outside but soft and vulnerable inside," he said. "Don't worry for it. Those gates couldn't keep out my grandmother. We'll be done here before noon."

Centurion Drusus then let out a long laugh which rippled throughout the maniple. Only Varro could not join in. He watched Centurion Protus at the fore of his century, hoping he could warn him about Oceanus. Optio Latro was set to the rear beyond any chance of reaching him until his line rotated out of the battle.

"This is will not go well," Varro said to Falco.

"At least we're not manning the battering ram," Falco said. "Look at the bright side."

A full century was rolling a huge battering ram toward the gate. It had a roof, and the soldiers had their long scutum shields to extend it against arrows from the walls. The general, Lucius Apustius, commanded from the center where the ram had been set. Varro could not see him, but did not need to. He simply had to obey his centurions, both of which were in clear view.

"I'm not talking about getting inside. It's what's supposed to happen in there. Nothing is going to go according to Latro's plan."

Falco hissed for him to lower his voice. He ducked his head down and looked around. Every grim face watched the brave men rolling the battering ram toward the gates. It had trundled halfway and the Macedonians were now appearing on their walls.

"Just stick with me, Falco. I'll feel better for it. I have an idea of what to do. I just don't know if it'll work."

"It'll work. By noon we'll have this town and we'll be done with all this other shit, too."

Falco turned to him. His face was tight with resolve.

"Silence!" Drusus shouted. "You keep your mouths shut or I'll shut them for you."

The battering ram reached the gates with no resistance. His fellow soldiers had raised their shields overhead, creating a multi-colored canopy over the crew and themselves. These were the breachers, the first to enter and the first to win the highest honors of this battle. While some of his fellows groaned about missed opportunities, Varro felt more practical about missing that assignment. He felt much safer out of bow range.

The first slam of the ram sounded like thunder. Varro leapt in shock. The heavy thud sounded as if it were by his ear rather than across the field. Dust shook from the wall and rained down on the battering ram as the crew hauled it back for another strike.

The Macedonians released their arrows now. It sounded like hail on a tile roof. Some screams mingled with the clatter of arrowheads on shields, but Varro did not see any change in the overall mass.

The ram struck again. The gates shuddered and a bright yellow slash of exposed wood shot through one door. The men on the ram cheered. More arrows fell among them.

"Looks like they'll break it open in no time," Falco whispered.

Before Varro could reply, a gout of fire spewed from the walls above the gate.

Even at this distance, he heard the whoosh of the flames as they splashed among the up-turned shields. Now the cheers turned to screams as men scattered from the flames. The roof of the ram caught fire, but it slammed home nonetheless. This time, one of the gate doors folded in.

"Forward!" Drusus called.

Varro's stomach clenched. The gates had not been broken, but they were already moving in. He could not see if the entire force had been ordered ahead, but enough marched along with them that he could only see Apustius's standard.

No one spoke or called out. No one hesitated at the order. But Varro did not believe he was the only one who would've rather fled than march toward flaming wreckage and screaming, burning men.

Yet the ram slammed the gate again, sending sparks and burning cinders into the air.

And now one door collapsed to reveal hazy light beyond. The way into Corrhagum opened.

"Double-time!" Drusus ordered.

The ground shook with their charge. The fire around the breachers had burned out. They were pushing into the broken gates to widen the entrance. The Macedonian archers shot into their ranks. But even Varro knew they could not remain on the walls now. They would have to pull back or else be swept off their perches to their deaths.

He was jogging now. Falco and Panthera were at his right. Gallio and Curio were at his left. Ahead, Protus and Drusus led them to their first battle. His mind was giddy with the promise of a true fight against enemies he had long imagined but never encountered. Would they be monsters, or would they be just like him? If the brigands were any indication, they would look like his friends and neighbors. But with every stride forward, those fears were pounded aside.

Centurions Drusus and Protus along with the best of their respective centuries led the way. Their maniple was the first to arrive at the gate, and being in the fore of the hastati, Varro was among the first to follow the breachers who were pushing into the gate tunnel.

The sickening stench of burnt flesh assailed him. He was a dozen strides distant when Centurion Drusus ordered them to slow. As Varro drew the final distance, what at first seemed like charred logs resolved into scorched corpses. The intense heat had burned them into twisted, agonized shapes. A bronze helmet with its feather ablaze sat like a ghoulish lamp beside its dead owner. Other men held their faces and screamed.

But the gates had collapsed in and the breaching team was now inside. Archers were prepared on the opposite side, and the hiss of their shafts was clear even over the cheers and shouts of the Romans pouring through.

Centurion Protus now pointed to Varro and his century. "Follow me! Deploy left once inside."

Varro could not visualize the plan. Protus turned and dove into the oily smoke rolling off the smoldering ram. Varro and the others followed. His heart thudded and his nose was raw with the smoke that rushed over him as he followed in line.

Coughing, screaming men rushed into the opening. True to Centurion Drusus's prediction, the gates had been defeated. Varro scaled over splintered and scorched wood to enter a short tunnel. Light vanished and the roar of chaos echoed in the stony dark. His feet raced, his companions at his side, the comforting bulk of his shield before him, and the heft of his pilum in hand.

He burst into Corrhagum.

But an orderly deployment to the left was impossible. Bales of hay had been stacked around the gate. Archers and spearmen hid behind these.

Centurion Protus ranged ahead, having already cast his pilum and now drawing his gladius.

But Varro understood what the hay bales meant beside cover for the enemy.

"Sir, look out!" Varro lurched ahead toward Protus, who hid behind his shield from the return cast of Macedonian skirmishers. A javelin clanked off Varro's shield as he raced out of line to join Protus.

"The bales are wet with oil, sir," he shouted, as he grabbed at Protus's arm. "It's a trap."

"Shit! Of course!" Protus regarded the wall of hay bales and waved his century back.

Yet in the smoky chaos not all flooding inside saw the

command. Varro shouted it back to the others, as did Falco and Gallio. But in the next instant he heard a rush of flame and heat burst over him.

Archers on the walls shot flaming arrows into the bales, which readily ignited. Now they faced a wall of fire looming over where they would have deployed. The century clogged the small area around the entrance, piling up behind each other while trying to clear the gate tunnel.

Behind them, another set of hay bales roared into flame.

"They're funneling us," Protus shouted. He squinted ahead while Varro and the others lined up behind him. Men pushed into Varro's back as they continued to enter through the gate.

"Clear the center," Protus said. "Follow me!"

Varro and Falco were shoulder to shoulder. To their left hot flames licked at them and to the front a line of long spears blocked the main street. These bristled from scores of round, ornate shields. It was a wall of spiked death.

And Protus was leading a charge toward it.

But then the bales of flaming hay shifted.

Gallio shoved him from the left, away from the bales. "They're pushing it onto us!"

Fiery bales tumbled off the wall and landed among the ranks, breaking up their charge and clogging the entrance with smoke, fire, and a press of Roman soldiers unable to spread into the town.

Men screamed as burning bales tumbled over them. Varro collided with Falco and both shifted to the right. Centurion Protus vanished behind smoke.

"We're not charging a wall of sarissas," Varro shouted as he bobbled into the press. "I thought we're supposed to go around them."

Falco shouted something back, but it was lost when a great cry went up behind them. Both turned to see a brilliant flash of orange from the gate tunnel.

"Shit! We're cut off," Varro said. He ranged his eyes over the ranks of soldiers now turned to see the fire closing their retreat.

"Good thing we don't need to retreat," Falco said. "Straight ahead, Varro. It's our only way."

"Shield ups and straight ahead!"

Centurion Drusus emerged from the smoke. His face was black, and a broken javelin shaft hung from his shield. But he stood in the center of the street as if this were a calm market day. He even smiled as he pointed ahead.

"There's not even fifty of them, boys. The day is ours. Let's claim it!"

The endless hours of training overtook Varro. He lined up again, despite the chaos, the black smoke, the tumbling bales of flaming hay, and formed up with his contubernium. Gallio touched his left shoulder and Falco touched his right. They raised their shields and gripped their pilums.

They stepped over the bodies of the remnants of the breaching team. Arrows and javelins stood up from their bodies. Those that had continued on seemed to have melted into the wall of pikes ahead of them. The Macedonians did not break, but crouched with shield and sarissa poised for the Roman charge. They anchored themselves in the main street with two buildings on their flanks. Varro's maniple had the unenviable job of unclogging the road into the town. But once the flames burned through the hay bales, other maniples would join in on the flanks and destroy them.

They only had to survive long enough.

"Cast!" Drusus let his pilum fly.

Varro drew back and let his sail along with the scores of pilum soaring toward the Macedonians.

Behind his shield, he saw the keen sarissa points waver with the impact of the cast. They cried out and cursed, but their wall remained. Their bronze shields and conical helmets caught the dim light that filtered through the smoke.

Then their lines collided.

It was like punching into a wall. The Macedonian sarissa was a long weapon held far from the line of action. Varro's heavy shield smashed the gleaming blades aside and he punched in with his gladius to stab a man in the front rank. His curiosity at the Macedonian's appearance vanished. He was blind with terror, and his reflexes delivered the attacks he laced into his opponents. He shoved forward and sarissa blades shoved back at him. One scored across his helmet, and another turned on his cheek plate.

From his peripheral vision, he saw Falco's shield and the feathers of his helmet waving above it. Beyond him, he saw men collapsing as the Macedonian pikes claimed victims.

He kicked and stomped on enemy feet, anything to drive them back. He punched with his shield and stabbed with his gladius. But he seemed to make no headway into the dark thicket of pikes, bronze helmets, and staring eyes. Blood pooled at his feet. Blood rolled from a cut above his brow down into his mouth. His ears throbbed with the crash and thunder of battle.

But the line did not yield.

At last Drusus sounded the rotation whistle. Along with all others engaged with the Macedonians, Varro shoved into the front to force open space for the change. His relief stepped into the new space with scutum raised to cover them both as he replaced Varro. Once he felt the shield at his shoulder, he stepped backwards to let his replacement slide in, then filed through the rear ranks.

Though bloodied and black with smoke, all of his contubernium were alive. Gallio winced, holding his old wound. "That was something," he said. "A real fight."

Varro nodded. He could not speak. His throat was parched and his hands trembling. But his sword hand was thick with blood, none of it his own. He stumbled along the ranks of soldiers waiting to press into the fight until he eventually found the rear. Falco remained with him, his face white and his expression blank.

"Good work," Optio Latro said, waving them into their positions. "Not bad for a bunch of recruits. Everyone still has their fingers and eyeballs, I see. Well done."

Varro did not recognize the place. The street no longer seemed clogged with bodies. The young velites were busy pulling dead and wounded to the sides. While black smoke rolled over the gate and surrounding areas, the walls of flaming hay had been shoved away. An endless stream of soldiers marched in through the gate tunnel, the flames there extinguished.

"The walls are clear," Falco said, squinting up.

"So they are. It doesn't look like there's any resistance." Varro turned back to the fight ahead, but all he could see were the backs of his fellow soldiers waiting their moment to fight. The triarii leaned on their spears and observed the battle, chatting as if watching a chariot race.

Panthera joined them, pointing to the side. "I saw a century moving around those buildings. Unless there's something else in the way, they'll hit these Macedonians on the right flank. It'll be over for them."

"That's right," Optio Latro said. "Battle is almost over. But your work will just begin. Got a whole town to round up. So get in line and save your breath for the real work. Understood?"

"Yes, sir," All of them answered in unison.

But Varro looked to his optio, who offered him the barest hint of a knowing glance.

The hunt for Oceanus would begin soon.

The roar and crash of battle washed over them, rolling with the billows of smoke and the sour notes of burned hay. The flush of battle now drained from him and he began to wonder where Oceanus was in this chaos. As promised, despite the ordered ranks and centurion whistles, the battle was confused. Men shoved into their positions, staring fixedly ahead at what might be their last looks at the world. The ordered blocks and ranks of maniples and legions broke down with the streets and buildings. Battle lines could not extend more than a street-width.

At last the Macedonian resistance at the center of their town broke. Lucius Apustius had commanded Rome to a victory. History would not mark this tiny town on the frontier of Macedonia, Varro mused, but it was his first proper battle and his first taste of the enemy he would face in the larger war to come. For him, he would not forget it.

The breaking Macedonians were easy to see from their sarissas. The long pikes raised into the air, shaking like a forest of trees in a storm. Many fell by the score as the Romans pushed in from the flank. The Romans to their front now surged ahead as men hunted down their enemies.

"They're done," Optio Latro said. "Now forward and fill in those gaps!"

He snapped his vine cane. The triarii stepped aside to let them through. There seemed confusion at this strange order, but there were no other officers at the rear to countermand Latro.

"This is it," Varro whispered to Falco as they marched forward. "What's your plan?"

"I don't remember," Varro said. "This battle was too much."

"Gods, Varro! You forgot? Well, the job's still the same. I'll be with you, no matter what. Just get over to Latro and avenge your father."

They were in a mass of soldiers who had not yet had their turn at battle. They were eager for blood, surging ahead to claim an enemy for themselves before every Macedonian soldier was slain. Varro and Falco bobbed among them and struggled to keep together.

He looked into Falco's sooty, bloodied face. He had hated this man for all his life, and begged the gods to send him an agonizing death. But Falco had cared for him while hospitalized and now thrice fought shoulder to shoulder to him. He had demonstrated true brotherhood, and Varro could think of no other he would trust with his life.

"If I am killed, take care of my mother and sister," he said.

"A bit late to ask that favor now, isn't it? We just ran through fire and jumped into Macedonian pikes. But certainly. I know you'll look after my mother if I die. But we're not dying, Varro. Not now. Go get to work."

Falco clapped Varro's helmet with his palm, then shoved him into the crowd. He slid sideways into the press, turned back to see Falco waving him on over the shoulders of eager soldiers. He then shoved his way toward Optio Latro who waited at the rear of the line with his fierce blue eyes flashing and a wicked smile creasing his face.

26

An ending battle was louder than one in progress. As Varro slithered between his comrades, all shoving forward into the narrow streets, his head pounded with the noise. Weapons clanged on shields, men screamed in pain or in glory, officers shouted, whistles blew, the enemy howled. He could not hear his own voice amid it. Far back from the battle line, he at least did not smell the blood or the bowels of the dead. But the air was heavy with acrid notes of burned hay and wood.

He at last popped out the rear of the press, where Optio Latro met him with a sneer.

"Sir, I've got important news."

"I'm certain you do." Though Varro was not clear if Latro said exactly those words. His voice was low and the chaos surrounding him overwhelmed all. He stepped close enough to smell Latro's pungent sweat.

"Sir, I met Oceanus before the battle. He won't come help me, but is going to find Centurion Protus instead. I haven't seen him either, sir. We should get to the centurion."

Latro cocked one of his wild eyebrows. His blue eyes seemed crazed in the shadow of his bronze helmet.

"Giving orders now, Latro?"

"No, sir, but the centurion did say we would have to adjust our plans as needed."

"Don't remind me of my orders. Mind your rank, Varro. I know what the centurion wants and you do not. We're following his plan as given. Do as instructed, and you'll get your reward."

Varro opened his mouth to protest again, but Latro tilted his head back as if to dare him to speak. His mouth closed. He had not seen either Protus or Drusus since the whistle. Finding them among the milling soldiers might be difficult even for Oceanus, whereas he and Latro were exposed in the road.

"That's better," Latro said. "Now to make this look real. We're going to round up enemies. You'll go with me, and we'll find a spot to ambush Oceanus. He'll come. His masters want your farm and you're in the way."

Varro could only swallow and acknowledge the order. He did not like Latro but admired his supreme confidence in all he undertook. If he said Oceanus would come, perhaps he understood more than Varro himself. After all, the optio and centurion worked together daily whereas Varro had not been invited into their confidence since their last meeting. He was the bait in their trap and nothing more.

Latro pulled men off the back of the press, which was fast dissolving as the forward ranks pursued fleeing Macedonian soldiers. These dumbfounded men had each complained and cursed their missed chances, but the optio silenced them with a look.

"You fools going to catch any glory up there? Your chances are gone, but there's more to be had in and between these buildings. We're getting our share of the loot while those glory-seekers waste their time."

The appeal to greed outweighed the chance at glory, which could be had at the next fortified town. Latro had pulled in four men Varro did not recognize. They noted his bloodied face. He was surprised and embarrassed to have them nod with approval. He was a real soldier now, at least in their eyes.

"Two-man teams," he said. "One to open doors and the other to watch his back. Don't think the women won't fight. Their brats will too. So don't be too kind. Take what you want and clean up any fleeing soldiers you find. Don't be stupid about it, either. I don't want to hear you got led into a trap. They lost the battle, but they'll be happy to kill even one more of us if they can."

Latro paired the men, then offhandedly tapped Varro's shoulder.

"Looks like I'm stuck with you. Now let's go."

He led Varro away from the main road while the other teams left in opposite directions. Varro glanced over his shoulder, but did not see Falco. He hoped he kept close.

"That was well done, sir. It seemed like a genuine plan."

"It is a genuine plan, you fool. We've got to take apart this town and grab whatever we need before we burn it down. Takes organization to do that much killing before the afternoon."

Slipping off the main road relieved Varro's ears of the battle, but the screams that now emanated from all around weighted on his heart. Soldiers no longer voiced these, but women and children. As he threaded the barren side streets with Latro in the lead, he heard the cries rising like the smoke in the distance. Some ended abruptly, while others dragged on without pause.

But Latro moved with purpose, passing into another wide road. Varro followed, glimpsing a woman with her child clutched to her chest at the far end. She paused as if to check for friend or enemy, and upon seeing Varro fled around the corner.

"Sir, where are we going? Oceanus won't be able to keep up if we move so fast."

"Don't overthink it, Varro. He may be older than you, but he's no old man. He'll keep up. Greed won't let him fall behind."

"But we're now two major roads away from the action, sir. Will he be out here?"

Latro did not answer, but paused in the street as if suddenly aware of how far from the rest they had ranged. Varro looked into the buildings, finding shuttered windows and closed doors. If they opened and disgorged armed citizens, they would overcome him and Latro. Varro hefted his scutum and adjusted the helmet strap under his chin. His sword still dripped blood. He prayed the inhabitants of this town would be too terrified to approach.

Yet Latro crouched in the road with his head cocked, listening like a wolf waiting for a rabbit to bolt. Varro drew close and was about to speak when Latro raised his arm to bar his speech.

He held his breath. Was Oceanus near and he did not see him?

Then a child cried, stuttering and muffled from behind a door in a small building where the plaster had crumbled to reveal ancient brickwork.

Latro whirled to face it.

The cry stopped, as if cut off, but then grew louder and more intense.

Latro stood up from his crouch and smiled.

"There we are."

"Oceanus, sir?"

But Latro did not answer. He waved Varro after him as he charged for the door where the child cried.

He hopped and kicked the door, hobnailed sandals clanking against the wood. The old door flexed and cracked. The child beyond screamed.

"Sir, Oceanus isn't in there."

"He'll be along," Latro said, then grunted as he slammed his heel against the buckling door.

The wood shattered and exploded in. Latro's leg followed into the darkness. Two children screamed now, along with a woman and another voice. But Latro smashed aside the remnants of the door with his shield, then plowed into the darkness.

"Follow," he shouted back.

Varro looked behind. No signs of Falco, Oceanus, or anyone else showed in the street. The clangor and smoke of battle rose above tile roofs in the middle distance. He ducked into the building after his optio.

The shift in light blinded him. But the screaming overwhelmed him. In the tiny space, Latro used his shield to press an old man against the wall. He feebly wielded a knife that scraped against the wood. Latro pointed his sword at a young woman with disheveled black hair.

"Surrender the children and you'll live," he shouted.

Instead she hurled a pot of water into Latro's face. He stepped back howling. Flecks landed on Varro's arm, hot but not scalding.

The woman swept two children out of hiding beneath a small table. She herded them to the rear of the house while Latro held his face and cursed. He lowered his shield, freeing the old man, who lurched for Varro.

"Hold on," Varro shouted, raising his shield. But the old man did not hesitate and struck for him.

Out of instinct, Varro punched with his shield, following with a thrust. But it was unnecessary. His shield blow alone had staggered the frail man and crumpled him against the wall, either dead or unconscious.

Latro had recovered and bounded after the woman. His sword ran through her upper back stopping at the hilt. She arched and let out a short gasp. But collapsed as Latro ripped out the sword with a curse.

"Better than she deserved," he said, spitting water from his face. "Get the children before they escape."

"Sir?"

"Gods, Varro! I'll do it."

The tiny room comprised all but one other room of the house. The sudden rush through it had sent ramshackle furniture flying, overturning everything not stored in a box or sack. The stove fire still burned. But the rear door flashed white as Latro ran outside. Varro followed.

A grandmother shepherded her two grandchildren, or so it seems to Varro, but she was aged and the children were not much older than six or seven. One boy and one girl. They clung to their grandmother who seemed to have forgotten the backyard was a pen for their chickens, which now clucked and jumped trying to escape through the fence.

Latro stamped forward, smashing the old woman with his shield. It was no blow to move her aside. It was a crushing blow that would've staggered the stoutest legionnaire. For the old woman, it broke her neck and dropped her to the dirt.

The two children hugged each other, screaming and crying. Fear had robbed them of their senses. They simply collapsed in horror beneath Latro's hulking form, lost in his shadow.

"Sir, what has this to do with Oceanus? These are civilians."

"These are the enemy, Varro. These are the people who fed the men that dropped flaming oil on our brothers, who built the spears that plucked out their eyes, and who stacked the flaming hay that nearly killed all of us. You want to feel sorry for someone? Go out to the gate and look at the good young men of Rome, all twisted and burned. Go ask their mothers if we should think kindly upon those who burned them alive."

Varro looked to the wailing children, faces red and shining with tears and snot. Their thin, white arms wrapping each other. Brown feathers floated through the air as the chickens struggled to escape. One alighted on the grandmother's cheek, her head bent at a sharp angle and her old eyes staring into emptiness.

"Sir, these are children. They had no part in any of that. Let's take them as slaves."

"That's the spirit," Latro said, smiling. "You can see reason when you want to."

"We should expect Oceanus, sir. But he couldn't have followed us back here."

Varro at last noted his surroundings. He faced a series of back-yards, all with pens and livestock. Some pens were opened and empty, while others still contained a goat or chicken. This home must have been the wealthier of the lot, Varro mused, with four chickens. Paths led between the yards and out to the street and a lone tree provided shade. He imagined cheerful conversations between neighbors here. Now he had brought them blood and death. He pushed the thought aside.

"Sir, we really can't take these children if we're to flush out Oceanus."

Latro nodded and Varro grew chill at his look.

"You're right, of course. So I've got an order for you, Varro. Kill them."

"Sir?"

"Kill the children, Varro. That is a direct order from your commanding officer."

Varro looked down at the sniveling children. They clung to each other, tears streaming over their red faces. Neither understood their speech, but they had witnessed the murder of all the adults in their lives. He had a hand in it as well, and the thought made him queasy.

"Sir, there is no need to kill these children."

"Your duty is to obey the commands of your officers, not to offer your opinions on what is needed." Latro's blue eyes flared and a terrible smile creeped across his face. "Now, I'm not going to repeat myself. You have your orders."

The girl cried again, pressed cheek to cheek with her brother. Varro pointed his sword at them and they both cried louder.

"I will not kill these children. My vow before the gods supersedes your orders, Optio Latro. If this means my death, then so be it. I would not go before the gods having broken my solemn promise."

"Now that's a real problem for a soldier," Latro sneered, pointing with his bloodied sword. "These are enemies, and you will not do as I've commanded. You know the punishment for that."

"I know, sir."

Latro nodded, then seemed to retreat into thought. The two children continued to sob, with the girl's wailing trilling Varro's nerves.

"Well, you won't kill children. It's a hard task, I admit. She looks like one of my girls at that age, too. If you clean all the snot and dirt from her face, that is. But you know what will happen if these children live? They'll grow up and fight against Rome. Maybe they'll kill your son one day, Varro. Wouldn't that be a trick of the gods?"

"Sir, Oceanus is out there and Centurion Protus needs our aid."

"You want to save these children, just like you did when Centurion Protus ordered you to capture those farmer brats. Well, this is payback for that disobedience. If you won't kill them, then you'll watch me do it for you."

Latro sliced down with his gladius, not in the trained stab of a soldier but in the careless slash of a murderer. The blade cut the children apart from each other, carving deep wounds into their faces. Both screamed in pain and terror as they flailed aside.

Latro pulled back to stab the boy.

Varro threw his weight behind his shield and bowled Latro aside. He crashed against the flimsy pen fence, flattening it beneath him. The chickens jumped into the air, then fluttered over the boards.

"Get out of here," Varro yelled at the children. But the boy had fallen to his knees, holding his face as blood poured between his fingers. The girl had fallen over. Latro's careless slice had also gashed her neck. She blinked silently as bright blood squirted across the dirt.

Latro laughed, rolling onto his side to regain his footing. His heavy mail coat hindered him.

"You saved the chickens," he said. "I hope it felt good. But I think they'll end up in one of our boys' cooking pots, anyway."

"Get up," Varro shouted at the boy. He hauled him from the ground, then shoved him across the now flattened fence. "Run!"

The boy stumbled, then turned to his sister, hand pressed to his sliced cheek. He froze in shock and did not move.

"They don't understand you," Latro said. He had recovered, now holding his shield and gladius ready. "Don't waste your breath."

Varro readied his shield and his gladius, then squared off with Latro.

"You're working with Oceanus," he said, having at last guessed why Latro had led him here.

"You had me right from the first," Latro said, inclining his head. "It's a late lesson to learn now. But always trust your gut. It's almost never wrong."

"But why? Didn't he kill your brother?"

"He did, and I helped him do it. We had to get rid of him for the same reason we had to get rid of your father. He grew soft and started talking about getting out. There's no getting out, Varro, except as your father and my brother did."

Varro widened his stance and crushed down on the hilt of his sword. His temples throbbed. His vision misted white. A terrible, burning hatred uncoiled in his gut, spreading fire through his body. His limbs quivered with it.

"There are other ways to get your farm," Latro said, shifting along with Varro as they prepared to clash. "But it's easiest if you're dead. You're not going to out-fight me, either. I taught you everything you know, but not everything I know. So, you might get a surprising lesson, even if it's your last."

Latro sprang and struck with his shield like a move from a combat drill. Varro absorbed the force, stepping back with it, yielding ground but keeping himself upright. His head blazed with heat and his neck pulsed with loathing for the man who had killed his father.

He punched back and stepped into his sword thrust, but even with all his hatred he was walking through a drill with his optio.

Latro laughed. "A few practice blows to warm up, eh, Varro? Now here comes a new lesson."

He raised the edge of his shield to Varro so that it exposed his entire body. But the shield now forced space between them while also becoming a battering ram. Latro slammed it against Varro's own shield.

The force of the strike was harder than he ever experienced. Worse still, he had not paid attention to the ground. As Latro's shield slammed him back, his foot caught on something and the force sent him sprawling.

He had stumbled over the dead girl. Crashing hard over her body, his scutum fell away and his helmet dislodged, rolling aside.

Latro followed on, swift and strong as mad boar. He slammed the edge of his iron-rimmed shield on Varro's sword arm. The crack of bone shuddered through his arm, unleashing a burning wave of agony that blinded him.

"Always know where you're standing," he said.

Latro shifted over him, raising his iron-shod shield once more and aiming it over his head.

"Can't make it look like a gladius killed you. But anyone can bash your head in. Go tell the gods about your vow. It's time."

He hauled back with his shield as Varro's consciousness returned. He instinctively snatched at his sword, but his broken arm did not move.

That lost moment gave his life to Latro, who snarled as his shield slammed down.

Then Latro screamed and stumbled aside. The shield instead skidded through the earth beside his head.

Falco called outside of Varro's sight.

"Get up, lily!"

27

V arro fought up from prone, but placed his weight on his broken arm. The blinding pain caused him to scream and he collapsed.

Latro screamed and cursed beside him. He lay atop his shield, back arched and eyes pressed shut.

"You fucking bastard! Gods, my fucking leg!"

Rolling onto his other shoulder, Varro tried to rise. Next to him, Latro squirmed in his chain shirt as he reached toward the back of his left leg. A javelin had pierced his leg beneath the hem of the chain armor. How badly he had been struck, Varro could not tell. He was too close.

Falco rushed to his side, hauling him off the ground.

"I said get up." His breath was hot in Varro's face. "Others will be following. You've got some time yet."

Varro now stood with Falco's aid. His right arm hung limp, showing a horrible bruise surrounded by swollen red flesh on his forearm. On the ground, Latro pawed at a javelin that had passed through his hamstring. Thin streaks of blood flowed around it, but the muscles had contracted tight around the shaft. As he writhed on the ground, Varro saw the point protruded from above his knee. If he recovered, he'd be lame.

"He's working with Oceanus," he said. "If we take him prisoner, Centurion Protus can interrogate him. He'll want to know how he deceived him."

Falco's heavy brow drew together. "You won't do it? Varro, he murdered your father. Avenge him."

He hated the man who writhed in crippled agony. Latro deserved a death as painful as possible. But a well-cast javelin defeated him, even with a chain shirt and his years of experience.

"There is nothing more for him," Varro said. "I will not kill a defeated enemy."

"Gods, you fool!" Falco turned to Latro, raising his sword. "If he lives he'll have both of us killed. He's an officer and they stick together no matter what."

Falco stood over Latro's writhing body. The dead girl lay nearby, her pooling blood creeping closer as if straining to grab him.

"You were a fucking bastard from start to end," Falco said. "If Varro won't take revenge for his father, then I will. Die, Optio!"

Falco leaned over to plunge his gladius into Latro's neck.

But Latro was not yet dead.

Like a striking snake, he shot out with his pugio and hammered it into Falco's inner thigh.

He stumbled back, grabbing his leg. Blood flowed down his thigh and over his sandal. Falco hopped on one leg, then crashed to his back. The pugio plugged his wound and his hands reached for it.

"Falco, don't touch it!" Varro crashed to his side, his one good arm bearing down on Falco's.

"Gods, Varro, I wasn't supposed to die."

"You're not dying."

But blood pumped around the pugio to run down his leg and

puddle beneath it. His skin had gone the color of ash.

"My heart is beating so fast. I can't breathe," he said. "I'm afraid."

"Hold on. I'll tie it off. You're going to be fine."

Falco nodded, but his face was now waxy and slick with sweat. His dark eyes were wide and staring.

Yet Varro had only one working arm.

"We each took a leg," Latro said, grunting as he forced himself upright. He collected his sword to him, using it to prop up his body. "But I'm not dying. Falco is. That's a good hit, right to his inner thigh. Better work fast. He's got a few dozen heartbeats then he's dead."

Varro patted Falco's chest, then stood up glaring at the optio.

"You can save him, maybe." Latro now sat up without support. His other hand grabbed for his shield. "Or you can try to kill me, maybe. Choose one. I can beat you even on my back, Varro. You were never that good of a fighter. You don't have it in you. You're weak."

"You killed my father and my best friend." The mist returned to his eyes. His temples throbbed. His broken arm twitched, yearning to latch onto the optio's neck and throttle him. "You will pay for it."

Latro laughed, then shoved up with his shield.

"Try it, if you th—"

Varro closed the gap, and in one deft draw gripped his pugio in his left hand. His body slammed Latro flat.

His pugio sliced into his throat.

Latro's wild, blazing blue eyes met his.

Varro sawed at his neck, spraying blood down Latro's chest and forcing it out of his mouth. He sawed until his blade reached bone.

All the while, Latro glared at him, hateful and mad.

Then the baleful glare of life from those crazed blue eyes dulled.

Optio Latro's head dropped into an ever-widening pool of his own blood.

Varro stood, heaving and shaking. His pugio, the gift from his mother, dripped Latro's blood back onto his corpse.

Falco coughed. "You killed him. At least I got to see it."

Varro rushed back to him. He tore off his gladius harness, braced it with his foot and used his good arm to cut the straps.

"I'm going to tie it off. You might lose the leg, but you'll live."

"You're such a fucking comfort."

"Are you dying?"

"Seems so."

"Then shut up while I save you." Varro worked the cut straps under Falco's leg. He was no doctor but knew enough to keep the pugio in place. The strike was close enough to Falco's knee that he would not have to contend with the big muscles of Falco's thigh.

"You must be as heavy as an ox. Can you lift your leg?"

Falco stared up into nothing. His only reply came in fluttering blinks. Varro shoved the strap under his thigh, then laced it over. He struggled to tie it with his left hand. Something wet splattered this working hand, then he realized he was crying.

He was not working fast enough.

"Varro." Falco's voice was hoarse and dry. "Nice try but I think you can stop now. Get away before you're caught."

"Shut up, you stupid brute." He braced the strap with his left hand, then bit the loose end. He pulled back to tighten the strap.

"I'm sorry about how I treated you."

Varro looked to the wound. It did not seem to bleed as much, but the strap slipped loose again.

"I blamed you for stuff I shouldn't have."

Varro bit down and pulled on the strap again, hauling back with his head.

"You're a good man, Marcus Varro. Don't change. Tell my mother I'm sorry."

"By the gods, Falco, silence! I am trying to save you here."

But Falco's head had fallen back and his eyes closed.

"No, no, you're not dying, Falco. Not now. We're getting thought this war together. Remember?"

He again hauled on the strap, his teeth and jaw sore from pulling the leather tight.

Then soldiers arrived along the backyard paths. Varro did not see how many. Instead, he stared at Falco's gray face. Tears blurred his sight.

"Over here!" The soldier's voice was familiar, but Varro did not look away from his friend.

Hobnailed sandals clanked over the destroyed pen wall. Shapes gathered around him.

"Dear gods, is he dead?"

Varro looked up to find Panthera and Curio hovering over him. Two others were joining from behind.

"Latro killed him." The words sounded hollow. "So I killed Latro."

Panthera stepped back in shock, looking from Falco to Latro to the dead girl and her grandmother.

"What happened here?"

Varro wept openly. He could not contain the pain welling inside. It strangled him from within, more painful than any broken arm.

Only Curio, not being much attached to anyone yet, leaned beside Falco. He put his ear to his chest, then pressed his fingers into his neck.

"He's not dead, just passed out."

Varro rubbed the tears from his eyes. "He's alive?"

"He has a pulse and he's breathing," Curio said. "Where I'm from, that is considered alive."

"But he bled so much," Varro said. "I thought he couldn't survive."

"He might not still," Curio said. "But if we can get him to the medical station, he has a chance."

The two soldiers now joined. One was Gallio and the other Varro did not recognize.

"He said he could take care of himself." Gallio crouched beside Falco's body, feeling for the same pulse Curio had detected. "Now look at this mess."

"Help me get him to the medical station," Varro said. "My arm is broken."

"What about Latro?" Gallio asked. "I mean, well, I guess he wasn't on your side after all. Do we take him?"

Varro looked to the stranger, a soldier from another century. He had wide-set eyes and horrible acne scars. But he waved both hands as if to say he did not want to know more.

"Don't worry," Gallio said. "A friend of mine. Trust him."

"If that's the case, then let Latro rot here. He killed this family, so let his ghost haunt this spot with them forever."

All the others spit as a ward against the curse Varro had made. But no one spared another look at Latro.

Curio and Panthera carried Falco between them. Varro took the boy with the slashed face. He had collapsed against the shade tree, alive but shocked into white-faced silence. He held Varro's hand and followed without a word.

They arrived at the medical station, where dozens of men in various conditions sat or lay in long rows. Their fellows bandaged them, or else aided as they could. It was not a hospital, but better than lying in the dirt and praying to live.

They found an open spot for Falco and set him down. He had not regained consciousness, but now Varro felt the faint pulse the others had detected. He sat next to him.

"My arm's broken," he said, showing it to Panthera and Gallio.

"You don't have to explain to us," Gallio said. "You belong at the aid station too."

For a moment, as healthy men worked down the line toward him, he felt a wave of relief.

Then he bolted upright.

"Centurion Protus. Has anyone seen him?"

"He was reorganizing the century," Gallio said. "We had to slip him to go find you and Falco. We're probably all in trouble."

Varro looked between Falco and the others. He could not abandon his friend, but Oceanus was still seeking Protus. The plan must have been for Latro to make the easy kill and leave Oceanus to the more expert attempt on Protus's life.

"I've got to find him. You stay with Falco and make sure someone sees him soon."

He did not wait on an answer, but sped up the main road where Roman units were reforming. Each footfall shuddered pain up his arm. But he had a duty to Protus.

An optio from another century shouted at him, but he sped past. He laced between old triarii leaning on their spears and scratching their heads. He bumped among the regular soldiers, forcing his way to where Protus and Drusus stood at the fore of their maniple.

Both centurions glared at him as he broke through the ranks. Black smudgy smoke formed a backdrop to them. Protus looked to Varro's broken arm, and his expression shifted.

"Is this all that's left of your contubernium?" Centurion Drusus stepped forward, pulling Varro back. "The hastati always take it hard, but to have only one survive? Protus, you should have rotated them out earlier."

"No, sir, there are others at the aid station." Varro withheld further elaboration, hoping to end the discussion and excuse his friends.

"And your arm?" Drusus asked. "You don't need to set that bone? I can see the lump."

He pulled free of Drusus and addressed Protus directly.

"Sir, I have important news for you."

The two centurions looked to each other, and Drusus shrugged. "Just because the battle is won does not mean we excuse the chain of command. Where is your optio? Go to him first."

"I'll handle this," Protus said, peeling Varro aside. They stepped into the shade of a building. Roman soldiers had stacked dead Macedonian soldiers like logs in the street. Others were delivering captive Macedonians to a central collection point for prisoners.

"Sir, Optio Latro was in league with Oceanus."

Protus's back stiffened and his eyes narrowed.

"I worked closely with Optio Latro and he raised no suspicion with me."

"Sir, I know you think I hated him. I did, actually. But I trusted him after you both explained things. Latro said he helped Oceanus kill his own brother because he was trying to get out. Whatever that meant. He said that's why they killed my father, and probably Tanicus. He led me to the edge of the town, then tried to get me to kill two children."

"Which you refused to do," Protus said, his jaw tight.

"Of course, sir. I won't kill children, even if Jupiter commands it. If you ever wish to order me to do so, sir, please just directly order my execution."

"All right, Varro, remain on point."

"Yes, sir. It ended up being his excuse to kill me. But he was just enjoying some sport before the deed. He led me off to be killed no matter what I said or did. Oceanus is coming for you, sir. Latro was supposed to kill me, and he'd eliminate you. Then their masters would be satisfied and they could go about their business."

Protus stared hard at him. Varro was not certain if he had convinced the centurion. But he pinched the bridge of his nose and shook his head.

"Your broken arm and the fact that you're here means you fought with and defeated Latro."

"Sir, you must watch out for Oceanus. If he thinks I'm dead, then he'll really want you out of the way. We need to get you to safety, sir."

At last Protus's hard face shifted to a bemused smile.

"I'd rather like to see what your plans are for my safety. And I thank you for placing my safety above your own. But Oceanus will not bother me today."

"Sir? Was he killed, or you defeated him already?"

Protus gave a sly smile.

"There's more going on here than you know. And I pray you'll never know. I've done one better to rid myself of Oceanus."

"Sir, I spoke to him only this morning. He must be close by."

"No longer," Protus said. "He is not dead, but he will not threaten us. At least, he is not dead yet. We'll see how his masters deal with him. For now, you should get to the aid station and have that arm set before it has to be broken again."

Varro stared gape-mouthed at Protus, who gave a light chuckle.

"Go now. I will find a way to reward your service. I will also do my own investigation into Latro. I rather wished you took him alive so I could've learned more about his methods. But he had years of experience over you. You either kill him or die. The gods were with you, it seems. With both of us. For if you had fallen, Latro would have done what Oceanus failed to do."

"Sir, there were no witnesses to my fight with Latro. I can trust that we are done with all of this? I'd like to just return to being a regular soldier."

"We are done. But as for being a regular soldier, you know more than most do. Keep yourself alive, Varro, and know I may call on you again. It will be worth your while."

"Thank you, sir."

Varro saluted and returned to the aid station.

Falco had regained consciousness and his bleeding stopped. The pugio remained in place, to be extracted later by a doctor. But he and Varro exchanged grins and laughed.

The clean-up after the battle lasted until late afternoon. Gallio, Panthera, and Curio were all that remained of their contubernium and being uninjured were taken to help execute all the men of the town and enslave the rest. Varro was glad to be spared that ghoulish work.

By late afternoon they picked up and marched toward a new campsite closer to the next target. Varro's arm was set in a sling, but he still carried Falco on his back. The town of Corrhagum burned behind them.

He and Falco, being wounded enough to not fight, spent the next two attacks in camp with the other wounded. More were added after each town was razed. Varro had one good arm, so was charged with caring for the more seriously wounded, like Falco. So he spent his time with this friend.

At last Lucius Apustius had devastated the Macedonian countryside and planned to take the battle on to the larger cities on the edge of the country. Varro wondered at how many could die and or be wounded and yet the legion show no signs of slowing or failing.

The night after sacking the third and final fortified town, the entire army celebrated with wine reserved for the officers. Centurion Protus joined Falco and Varro at the hospital and drank to their health. He thanked them again both in private and confirmed that Latro was in league with Oceanus.

How he got this information so far out in Macedonia, Varro did not know. Nor did he care. It seemed he was freed to be a regular soldier. Nothing pleased him more.

"It seems Falco knows more than he should," Protus said with a tight grin. "But do not involve any others in this. Varro, you may be out of immediate danger, but you've earned enemies."

Varro shuddered and looked to Falco lying on his blanket in

one of the hospital tents. He curled his lip in disgust.

"And you've earned new allies," Protus said. "These should balance out. Your farm is only worth something if it is easy to take, which you've shown it is not. And there's the natural course of the war too. If you fall in battle, it is the same outcome for them. Your enemies can be extremely patient, Varro. Remember this well. For one day you might find yourself in their shadows long after you've forgotten them."

"Sir, there is nothing more you can tell me?"

He waved dismissively.

"In time and only if needed. For now, we will send the wounded back to camp when replacements arrive tomorrow. You two will be leaving. And since your contubernium is under strength, they will go with you. Plenty of fresh and eager young men will come up. These fights will be longer and deadlier. We need complete fighting capacity."

"Deadlier?" Varro rubbed his arm over the splint. "This wasn't deadly enough, sir?"

Protus leaned back and laughed.

"Only a recruit would ask such a question. Surely your father or grandfather had stories for you? There is more to come, Varro. But for now, you've nothing to worry for. Do your duty, drill and march, never be idle, and you will have done all you can to ensure your survival. The rest is for the gods to decide, if they decide at all. Now, I'll be missed soon enough. You two enjoy your wine and be ready to depart tomorrow."

After the centurion left, he and Falco sat in the cool shadow of the tent.

"I can't believe it," Varro said. "It's over. Back to normal soldiering. I'm so relieved."

Then, the next morning, he learned that Centurion Protus had died in his sleep.

And he realized his life would never be normal.

28

Varro's eyes fluttered open from a deep sleep. He had been dreaming of something awful. Clanging swords, screaming men, and torrents of blood. Smoke and ash swirled through his dream world, blinding him as he staggered ahead in isolated confusion.

But now he stared into the darkness of his barracks room. He was on the top bunk, and Falco snored beneath him. With no view of the outside, he guessed it was the predawn hour and soon they would be up with the sun. He had sacrificed extra sleep he would have treasured. With a short yawn, he tilted his heavy head to the side.

Gallio slept on his bunk across the way, and Curio beneath him. Panthera snored out of view, and three bunks remained empty. Varro closed his eyes and hoped for sleep again, even if it would bring him back to the nightmare world of enemy pikes jabbing at him from blinding smoke. His arm remained broken, but officers found labor for him, nonetheless. Idleness was a crime no officer could ignore. Varro needed all his sleep.

Lucius Apustius was to return during the upcoming day.

Consul Galba had announced a special welcome for his victorious lieutenant. For Varro, this meant polishing his helmet and sword, repainting his scutum, and doing everything to look his best. It meant little else besides a chance for another drink of that delicious wine the officers hoarded.

Sleep crept up on him. His breathing steadied and strange visions flitted about his mind. The edge of slumber was bright and cool, but then something shook him awake.

His eyes shot open.

Again he stared up into darkness. The same deep gloom barely showed the hints of rafters. Had someone touched him? He held his breath, listening but only hearing the beat of his own heart.

But then he felt it.

Something heavy coiled on his chest shifted.

A snake!

Varro shot up with a shout, batting the snake away. He kicked back up against the cold wall.

But the snake did not hiss. Nor did it strike or make any movement.

Gallio rolled over with a grunt and Panthera's snoring stuttered. But otherwise no one had awakened to his shout. He remained still, wondering if the snake was merely stunned.

Without light, the snake remained hidden and silent in his bed. His heart raced.

"What are you doing up there?" Falco's sleepy, irritated voice floated up in a harsh whisper. "Nightmares again?"

"Falco, there's a snake in my bed."

"What?"

He heard Falco's naked feet thump on the wood floor. His head bumped on the bottom of the bunk and he cursed.

"Don't frighten it." He curled up tighter, but as his sleepy numbness faded, he doubted his senses.

Falco's head now appeared from beneath the bunk, a mere outline in the dark.

"Where is it? Did it bite you?"

"No, and I hear nothing. I don't know where it is."

"Gods, Varro, you were dreaming again." He let go a long sigh and dropped back to the floor. "I hope you get over this soon. The rest of us need sleep."

Gallio again grunted and flipped angrily in his bunk. Neither Curio nor Panthera reacted.

"But I felt it on my chest, heavy, and I did hit something." Varro swept his hand across his narrow bunk. It was not large enough to hide a snake without his feeling it.

His hands bumped something. He recoiled in shock, but did not cry out. Now awake, his logical mind had come to the fore. His fingers brushed the alleged snake again, finding something hard and cold, but coiled like a snake.

"Falco, there is something here," he whispered. "I've got it."

He collected the hard length of the object into his hand. He felt around, and realized something had fallen into his lap when he had shot up. It was light, and felt like a bark strip used for simple notes.

"Light the lamp and let's see what this is." He weighed the object in his hand, wondering at this heft and relieved it was not alive.

Falco had crawled out of bed with a groan, but shuffled into the front room where their gear was racked. Varro dropped behind him and followed.

The lamp flame fluttered open, and Falco adjusted it so a dull yellow globe illuminated the desk in the tiny room.

Varro's heart pounded, wondering at what he held. He tipped his hand over the table beneath the lamp.

A long chain of thick gold links chimed together as it rolled from his palm. One of the links had been snapped.

"Artas's chain," Varro said with a gasp. "This is the chain I told you about."

Falco whistled faintly, leaning down for a closer look. He extended his thumb and placed it next to the links.

"You weren't lying. It's as thick as my thumb. Varro, you're rich."

"We're rich."

"If you're going to argue about it, then I'll concede." Falco's heavy brow raised, exposing points of golden light in his eager eyes. "But you don't mean the others, right? This is just for us two good Sabine boys. A little reward for all the pain."

"That makes sense to me," Varro said. "I'll hold it for now."

But as he made to collect it, he realized he still held the bark slip.

"This was with it too." Varro set the bark slip under the lamplight.

He stared at the single word, inked with precise strokes.

Peace.

He looked to Falco, who stood back as if now presented with the venomous snake.

"I didn't hear anyone enter."

Varro snatched up the bark slip and the chain into his hand.

"I woke from a dream, then faded back to sleep. That's when I felt the weight of the chain on my chest. But whoever placed it there must have done so when I first awakened. He was gone before I cried out."

"It wasn't one of...."

Varro shook his head. "The others were all asleep."

"They could have been faking," Falco said, now narrowing his eyes at the other room. "It's Curio. He was Latro's man, and I bet he still is."

"He would have had to fly like Mercury to place the chain and jump back into a top bunk. I don't think it's any of ours. It must be from whoever poisoned Centurion Protus while he slept."

They both stared at each other, their mouths open. Falco raised his finger to point.

"You could've been killed as easily as Protus had been. But instead whoever was here left you the chain he took from Latro."

"Meaning he knew everything Latro did. Otherwise, why give me the chain?" Varro raised his hand again, crushing down on the chain and bark note. "My enemies have offered peace."

Falco stared down at his fist.

"Are you going to accept it?"

"For now." He rolled his fingers, crushing the bark into flakes.

"But there will be a day of reckoning, Falco. One day, I will destroy them."

HISTORICAL NOTES

The Roman Republican Army at the end of the Second Punic War was not yet the professional army commonly seen in movies and television. It consisted of citizen-soldiers liable for military service from ages seventeen to forty-six and who also owned a certain amount of property. The soldier payed his own way, buying all his gear and maintaining it himself. He would be eligible for up to sixteen years of service (ten for cavalry, the wealthiest of citizens) though during the time of this novel most served six years' continuous service and then remained eligible to be recalled if needed.

The Romans divided their army into legions, of which there were four, two for each consular army. A legion comprised roughly four thousand infantry and two hundred cavalry. The heavy infantry divided themselves into hastati, principes, and triarii, and in that order. Ahead of them went approximately 1,200 light-infantry skirmishers, the velites. The legion further broke down into maniples and centuries. A century had sixty soldiers in total, with a centurion to command and an optio as his second. A maniple was formed of two centuries and commanded overall by the most senior of the two centurions. The maniple was Rome's key fighting unit. It provided tactical flexibility and was an innovative formation for its day.

This story begins in March of 200 BC. The Second Punic War had ended, and Rome turned its attentions to Carthage's allies. Chief among these was Philip V of Macedonia. Rome wished to punish those who allied with her enemies. Trouble had already been afoot between Athens and Macedonia, and at last Philip sent two thousand men to besiege Athens. Rome had found its excuse and rallying cry.

Newly elected Consul Publius Sulpicius Galba Maximus was serving his second term in this role. His priority was to make a case for war against Philip, but the Centuriate Assembly rejected his proposal. The Second Punic War had ended and the Roman people were tired of warfare. But Consul Galba brought the same proposal to the Assembly's next meeting. This time he raised the specter of an invasion by Philip akin to Hannibal's. His cautions were heeded.

The Second Macedonian War was underway.

Galba had clashed with Philip ten years earlier during the First Macedonian War. After enjoying some easy successes, Galba's military action fizzled over the course of his term which ended with his hardly participating in the war. Perhaps he was eager for a new chance to defeat Philip in 200 BC.

He raised his legions and settled near Brundisium (modern day Brindisi) to prepare to cross the Adriatic Sea with plans to land in Apollonia. While in Brundisium, Galba was allowed to recruit from veteran troops returned from the Second Punic War. These men were not coerced to serve, and many were willing to continue fighting. With his troops assembled, Galba made the crossing.

Upon reaching Apollonia, he was met by Athenian ambassadors who begged swift action for their besieged city. Galba's plan was to invade Macedonia overland from the west. But seeing an opportunity to aid Athens, he dispatched twenty ships and one thousand men to relieve the besieged city.

With the end of the year coming, Galba settled winter quarters along the Apsus River (modern day Seman River). He mounted a short campaign against fortified towns and cities in the area, assigning a portion of his army to the task under the command of Lucius Apustius. After terrorizing his enemies, Apustius's reputation caused some heavily fortified towns to surrender without resistance. Yet others had to be taken by siege. After satisfactorily smashing the fortifications of the Macedonian frontier and garrisoning some captured points, he began his return to Galba's camp. However, on the return trip his marching column was surprised by a rear attack. Yet Apustius wheeled his men around and vanquished his enemies, thereby increasing the booty and slaves he returned to Galba.

So now the stage is set for the proper invasion of Macedonia to begin in 199 BC.

Marcus Varro and Caius Falco and all their families are fictional. So it is with their companions and officers. The skirmishes they fought and the setbacks they faced along the way may be forgotten to history, but certainly the Romans faced pockets of resistance and ill-luck along their march to war.

Our young citizen-soldiers, Varro and Falco, may have discovered more than expected serving in the legion. They have many years to go and many battles to face. Some will be on blood-slicked plains or rocky slopes littered with the detritus of combat. Other battles will be staged in the shadows, beyond the eyes of history and forgotten to all but those who bled and suffered through them.

There is time yet for Varro and Falco to learn the price of Roman conquest and to become the great men they both aspire to be.

NEWSLETTER

If you would like to know when my next book is released, please sign up for my new release newsletter. You can do this at my website: http://jerryautieri.wordpress.com/

If you have enjoyed this book and would like to show your support for my writing, consider leaving a review where you purchased this book or on Goodreads, LibraryThing, and other reader sites. I need help from readers like you to get the word out about my books. If you have a moment, please share your thoughts with other readers. I appreciate it!

ALSO BY JERRY AUTIERI

Ulfrik Ormsson's Saga

Historical adventure stories set in 9th Century Europe and brimming with heroic combat. Witness the birth of a unified Norway, travel to the remote Faeroe Islands, then follow the Vikings on a siege of Paris and beyond. Walk in the footsteps of the Vikings and witness history through the eyes of Ulfrik Ormsson.

Fate's Needle

Islands in the Fog

Banners of the Northmen

Shield of Lies

The Storm God's Gift

Return of the Ravens

Sword Brothers

Descendants Saga

The grandchildren of Ulfrik Ormsson continue tales of Norse battle and glory. They may have come from greatness, but they must make their own way in the brutal world of the 10th Century.

Descendants of the Wolf

Odin's Ravens

Revenge of the Wolves

Blood Price

Viking Bones

Valor of the Norsemen

Norse Vengeance

Bear and Raven

Red Oath

Fate's End

Grimwold and Lethos Trilogy

A sword and sorcery fantasy trilogy with a decidedly Norse flavor.

Deadman's Tide

Children of Urdis

Age of Blood

Printed in Great Britain
by Amazon

78868176R00182